"Torm save me," Abdel called and sliced his sword back to his left, then right. The spider paused, and Abdel rolled all the way over to one side, hoping to escape the web. Hair was pulled painfully from his arm, and a strand of web stuck to his neck. He was a fly now, a meal for this eight-legged predator, and like a fly, his desperate struggles only served to cement his captivity in the sticky web.

"Hold still," the spider said, and Abdel flinched at the sound of its voice. It was a sound like glass being drawn across steel, and it set Abdel's hair on end as much from the sound of it as from the horror that such a creature had the power of speech at all. "Hold still, human, and let Kriiya drain you. Let Kriiya drain you dry."

FORGOTTEN REALMS

Exciting novelizations of best-selling computer games!

Baldur's Gate™
Philip Athans

Baldur's Gate II: Shadows of Amn
Philip Athans

Baldur's Gate II: Throne of Bhaal
Drew Karpyshyn

and coming soon . . .

*Neverwinter Nights
An Anthology*

Baldur's Gate™

Philip Athans

BALDUR'S GATE

©1999 TSR, Inc.
©2001 Wizards of the Coast, Inc.

Distributed to the hobby, toy, and comic trade in the United States and Canada by regional distributors.

Distributed worldwide by Wizards of the Coast, Inc. and regional distributors.

FORGOTTEN REALMS, BALDUR'S GATE, WIZARDS OF THE COAST, and their respective logos are trademarks of Wizards of the Coast, Inc., in the U.S.A., and other countries.

All Wizards of the Coast characters, character names, and the distinctive likenesses thereof are trademarks of Wizards of the Coast, Inc.

Printed in the U.S.A.

First Printing: July 1999
Library of Congress Catalog Card Number: 99-62582

9 8 7 6 5 4

ISBN: 0-7869-1525-0
620-21525

U.S., CANADA,
ASIA, PACIFIC, & LATIN AMERICA
Wizards of the Coast, Inc.
P.O. Box 707
Renton, WA 98057-0707
+1-800-324-6496

EUROPEAN HEADQUARTERS
Wizards of the Coast, Belgium
T Hofveld 6d
1702 Groot-Bijgaarden
Belgium
+322 467 3360

Visit our web site at **www.wizards.com**

For my two girls.
(I'm still a regular person.)

Acknowledgments

Abdel is all mine, but every other character in this book, the beginning, almost all of the middle, and the end of the story is based on the brilliant work of the creators of the *Baldur's Gate* computer game from BioWare: James Ohlen, Lukas Kristjanson, Rob Bartel, Ray Muzyka, John Gallagher, Scott Greig, and the rest of the BioWare *Baldur's Gate* team. And thanks to Interplay's Black Isle Division. Thanks guys, it was fun!

And, I must of course acknowledge my editor Jess Lebow. (Okay, I put your name in the book. Now where's my five bucks?)

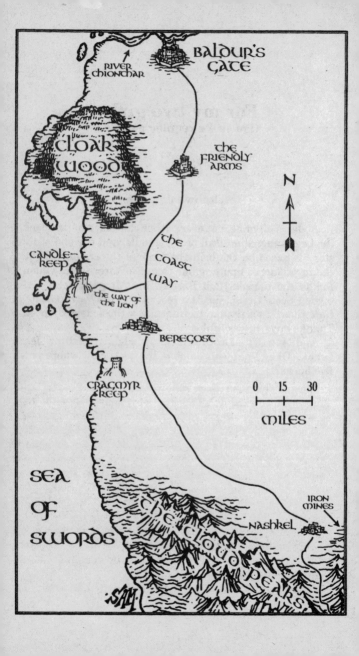

Chapter One

The blades came together so hard they threw out a blue-white spark bright enough to burn its gentle arc into Abdel's vision. The impact sent a shudder through the heavy blade of his broadsword, but he ignored it and pushed back in the direction of the attack. Abdel was strong enough and tall enough to seriously unbalance his opponent. The man stumbled backward two steps and brought his empty left hand up to keep from falling. Abdel saw the opening and took full advantage of it, flashing his sword across his opponent's open midsection and slicing deeply through chain mail, flesh, and bone.

Abdel recognized two of the four men who were trying to kill him. The men were sellswords—hired guards and thugs—just like Abdel. They had obviously been paid, but by whom and for what reason, Abdel couldn't fathom.

The man Abdel had killed took ten or twenty seconds to realize he was dead. He kept looking down at the deep gash that had nearly cut him in two. Blood was everywhere, and there was a hint of the yellow-gray of entrails. The expression on the man's face was nearly comical: surprised, pale, and somehow disappointed. The look of it made Abdel's heart leap, and he couldn't tell if it was from the horror or the pleasure of the sight. The pause was enough, though, to allow another of the bandits to step in and nearly gut him with one of the two small, sharp axes the mercenary spun madly in both hands.

"Kamon," Abdel said as he skipped back half a step to

1

avoid the second axe. "Long time."

He'd worked with this one before, a year ago, guarding a warehouse in Athkatla that was storing something a very long and increasingly bizarre parade of thieves were intent on stealing. Kamon's trademark was this fast and furious, though not terribly exact, twin axe attack. A short, stocky man, he was a fighter many less experienced opponents underestimated. Anyone who'd been fighting as long as Abdel had, though, could tell by the man's quick, crystal blue eyes that he was a smart and capable fighter.

"Abdel," Kamon said. "Sorry about your father."

It was an old trick, older even than Gorion, who sometimes seemed to Abdel to be the oldest man ever to walk the streets and trails of Faerûn. Abdel could see his foster father out of the corner of his eye. Gorion was on his feet, fighting, but as usual trying not to kill the bandit—who was obviously not as considerate as the older man. The dark complexioned bandit with the elaborately covered headscarf was coming at Gorion with a scimitar too fast, too out of control. Gorion was able to keep him at bay with his heavy oaken staff, but for how long?

Abdel let Kamon come in with his right-hand axe and caught it with his blade just under the head. The broadsword's sharp edge cut into the axe handle, and Abdel pulled up but not out, and the axe came out of Kamon's hand so quickly it left a red burn on the bandit's palm. Kamon cursed and backed up three quick steps. The loss of one of his weapons surprised him, caught him off guard maybe, but Kamon was experienced enough to keep his eyes open. The axe was still stuck on Abdel's blade.

Abdel knew he shouldn't stop to try to pull the axe off, but when he heard the crunch of gravel behind him he did it anyway. He was hoping Kamon would do the obvious thing, and Kamon obliged. The bandit came in fast with the other axe, swinging low to cut his victim at the waist.

Abdel pulled his knees to his gut, keeping his sword across his chest to protect him. His feet came off the ground, and he fell onto his backside at the same time the big halberd blade came down from behind him. The crunch of gravel was the heavy step of Eagus, the first of the bandits Abdel had recognized when they first presented themselves on the road. Eagus still bore the scar on his face from that bet he'd lost to Abdel in Julkoun eight months ago. The memory made Abdel smile even as he was suddenly drenched in thick, hot blood.

Eagus's blow, meant for Abdel, had split Kamon's head in half from crown to chin. Abdel was disappointed only because now he wouldn't be able to ask Kamon if he ever found out what it was they'd been guarding in that warehouse.

Still curled in a ball, Abdel swung his feet up and brought his sword back, the hand axe still stuck awkwardly to the blade. He was hoping to gut Eagus from behind while the halberdier still had his weapon stuck in his friend's head. Halfway up a burning pain drove the breath from Abdel's lungs, and he instinctively dropped to his left.

The fifth bandit, the one who had been hanging back, had fired a single crossbow bolt into Abdel's right flank. Abdel tore it out, pulling some links loose from his chain mail tunic and roaring at the pain. He made eye contact with the crossbowman just long enough to send the man scurrying backward in fear. The sellsword could only hope the crossbowman was scared enough not to shoot him again. Abdel had more immediate problems.

Eagus swore as he worked at wriggling the blade of his halberd out of Kamon's head. He had to stay close to the halberdier, but Abdel gave himself a handful of seconds to check his father's progress. Gorion was holding up well. He was letting his opponent tire himself out with one hopeless lunge of a scimitar after another.

"We can go on like this forever, Calishite," Gorion said, guessing the man's origin by his peculiar dress and choice of blade, "or long enough for you to tell me who hired you and why."

Abdel grabbed Kamon's axe free of his sword, keeping track of Eagus's hurried progress with one eye while keeping the other on his father.

The Calishite sellsword smiled, revealing a tarnished silver tooth, and said to Gorion, "We were paid extra, sir, not to say. You can give us your ward, though, and maybe live."

There was a sound as if someone had tossed a maidens-thigh melon from a guard tower, and Eagus's halberd was free. He swung the polearm up and around, spraying Abdel and the road with more of Kamon's blood. Abdel threw the axe, and Eagus dodged it easily. The throw wasn't meant to kill but to force Eagus off balance, and Abdel knew there was only one way, and one second, in which to test the success of this method.

Abdel came in fast, leaping really, his feet leaving the ground for a risky half second. He speared at Eagus and felt his blade sink home through a gap in the bandit's rusted armor before he tucked his feet back under him. He meant to stand and drag his blade up through Eagus's guts to disembowel him, but Eagus wasn't quite as off-balance as he could have been. The bandit slipped gingerly off the tip of Abdel's blade. There was blood, and Eagus was obviously in pain, but he fought on.

The halberd came down hard again, and Abdel almost didn't have a chance to get his sword up to block it. His broadsword blade bit deeply into the thick wood of the halberd's pole, and this time it was Abdel who was disarmed. Eagus, his yellow teeth showing through the brown and gray mass of his ill-kept beard, had the advantage of leverage. Though the act of twisting the long, heavy weapon out of Abdel's strong grasp obviously caused Eagus pain, opening his wound yet wider, the sword came free of Abdel's grip.

Eagus allowed himself a coughing laugh when the broadsword fell from the halberd. He wouldn't be as encumbered as Abdel had been, and he took full advantage of it. Abdel could still hear the ringing of steel that meant his father was yet engaged with the Calishite swordsman. He would have to fight Eagus alone, and without his sword.

Eagus, maybe a bit fatigued now, maybe having lost too

much blood, came in too slowly, too clumsily, and Abdel was almost disappointed when he easily batted the halberd away with his arm. The force of Abdel's blow meeting Eagus's nearly broke the young sellsword's right forearm. It hurt, but Abdel ignored the pain and kicked up with his left foot, slamming the toe of his sturdy boot into Eagus's seeping wound.

Eagus shrieked and dropped, his knees falling out from under him like dry twigs. Abdel pulled out the dagger Gorion had given him as a coming-of-age gift, the one with the silver blade. He cut Eagus's throat, watching the man's eyes as his life fled him. Abdel smiled at the sight, though he knew Gorion wouldn't approve. That's when he realized Gorion was still fighting and there was—

The crossbowman stepped out, dark eyes slitted against the midmorning sun, padded leather vest creaking with every movement. His long red hair fluttering greasily in the breeze. He aimed carefully at Gorion.

Abdel screamed out, "*Fa—*"

The crossbow released, and the heavy steel bolt shot through the air with a hiss.

"*—th—*"

Embedding itself deeply into Gorion's eye.

"*—er!*"

Abdel knew, before Gorion's twitching body hit the gravel road, that the only father he had ever known was dead.

Red filled his vision, a ringing filled his ears, there was the stinging taste of copper in his mouth, and Abdel went mad. He ran at the Calishite swordsman first, simply because he was the closer of the two surviving bandits. Abdel's heavy silver dagger was out in front of him just swinging back and forth as if he was working a field with it. The Calishite danced back and brought his scimitar up.

There was a clang of metal, and the Calishite pronounced the first syllable of the name of some forgotten god as Abdel's sturdy blade slashed through the finely wrought scimitar. Two thirds of the curved blade spun wildly off into the brush at the side of the wide gravel road, and the Calishite couldn't help but watch it spin away as he continued to back up and out of the reach of the slashing dagger.

The Calishite's foot dropped an inch and a half into a wagon wheel rut in the road, and he fell backward, off balance, enough to be saved from the next slash that might have taken his throat out.

Growling in feral, incoherent rage, Abdel came forward and slashed again. His arm vibrated from the sudden resistance along the blade of the heavy dagger.

The Calishite probably saw his broken blade bounce once after it hit the ground before the world spun and something wet and sticky splashed across his face. His severed head might have lived long enough to experience that, but he was dead before his head and his body hit the ground.

The crossbowman didn't bother to wait long enough to curse or beg or be horrified. He wasn't the smartest man on the Sword Coast, far from it, but he was more than smart enough to know when to turn around and run for his life.

Abdel, still wild with a murderous frenzy now wholly out of his control, chased the man down and butchered him into a mound of bleeding meat. Finally spent, the foster son of Gorion of Candlekeep collapsed onto a pile of leather, gore, and crossbow parts, and he wept.

* * * * *

Abdel had been selling his strong sword arm and experience up and down the Sword Coast for years, and had spent the last tenday escorting a merchant caravan from Baldur's Gate to the library at Candlekeep. The massive monastery had been his boyhood home, the closest thing to a real home Abdel had ever known. It was there that Gorion, a kind but stern monk, had raised Abdel in the worship of Torm, god of the brave and the foolish, and had tried to instill upon Abdel his own love of the written word and the history and traditions of Faerûn.

Abdel had studied hard, but his mind wandered, and

both he and his adopted father soon came to realize that he would never live the life of a monk, cloistered away copying the great texts, storing away the knowledge and experience of others. Abdel sought his own knowledge, his own experience, and he found it in the world outside the protective walls of Candlekeep.

It seemed to frighten Gorion somehow, Abdel's need to fight, to kill, but he seemed also to have some deeper understanding of it, as if he expected it of his foundling son, though he could never really condone it.

Abdel looked nothing like this man who was not truly his father, and it seemed to surprise no one who knew them well that they didn't think much alike either. Where Gorion was thin of frame, bookish, and rigid of posture, Abdel was powerfully muscled, with chiseled features and ink black hair he kept long to flow with the same fluid grace as his body. Abdel was nearly a foot taller than his adopted father, almost seven feet tall, and probably outweighed the monk threefold.

They hadn't spoken much in the last several years, but when Abdel was offered the spot on the caravan from Baldur's Gate he jumped at the chance not only because his purse was growing light from some lean times, but because he truly wanted to see his father again.

Their meeting had been oddly emotional from the moment Abdel stepped through the gates of Candlekeep. Gorion was happy to see him. Maybe Abdel had spent too much time with sellswords and hired killers, but it seemed to him that Gorion was almost too happy to see him. They had talked of many things that first evening. Gorion was always curious to hear Abdel's stories of battles fought and won, of greedy merchants and marauding orcs, or seaside taverns and the warrior's camaraderie. This night, though, Gorion seemed detached, preoccupied, and nothing was more unlike Abdel's father. The young sellsword got the feeling his father needed to tell him something.

Abdel, as he was wont to do, simply asked his father what was on his mind. Gorion had smiled and laughed.

" 'And hid his face amid a crown of stars?' " Gorion asked, quoting some bard Abdel vaguely recognized.

"Staey of Evereska?"

"Pacys," Gorion corrected, "if memory serves."

Abdel only nodded, and Gorion asked him a simple question: "Will you come with me somewhere?"

Abdel sighed deeply. "I can't stay, father, and you know I'll have no more of your books and scrolls—"

"No, no," Gorion cut his son off with a heavy, worried laugh, "none of that. I meant somewhere outside the confines of Candlekeep. A place called the Friendly Arms."

Abdel had to laugh. Of course he'd passed through this legendary roadhouse on more than one occasion. He'd gone there a few times to find work, or wine, or women, and had never failed to find at least one of the three. What his father might want there, he couldn't hazard a guess.

"There are two people there . . . people I must meet," Gorion said, "and the road is treacherous."

"Is this something to do with my parents . . . my mother?" Abdel asked, though he had no idea why, and even tried to stop the words as they passed unbidden through his lips.

Gorion's reaction was the same as every time Abdel brought up the subject of the mother and father he never knew. The old monk was pained by the thought.

"No," Gorion said simply. Then there was a long, strained, awkward pause before he said, "Not your . . . not your mother."

He wanted to go to the Friendly Arms to meet some people who had some information for him, that was all. Gorion's life had been centered around the gathering of other people's information, so Abdel was hardly surprised by the request. He agreed, of course, since he'd probably have wandered into the Friendly Arms on his own anyway. Having his father along for company on the road would be a pleasant change of pace.

So the two of them walked out of Candlekeep together for the first time that next morning, and they'd made it well past highsun of the third day out of Candlekeep, following the wide, well-traveled Coast Way road, before finding their way blocked by a band of cutthroats.

* * * * *

Abdel rushed to the side of his fallen father at the first sudden sign of life.

It was a ragged, gurgling intake of breath, and Abdel crawled toward it like a drowning man to a floating barrel. His wounded side sending brilliant flashes of pain from his waist up to his neck and into the space behind his eyes, Abdel fell to the ground more than sat. He tried to say "Father," or something else, but the sound stuck in his throat, lodged there painfully until he thought the word itself would choke him.

His father's one remaining eye wandered, searching blindly, and his left hand fumbled in a pouch at his belt. His right hand was twitching with painful spasms, clawing at gravel as if trying to push the pain away.

"Mine—" Gorion managed to say; just that one, clear word.

"Yes," Abdel breathed, his throat tightening again to cut off any more words, and his eyes once more filling with tears at the sight of his bleeding, dying father.

"Stop it," Gorion said, again in an unbelievably clear voice. He said something else then, something Abdel couldn't make out.

The old monk's hands came up, and Abdel blearily realized he was working a spell. Gorion touched him roughly, the dying man's hand falling more than reaching to the young sellsword's side. A wave of warmth washed over Abdel's midsection, and the burning pain abated all at once. Gorion hissed out a long, pained breath and Abdel, the wound in his side now closed, almost completely healed, said, "And now you."

Gorion didn't begin another casting. "Last one," the monk croaked out.

Abdel wanted to spit his anger at his foster father for wasting his single healing prayer.

"You're dying," was all he could say.

"Stop the war . . . I'm not—"

Gorion's body shuddered with a wracking cough, and his left hand came up with a sudden jerk that made Abdel flinch. Gorion was holding a tattered scrap of parchment in his hand, and it tugged in the goosefeather-fletched quarrel still protruding from his ruined eye. The parchment picked up some blood. Abdel reached out to catch his father's hand, and Gorion let go of the parchment.

"I'm taking you back to Candlekeep," Abdel said, shifting noisily in the gravel as he made to lift Gorion in his arms.

"No," the monk grunted, stopping him. "No time. Leave me . . . come back for me . . ."

Gorion's body was seized by a shuddering wave of pain, and Abdel sighed at the sight of it.

"Your father—" then another cough. A single tear dropped from the only eye that Gorion had left to cry with, and he managed to say, "Khalid," and, "Jahi—" before his last breath hissed away and his eye turned skyward.

Abdel cried over his father until Gorion's right hand stopped twitching. The sellsword's hand brushed the parchment, and without thinking he took it in his grip. He sat there for a long time on the road, surrounded by the dead and the call of crows, until he could finally stand and begin to prepare his father's grave.

Chapter Two

Tamoko could not see what her lover saw when he stared into the empty frame. There might have been a picture in there once, perhaps a mirror of silvered glass, but now it was just a frame, hanging by small brass chains from the ceiling of Sarevok's private chamber. Sometimes he would stare at the thing for hours at a time, occasionally muttering a curse or jest to himself, or taking scribbled notes down in an expensive notebook bound in gem-encrusted leather. Tamoko could not read the language of Faerûn, was uncomfortable even with the intricate characters of her native Kozakura, so she had no idea what he was writing. She knew only that Sarevok saw things in that frame, kept track of things, kept watch on his pawns—and he had many pawns.

She sat with her legs folded on the wide, too-soft bed—a silk sack eight feet on a side stuffed with feathers—and tried to meditate. Something was prickling the back of her neck, though, and it was distracting her.

The smooth silk of Tamoko's black pajamas hissed against the silk of the bed and sent a chill of goosebumps up her thin, strong arms. She was a small woman, not even five feet tall, with the smooth skin of a pampered lady and the strength of a berserker. A life of constant training made her what she was: a killer, in every sense of the word.

She didn't bother to close her eyes, but kept her tongue

11

on her palate and concentrated on her breathing, and on the blood flowing quickly through her veins.

The room was dark and the air still, two things that normally helped her to center herself, but not today. Today the air in Sarevok's private chamber, deep in a complex of rooms few ever saw the inside of, felt heavy and dead. The steady orange candlelight, barely flickering in the still air, made her blink. The dampness made her silk garments stick to her every modest curve.

Minutes dragged on, and she continued to struggle to meditate. When Sarevok stared this intently and seemed this disappointed, it usually meant he was going to ask her to kill someone, so she would need her concentration.

"My brother," Sarevok said suddenly, so suddenly a lesser trained assassin might have flinched, but not Tamoko, "is on the path."

"Your brother?" she asked, too quickly, and Sarevok took a long, unsettling time to turn around.

"I have at least this one brother, yes," Sarevok told her in that voice she often thought was—not seductive—maybe seductive. . . .

A cold chill ran down her spine, making her angry with herself. There was something about Sarevok, to be sure, that she knew she should be on her guard about. He wasn't a man, not a human, that was certain. Even the barbarian men of Faerûn were more like her own kind than Sarevok was. She had no idea what he was, but she liked it. He wore power around him in a haze like Faerûnian women wore perfume. She could imagine him steeped in it. He was decisive and sure, not blundering about at the whim of a god, nor blindly attached to some infantile cause, nor forever in search of shiny metal disks. Sarevok wanted power—power and something else. As afraid as Tamoko sometimes felt in his presence, she couldn't help but admire him. The fact remained that when they were together, in the dark, with nothing physical coming between them, even then he could tell her only what he wanted her to know, and he never wanted her to know much. He was in control, always.

"The nature of his death?" she asked, meaning two things: that she knew she was here to kill for him, and that she was loyal enough not to ask why.

Sarevok laughed, and the sound made Tamoko smile—not because his laugh was particularly pleasant, but because it wasn't at all pleasant. Indeed, this was no mere man.

"Then he will live?" she concluded.

Sarevok continued to smile his dire wolf's smile and leaned forward, then rose and slithered onto the bed, coming slowly toward her. For the briefest fraction of a heartbeat, she wanted to back away, to escape the hard, tight, masterful embrace she knew was coming, but that was her mind's reaction. Her body's was something else entirely.

They slid together easily, and the touch was warm, welcoming, and full of the promise of danger that drew her to him in the first place, kept her coming back, and finally made her his slave. She'd killed for him ten, twelve, fifteen times—she'd allowed herself to lose count—and would easily kill a hundred more if he would look at her like that, hold her like that, move into, through her, then past her like that, just one more time.

"This one," he breathed into her ear—the sound seemed made more of heat than air— "will live . . . for a time."

He pulled away suddenly, and she heard herself gasp. She was disciplined enough to keep herself from blushing, but a twinkle in Sarevok's eye told her he noticed. Sarevok always noticed.

"The two Zhentarim," he told her, "will live for a time as well, but only for a time. I will bring them here from Nashkel."

"They have been useful to you," Tamoko said, her voice sounding small next to his, "so they shall die quickly."

Sarevok laughed again and Tamoko had to work hard to suppress a shudder. It wasn't excitement she felt this time.

"Let us not jump to any hasty conclusions, darling girl," he said. "They have the ability to fail me—especially the little one."

Chapter Three

During the days of the Avatars, the Black Lord will spawn a score of mortal progeny. These offspring will be aligned good and evil, but chaos will flow through them all. When the Murderer's bastard children come of age, they will bring havoc to the lands of the Sword Coast. One of these children must rise above the rest and claim their father's legacy. This inheritor will shape the history of the Sword Coast for centuries to come.

Nonsense.

Abdel couldn't believe it, but there it was. The sheet of stiff parchment his father had thought so important that he clutched it with his last quiver of energy in a dying hand, that he smear it with his own blood, was a disconnected bit of rambling about—what? Some dead god, maybe, if the reference to Avatars was indeed about the Time of Troubles when gods walked Toril like men, and, like men, died there.

When he'd first started to read it, over the still form of his father, Abdel had been certain it was some personal message, some secret his father had been keeping from him. When he first unfolded it and turned his still weeping gaze up to the graying sky, he thought it must have been about his mother; maybe a message from her, a letter she'd written to her infant son moments before she died, or gave him up, or sent him away, or sold him, or anything—anything that would provide some explanation for why he never knew her.

14

Instead it was just nothing, a scrap of words that formed a bit of some prophecy, that may or may not come true, but wouldn't, Abdel was sure, have anything to do with him.

"Whatever is to come to pass, old man," Abdel said to his father, just before he laid him into his shallow grave, "you won't be around to see it. Maybe I won't be either."

He wanted to say something else. He searched his mind and his heart for some prayer, for some line of verse or story, for some memory. He struggled to find words, some marker to the winds that this man had passed from its breath, but there was nothing.

The rain started as he filled dirt and gravel over the dead body of his father, and Abdel let the rain wash away his tears. When he was done he stood to his full height and turned his face up toward the cold droplets. He ran one hand through his thick black hair and closed his eyes, letting the rain wash away Gorion's grave dirt and blood.

His father had tended to the wound in his side. It had been deep, but it was now almost healed. He refused to feel the lingering pain, but it was difficult.

He wouldn't live with a wounded heart. His father was dead at the hands of bandit sellswords. Someone paid to kill him and probably paid well. It was business, that was all, but by failing to kill Abdel too, it was business left undone—left for Abdel to finish himself.

Abdel, son of Gorion, adjusted his chain mail tunic, scuffed his hard leather boots on the gravel to clear away some of the mud, shifted his shoulders to center the weight of the big broadsword that hung from his back, found a stick, and set it upright in the disturbed earth. He hung on the wet wood the tiny silver gauntlet that his father had worn on a thin gold chain around his neck, knowing some anonymous traveler would be along soon enough to steal it.

"I'll be back for you," he said, then turned his back and walked away.

* * * * *

It was impossible to tell what made the horrific sound that snatched Abdel out of a restless sleep, or how far away the source of it was, but he was on his feet in an instant.

He had buried his adopted father that day and made it to where the Way of the Lion from Candlekeep met the long, well-traveled Coast Way road. A stone marker had been erected there. Intricately carved from a solid block of granite, it had been a welcome sight when he'd seen it, days ago, on his way back to Candlekeep. Now, it was a reminder of all he had lost since then. With Gorion gone, Abdel wasn't even sure he'd be allowed back into Candlekeep.

Now there was little time for those thoughts. The sound was getting closer, and getting closer fast.

It was like a chorus of angry dogs competing for attention with a thousand bards whose tongues had been cut out so all they could do was wail and mutter, grunt and shout. The sound made Abdel afraid, and that was a rare thing.

He had to force himself back against the stone marker, so strong was his urge to slash out into the night at that fear. Abdel assumed he was in for a fight with whatever was making that godsforsaken racket. Whatever it was it sounded like a lot of somethings, and he'd have to fight as much with his mind as with his arm to make up for the odds.

The stone felt rough and wet against his back, and he realized he'd removed his chain mail tunic when he lay down to sleep. The night was dark, still overcast from the afternoon and evening's rain. Abdel set his eyes to slits to try to cut through the darkness and see what was making this noise, which was now so loud the sellsword's ears began to sting. The chorus of incoherent vocalizations threatened to drive Abdel mad with fear and rage.

He saw the whole thing first as a mass of shadow, like it was one thing, huge, moving along the ground to the south of the crossroads. The mass hit a tree—not a huge tree, but sizeable—and seemed to suck it under without hesitating. Then the mass started to take on shapes inside it, and Abdel realized to his horror and frustration that this loud gibbering mass was a horde of individual creatures—hundreds of them—that walked like men.

Abdel drew in a breath slowly, his jaw slack so he wouldn't hiss and give himself away. Though the moon was tucked behind a mantle of cloud and not a single star was visible, Abdel was thankful suddenly that he wasn't wearing his armor. A reflection might have attracted the attention of any one member of this impossible swarm and sent the entire horde in his direction. Even Abdel couldn't possibly defend himself against this tide of dark-skinned bodies. Just then Abdel saw the glint of steel among the shadows of the horde. They've got swords, he thought, they're armed with swords. This made him realize he was holding a lot of telltale steel himself, and he silently slipped the broadsword blade behind his back.

He didn't gasp when he heard he rustle of gravel behind him, on the other side of the crossroads marker. He tightened his grip on his sword and tried to think of a prayer to Torm. The sound behind him stopped, but he didn't dare turn around.

His attention behind him, Abdel didn't hear the thing approach from his left side, but he could smell it. Before he even realized what he was doing, he brought his blade back around in front of him, twisted his wrist, and slashed low across his left side. The blade met with resistance, and though Abdel couldn't see the beast in the darkness, he knew by the fact that it didn't scream that he'd killed it instantly. There was a flurry of babbling, yelling, guttural throat noises that burst into Abdel's hearing right after that though, and he realized there were more, lots more, and they'd seen him.

As much trouble as Abdel was having seeing anything but the vague outline of his enemy, the horde things seemed to have no trouble seeing him. Rusted, pitted, jagged blades slashed at Abdel and the noise was deafening. He flicked back one attack after another, killed one of the things, then another, all the time keeping his back against the stone marker.

He kept his blade slashing in front of him to make a sort of wall of steel, but the occasional slice got through. The wound in his side began to hurt again, but he had to ignore it and keep fighting. When he killed another one of the screaming, babbling things another stepped on the back of its fallen hordemate and came at Abdel anew. Abdel began to realize he was going to die that night.

There was a subtle change in the tenor of the mass sound and after a few seconds of an altogether different keening wail, the horde turned as one and came north. North, to Abdel.

Abdel kept batting them away, one after another until he was covered in blood, some of it his. It seemed like hours, like forever, but only seconds passed before a sudden burst of light blinded the sellsword.

There was no noise, no thunder, but Abdel was sure it must have been lightning striking the stone over his head. He'd had his eyes wide open, drinking in any meager scrap of light he could, when the yellow flash came out of nowhere. He screamed in pain and clenched his eyes tight. Tears streamed down his gore-spattered face, and the rhythm of his defensive slashes faltered.

The sound the horde of creatures made in reaction to the light was deafening. A thousand varieties of keening wail sent shivers through Abdel's body. It sounded like a whole village being slaughtered at the same time. They stopped attacking, and as Abdel blinked past huge amorphous blobs of purple and electric blue that filled his vision, he saw the horde retreat. The creatures—ugly, naked humanoids with sickly purple hides stretched over taut muscles and heads like distorted lions with wiry black manes—fled the light that still burned brightly, but with no heat, above Abdel's head.

Exhausted and relieved, Abdel slid down to his knees, the stone scraping through his thin chemise. He was panting, almost gasping for air, and his sword seemed to weigh a thousand pounds.

"Good enough," a reedy, gruff voice said, "ye can stop that damn light."

Abdel wanted to spring to his feet and whirl into a defensive stance against this stranger, but he just couldn't. He decided to wait until whoever spoke those words came close enough that he could kill him without standing up.

"It'll go away on its own, right?" another voice asked. "Let's get a look at our new—our new friend."

Footsteps came around the stone marker, two sets, and Abdel did manage to stand to meet them, though his chest still heaved. He closed his eyes tight again, holding his sword out in front of him with both hands. He was looking down when he opened his eyes. He saw, past smaller purple flashes this time, a pair of bare, wide feet, covered on the instep with thick, curly red hair. The boots that stood next to those feet were finely made of shiny black leather.

One of the newcomers chuckled and said, "How ye fairin', boy?"

Abdel had to laugh. He wasn't fairing very well at all.

"That's the second time this day," Abdel said, blinking his watery eyes to finally clear his vision, "that I've had to fight for my life. Do you intend to make it a third?"

"Ha!" the one with the hairy feet—Abdel could see now that he was a halfling—exclaimed. "We intend no such thing, lad."

"By all means, no," the other one—a tall, thin human draped in black robes—added. "Rest easy—rest easy."

Abdel studied these two unlikely rescuers. The halfling was odd for his kind, though he was as short, stocky, and fair of complexion as most of his race. He had a devilish quality to him, though, that Abdel had seen in a long parade of sellswords, toughs, thieves, and rogues, but not many halflings. He was wearing thick, reddish-brown leather worked into armor to protect his vitals but cut to leave his arms free. A long sword of excellent make, an imposing weapon for one as small as he, hung at his side in a gold filigreed scabbard. The halfling wriggled his pug nose and smiled back at Abdel's stare.

"G'day, young sir," he said in an odd accent that might have been—Waterdeep? Some city, Abdel was certain, which was again unusual for a halfling. "Name's Montaron, an' my travellin' companion 'ere is Xzar . . . that's 'im set that godsawful bright light up there to interrupt that little party ye were throwin'."

Abdel nodded to the halfling and turned his attention to the human. The one called Xzar was tall, thin, and twitchy. His face kept moving like there were worms under his skin, and his mouth worked as if he were talking to himself silently all the time. Every once in a while he'd twitch his head violently to one side, as if to shoo away a fly that wasn't really there.

"Gibberlings," the human said, "are not quite at all—" a twitch made him pause "—fond of light . . . at all."

"Gibberlings?" Abdel repeated, understanding that was the name of the horde of beasts. An apt name for all their incomprehensible vocalizing.

"An' ye are?" the halfling prompted.

"Abdel," he said, shifting his sword to his left hand and holding out his right. "I am Abdel . . . son of Gorion."

Montaron took Abdel's hand, and his grip was firm. He smirked a little, as if at some private joke. Xzar rubbed nervously at his own face, absentmindedly tracing lines around the rather prominent tattooed mask surrounding his eyes. When the halfling's hand fell away, Abdel turned his open palm to Xzar, but the human twitched away from it and made a quarter turn as if to wander off.

"Ye'll 'ave to excuse my friend, there," the halfling said, nodding to Xzar, "'e's not the friendliest sort, but 'em casties he does makes 'im might 'andy in a pinch."

Abdel thought nothing of it. This Xzar was a strange one, but he'd met stranger.

"I should thank you," Abdel said to the halfling.

"Aye, ye should," Montaron chuckled, "if ye 'ad any manners. I don't myself, so tend not to expect 'em in others. This road ain't an easy walk. Maybe we could offer ye a chance to return the favor, eh?"

"I'm bound for the Friendly Arms," Abdel said, raising his eyebrows to wait for a response.

Xzar grunted, but Montaron only continued to smile blankly.

"Ye'll find more work in Nashkel," the halfling said.

"Nashkel?"

"Aye—" Montaron started when suddenly it was dark again.

The magical light went out all at once and seemed to take the sound of the receding horde of humanoids with it.

"Thank the Lord o' Three Crowns," Montaron said, his voice suddenly edged with a surprising glee, "I was beginning to think that would never fade away. Things are clearer in the dark, ain't they Abdel?"

The sellsword only blinked, hoping not to go blind from all the sudden changes in lighting.

"Anyway," Montaron added, "there's work fer the taking in Nashkel."

"I have business at the Friendly Arms."

"So ye're not in need o' work?"

Abdel was, in fact, quite in need of work, but promises had been made, and there was this Khalid and another waiting for Gorion at the Friendly Arms. The gnome-run roadhouse was three days' travel to the north, and Nashkel was a full tenday in the opposite direction.

"What kind of work?" Abdel asked.

"The kind o' work I'm guessing ye're in," the halfling said, "an' lot's o' it. Word around the campfires is there's some trouble in the mines there."

"I have to go to the Friendly Arms first," Abdel said flatly. "There are people waiting for me there, but I will be in need of work."

"So the roadhouse first, then?" Xzar asked matter-of-factly, and in the darkness Abdel couldn't tell if the mage was talking to him or to the halfling.

Montaron solved the problem by answering, "Aye, the Friendly Arms first, then Nashkel. I could use a night's sleep in a real bed anyway."

Chapter Four

After spending three days with Montaron and Xzar on the road to the Friendly Arms, Abdel had to admit he kind of liked the gruff halfling. The little guy was odd, to be sure. He would complain incessantly all day that the sunlight was too bright, even though the sky was overcast and dull gray most of the time. His aversion to light was sometimes silly, other times it was disturbing. Montaron seemed amused by his human companion, Xzar, and often teased him by tossing pebbles and twigs at the tall mage's head as they walked.

Abdel was ready to do more than tease Xzar. Abdel was beginning to think about killing him. As the halfling joked, and the mage pontificated, and the hours dragged on, Abdel would devise elaborate plans to murder Xzar, just to pass the time.

Xzar had a way of speaking that confused and irritated Abdel. He would rearrange and repeat words for no good reason, would remain silent when he should speak and speak when he had nothing useful to say. The mage twitched literally all the time, and though Abdel felt sorry for the obviously disturbed man at first, eventually he couldn't think about anything but how much he wanted to slap him.

He was able to ignore the twitchy mage for the first day's walk, but when they'd settled into camp, Xzar told him the one thing Abdel always wanted to hear.

"I know," Xzar told him, "who your father—your father is."

Abdel sat up straight and Montaron, who had been chuckling happily in the darkness went suddenly bone still.

"What did you say?" Abdel asked, the only way he could think of to ask the man to continue.

"Xzar," Montaron started, then just said, "Xzar. . . ." again.

"Your father," the mage said to Abdel, ignoring the halfling, "your father was—"

"*Enough!*" Montaron said sharply, and the mage spun to lock eyes with him. "Can't ye see the boy's a mite sensitive 'bout that?"

"How would you know this?" Abdel asked Xzar, ignoring the halfling. "You don't even know me. You don't know who I am, how could you know my father?"

Montaron reached out and put a hand on Xzar's forearm. The mage jerked away violently.

"He should be happy," Xzar said to no one in particular, "he should be happy to be the son of a god—of a god."

Abdel sighed. The man was insane.

"I am the son of a god?" Abdel asked, anger making his voice tight and quiet.

"Oh," the mage said, his voice dripping condescension, "oh, yes, oh, yes, you most certainly are."

"My friend," the halfling said to Abdel, "is obviously a madman, but 'e can make fire shoot from 'is fingertips, so I keep 'im around."

"Shut your . . ." Xzar scolded, ". . . your . . . your—he's the son of Bhaal."

Abdel sighed again and lay down to go to sleep. Xzar muttered to himself for a little while, his voice eventually fading into the sound of the crickets.

"I buried my father," Abdel said, more for himself than for the delusional mage or the halfling, "the only father I'll ever need, the day I met you two. He was no god, and neither am I."

"An' what if ye were?" Montaron asked, his voice soft on

the night's quiet breeze.

Abdel looked up at him, and even in the darkness he could tell the halfling's face was set, serious. This made Abdel laugh.

"I'd wish myself a thousand times a thousand pieces of gold, for one," Abdel answered. This made Montaron laugh. "I'd drop the Sword Coast into the sea just to see it sink and make zombies of everyone who ever spoke ill of me."

"Make me lord o' Waterdeep?" the halfling joked.

"Aye," Abdel said, mimicking Montaron's peculiar brogue, "ye'll be king o' the world."

The two of them laughed, and when Montaron finally settled down to sleep he said, "Sometimes, lad, things 'ave a way o' surprisin' ye."

"Yes," Abdel said, yawning, "they do at that."

* * * * *

Abdel had visited the Friendly Arms over half a dozen times in the past several years, but the sight of it always surprised him. It had been a rather well-built fortress in its day, constructed by a cult of the now-dead god Bhaal. The story was that the band of gnomes who ran the place had run afoul of the cultists, and after years of fighting back and forth the gnomes drove the Bhaal-worshipers out. This seemed unlikely to Abdel, though, as he'd met a few gnomes in his day and found it difficult to believe that people who barely reached his knee could drive anyone out of anywhere.

Abdel didn't know anything about this god Bhaal, but if it was true that his worshipers were driven out of such an imposing stone fortress by these tiny forest folk . . . well, no wonder the god didn't survive the Time of Troubles.

Xzar's delusional ramblings weren't lost on Abdel either. The fact that the mage had used Bhaal as the focus of his fantasies about Abdel's parentage must have meant that Xzar had heard the story of the origin of the Friendly Arms as well. If they'd been in the Dalelands his father might have been Elminster, or maybe he should move to Evermeet and take on Corellon Larethian as his sire.

The Friendly Arms was a little village as much as it was a fortress. Within the high curtain walls of gray stone was a collection of buildings devoted to any number of purposes but all serving travelers in one way or another.

Abdel and his two companions approached the front gate and a heavy wooden drawbridge was lowered over a moat. Coming in from the south they could see that the moat didn't make it all the way around the keep yet, and there were teams of diggers and other laborers halfheartedly wandering about. The moat was a new addition, then, and certainly more for show than for defense. The Friendly Arms never locked its gate, and everyone was welcome inside, so the likelihood of siege was hardly pressing.

They passed over the drawbridge and made their way with no wasted time from the pillared entrance to one of the biggest buildings in the broad, open bailey. Even if Abdel had never been there before, the sound of revelry leaking into the early evening air would have told him that this was the inn proper. It was a long walk to the high oaken door, and as they crossed the bailey they passed a group of gnome guards. The sight of the tiny fighters made Abdel smile. The three guards, each no taller than two and a half feet, were dressed in fancy but functional ring mail. Their short swords were smaller and no doubt lighter than Abdel's dagger. One was holding a spear from which fluttered the banner of the Friendly Arms, less heraldry than advertising. The three little men nodded to Abdel and returned his smile, then turned their attention abruptly to the inn.

Abdel noticed a sudden change in the tavern sounds. Montaron stopped too and held out a hand to gently block Xzar.

The mage twitched away and shouted, "Stop *touching* me!"

"Shhh," the halfling warned as the gnome guards began moving slowly toward the inn.

There were pauses in the steady sound of laughter and frivolity, that was what first alerted the guards, then came loud cheers, a crash, and breaking glass followed by a loud grunt.

Montaron laughed and said, "Sounds like my kind o' place!"

The three travelling companions followed the gnome guards to the door. Abdel stood behind the gnomes as one of them opened the door, and he was hit with the blast of sound from inside just a fraction of a second before the chair hit him in the face. Down the big sellsword went, never seeing the three little gnomes wade into the crowd. The guards' fists were small, but when they brought them into play at their own eye level, taller men dropped like sacks of flour.

Abdel, angry, bleeding from the nose, stood up, grabbed the broken chair, and surveyed the dark room full of doubled-over men. He gave up hope of finding the one who threw the chair, but he gave the room an icy glare all the same. Laughter started, and Abdel turned red before he realized they weren't laughing at him but at the man being carried out by the three gnomes. They were dragging the dirty, vile-smeiling commoner more than carrying him, and the big man made a small sound every time his head bounced against the rough wooden planks of the floor.

Abdel looked at the now unconscious man with undisguised fury as he was dragged past. Montaron grabbed the chair when he saw Abdel jerk forward.

"Leave 'im," the halfling said. "Looks like 'e's paid in full."

Abdel stood stock still and tried to let the anger pass, but it wouldn't. He wanted to kill someone. Montaron was looking at him curiously.

"See?" Xzar stage-whispered.

The halfling pushed the mage away and pulled gently on the chair. Abdel let him take it.

"Ye'll be needin' a drink," he said, and Abdel nodded.

A gnome woman climbed up on top of the bar and called to the room, "Next one throws a chair gets my fist in his danglies. This—" and she paused long enough to belch resoundingly— "is a class establishment."

A cheer followed this warning, and the crowded room fell back into the general chaos of a night at the Friendly Arms.

* * * * *

The ale was good, and after three pints of it Abdel was starting to relax. He sat at the bar and kept his head down, ignoring the tussle and bluster of the ever more crowded barroom. He'd not spoken since he'd been hit by the chair, and though his nose hadn't bled much, he refused to wipe the blood away. The big sellsword was quite a sight. He'd been rude and sullen enough that Montaron soon left his side, disappearing quickly into a crowd that naturally towered over the little halfling. Xzar was easier to get rid of, the mage having found a dark booth, in a corner, in which to sit and mutter to himself.

Abdel didn't do much thinking, he just sat there and drank. He wasn't one for self-pity, but it had been Nine Hells of a tenday. The thought of leaving again in the morning with the halfling and that damnable muttering mage didn't appeal to him in the slightest. His purse was light, though, and not getting any heavier. The trip to Nashkel, if he took it, would be a lean one. He'd decided to let Montaron and Xzar go on their way without him, decided to look for some paying job here at the Friendly Arms, when he remembered why he'd come here in the first place. Gorion, with his dying breath, had sent him here to look for—and Abdel couldn't remember the names.

"Damn it all to the Abyss," he mumbled to himself. "What does it matter anyway?"

Abdel ordered a fourth pint from the pleasantly gruff gnome woman who was tending the bar. He'd paid her every time from a dwindling supply of coppers.

"Nah," the gnome told him when he slid another four copper pieces across the wet bar, "this one's for the smack on the beak."

Abdel nodded, accepting the woman's drink, then accepting the wet rag she held out to him. He wiped the blood off his face and allowed himself a short laugh when he realized the gnome woman hadn't gone away but was just standing there staring at him.

"You should put a window in that door," he said, "so a guest can see what's coming before he opens it."

The gnome laughed, said, "I'll pass the suggestion along," while waiting for him to finish the pint in one swallow, standing ready with a fifth pint. This time she took his copper.

"Well met, good sir," a richly Amnian-accented voice next to him said.

Abdel turned slightly to his right and glared at the lean Amnian with a look that would give the man no illusions that his company was welcome. The Amnian flinched at the stare.

"You are Abdel," he said, "Abdel Adrian."

"Gods," Abdel breathed, was this the man Gorion had come to see?

"You are," the Amnian said. "Where is Gorion?"

"Dead," Abdel said simply, then his throat caught, but he didn't cry. "Who is this Adrian?"

"You are not Abdel Adrian?" the Amnian asked.

"I am Abdel, son of Gorion, but I go by no other name."

The Amnian's response to this was simply a puzzled stare. The man was obviously a half-elf. His long, thin face and ears just barely too round to be called pointed would have been proof enough of that, but the bright violet of his eyes was a sure sign of elf blood. The human part of him was surely Amnian; he had a large, long nose and dusky olive skin. He was dressed as if for battle, in dented armor that he was obviously uncomfortable in. He was wearing a helmet, which, considering the surroundings, seemed a wise idea. His lips curled and twitched. He was nervous.

"You have come here to meet me, though," the Amnian said. "I am Khalid."

That was it. Khalid—the last word his father spoke as

his life drained from his punctured eye, then Abdel remembered that there was another.

"Jah," he said, "I was to meet Khalid and Jah."

"Jaheira, yes," Khalid said, grinning ear-to-ear, but still nervous, "she is my wife. She is here."

The Amnian turned instinctively toward a table on the other side of the room, but the crowd blocked his view.

"Come," he said, "sit with us, and tell us what befell your father. He was a great man, a hero in his own way, and he will be missed."

"What do you know of it?" Abdel asked, bile suddenly rising to the back of his throat. His voice was full of menace. "What was he to you?"

Khalid stared at Abdel as if the sellsword had suddenly transformed into a cobra. He was scared of Abdel, and he was not at all able to hide it.

"He was a friend," Khalid answered, "that is all. I mean no disrespect."

Abdel wanted to say something rude to the Amnian, but he couldn't. Instead he fished in his pouch for money for a sixth pint of ale. He came out with only three coppers.

"*Bhaal!*" he cursed loudly, stood, and threw the coppers into the crowd.

A drunk somewhere muttered something mildly offensive after having been clipped on the temple by one of the hard thrown copper coins. Abdel shot to attention, and more than one man, even innocent ones, scurried off to darker corners. Sweat broke out visibly on Khalid's upper lip.

"Gods," the Amnian said, "what did he tell you?"

Abdel looked down at the Amnian but said nothing.

"I will be happy to buy you a drink," Khalid said. "Please, come with me. We don't want any more attention do we?"

Abdel grunted and let himself be led through the crowd. He caught sight of Montaron for only the briefest of moments. The halfling was holding a silk purse, and Abdel was sure the little man winked at him.

Abdel took a couple of deep breaths to try to calm himself,

and when Khalid said, "Here she is," Abdel looked up, and his breath caught.

Jaheira was beautiful. Half-elf like her mate, she too must have had a human parent from Amn. The two looked oddly alike, but both the elf and human sides favored Jaheira the more. Her face was wide and dark, her lips full, and her eyes bright—nearly the same violet as Khalid's—and they sparkled with intelligence. Her face was framed in thick hair that might have been black if she were all human, but her elf blood highlighted it with streaks of fiery copper. Even though she sat, Abdel could tell she was strong of build, rugged even. She wore a bodice of hard leather that was scratched from what might have been blade strikes. She was armored.

When her eyes caught his, he saw rather than heard her gasp. Abdel sat without looking at the chair. He couldn't pull his eyes away from hers, and she did nothing to discourage him. Her full lips twitched like her husband's. She was nervous too, and though Abdel would never come between a man and his wife, he couldn't help hoping that she was nervous for different reasons than Khalid was.

"Why was I sent here?" Abdel asked them both, though he continued to look at Jaheira. "My father didn't live to tell me."

"How did Gorion die?" Jaheira asked.

"Sellswords," Abdel said, "like me. We were ambushed on the Way of the Lion. I killed the men who attacked us but not soon enough."

"There are forces that didn't want us to meet," Khalid said, "Gorion knew that. It was . . ." the Amnian hesitated, and Abdel thought he might be lying, "it was why Gorion wanted you to come with him to meet us."

"My father was a monk," Abdel said, "a priest, a man of letters and such. What could he have been caught up in that would set such forces against him? What are you people about?"

Abdel was growing angry again. He hadn't been able to blame the mercenaries for Gorion's death. Those men were just doing what he himself had done all his adult life. Someone had paid them, and it took real money to hire five experienced killers for a wilderness ambush.

"There are . . . forces," Jaheira said, her voice barely audible in the crowded room, "who want to bring war."

A comely servant girl set down two pints of ale. Abdel kept his eyes on Jaheira as he downed his, again in one swallow.

"So what else is new?" he asked sarcastically. "I've made a living from one 'force' or another wanting war. It's what people do."

Jaheira was sincerely confused by his last statement, but when she turned a questioning gaze on her husband, Abdel knew she was asking something else, something more important and more frightening to her. Khalid nodded, and Jaheira turned back to Abdel.

"This is different," she said, her voice even quieter, and Abdel had to strain to hear her. "This is your bro—"

A glass bottle disintegrated against the back of Abdel's head, and Jaheira had to flinch away from the shards of glass. Abdel didn't bother to wipe the residual wine off the back of his head or pick the glass from his black hair. He stood up and turned, and the crowd parted as if they were puppets attached to his joints. At the door, a far throw away, was the man who'd been dragged out by the three gnome guards. The chair thrower.

The big, stinky man was so drunk he could barely stand. Abdel stared hard at him, and the world around him seemed to slip away into blurred, echoing inconsequence.

Abdel heard only the drunk, who said bluntly, "What."

The sellsword's dagger flashed across the room like a sliver from a lightning bolt, and Abdel's blood rushed through his head at the heavy *thunk* of the wide silver blade burying itself in the drunk's chest. The force of it knocked the man over, and though he twitched once, then a second time, he was dead before his head hit the floor.

Abdel smiled and let the ecstasy of the kill wash away the anger and tunnel vision. When he came out of whatever trance it was he'd found himself in, it was as if the inn had plunged into pandemonium.

Khalid pushed him from behind and said something like, "What have you done?"

Inn patrons scattered, and serving wenches dropped their trays, spattering ale and wine over the fleeing or stunned revelers. Strangely, the serving girls advanced on Abdel, and he thought for a moment that it might be true what they said—that the serving girls here were really golems in disguise. Abdel smiled broader still. He didn't care.

"Wait!" called a familiar voice.

The gnome woman at the bar let out a shrill whistle, and the serving girls stopped. Even Abdel paused as he went for the sword at his back. The voice had been Montaron's.

"Thief!" the halfling called again.

Montaron was kneeling over the body of the drunk and producing one purse after another from the dead man's pants.

"He must have been picking pockets all ni—here's mine!" Montaron said, his voice loud enough for everyone in the room to hear.

"Fortunate for you," Khalid whispered to a still uncaring Abdel. "It would have been murder otherwise."

Gooseflesh whispered up the backs of Abdel's arms at the sound of that word: murder. He shook his head and approached the halfling, Khalid and Jaheira following closely.

"We'd better be goin'," Montaron said when Abdel was close enough that only he could hear the halfling's whisper.

"Aye," Abdel said. "My dagger."

Montaron smiled weakly and handed the wide-bladed knife to Abdel. No blood dripped from it, though Abdel didn't even remember seeing Montaron pull it out of the man's chest, let alone wipe the blood away. Even drunk, reeling from the kill, Abdel admired Montaron's finesse.

The sellsword was only barely sober enough to realize he wouldn't find work here now, even if the drunk was a thief, and he'd thrown his last three coppers to the crowd.

"Nashkel?" Abdel asked.

"Yes," Khalid said, his voice edged with incredulity, "yes, Nashkel. Gorion knew that was where we were planning to go?"

Abdel turned to look down at the Amnian, then to the halfling who was regarding Khalid with a face like a stone mask. Khalid returned the stare with a questioning glance.

Xzar came out of nowhere and said, "Five, then? Who are they, these two?"

Inn patrons started making advances toward the purses now displayed against the bloody chest of the dead drunk, and Abdel let himself be both pulled and pushed out of the inn. He smiled, though he wanted to cry. For his sins, he would let himself be pulled and pushed all the way to Nashkel.

Chapter Five

"We won't be the only ones trying to help," Jaheira told Abdel as they walked the seemingly endless miles to Nashkel.

"I'd say not," Montaron piped in.

Jaheira spun on the stout halfling, obviously not appreciating this intrusion any more than she'd appreciated the numerous others from both Montaron and Xzar over the last seven and a half days.

Montaron only smiled at her and said, "Sun's bright t'day, eh girl?"

Abdel pretended not to see the fire of warning in the halfling's eyes. Abdel was confident that Montaron was smart enough to keep his hands off Jaheira.

"This iron shortage," Jaheira continued, trying to ignore Montaron, "could well lead to war between my people and yours."

Abdel stopped, and the others hesitated in their steps, but all except Jaheira continued on.

"My people?" Abdel asked. He turned to face Jaheira, and it was the first time in the days since they'd met at the Friendly Arms that he'd looked her in the eye. Abdel, unsure of himself in many ways, was nervous around this strong, beautiful woman, and it embarrassed him. They were traveling with her husband.

"Amn, and . . ." she stopped, realizing she wasn't sure where he was from. "Gorion was from Candlekeep. He raised you as his son there, yes?"

"He did," Abdel said, again embarrassed though he didn't quite know why.

"Then perhaps . . ." she started again. "Well, a war between Amn and Baldur's Gate, for one . . . with Candlekeep caught in the middle."

"Candlekeep can take care of itself," Abdel stated simply. He turned and started walking again, but slowly, allowing Jaheira to stay at his side.

They were several paces behind their companions now, and Abdel surveyed the unlikely crew. Xzar kept swatting at something though there were few if any insects about. The mage muttered to himself constantly, though since Jaheira had joined them, Abdel was distracted enough by her not to be troubled by Xzar. Montaron would glance back at them from time to time, apparently feeling left out or, for reasons known only to himself, afraid. Khalid walked purposefully onward and spoke little. When he had spoken over the last seven and a half days it was about what he called "the mission."

Abdel, Montaron, and Xzar were headed for Nashkel to seek work guarding the iron mines there. For Jaheira and Khalid, there seemed to be some more noble cause, and as much as the woman tried to turn Abdel's heart to it, he just couldn't understand her urgency.

"Men fight," he told her, ignoring her grunt of protest. "Amn and Baldur's Gate, Amn and Tethyr, Tethyr and Tethyr . . . it is the way of things, the way I make a living."

Jaheira sighed and said, "It doesn't have to be."

"It doesn't have to be what?" He asked, smiling, "The way of things, or the way I make a living?"

Montaron laughed from in front of them, and Abdel realized the halfling could hear them. This made Abdel smile.

"Someone is deliberately sabotaging the iron supply at Nashkel and other mines," Jaheira pressed, though something in her tone made it clear she'd say a little more, then let it rest until at least the next day. They were still more than half a tenday north of Nashkel.

Montaron stopped and, smiling, turned around. "An' what o' that, fair Jaheira," the halfling asked. "Let 'em sabotage away, I say, an' when we get there, we'll find the culprit an' turn 'im in fer a great, 'uge reward."

Jaheira didn't even acknowledge Montaron as she passed.

"Reward?" Abdel asked.

"Sure, lad," Montaron said, clapping the big sellsword on the forearm, "what'd ye think we were walkin' fer a tenday an' three fer, justice?"

Jaheira spun on the halfling and spat, "What would you know of justice, thief?"

Montaron's eyes hardened for just a fraction of a second, and Jaheira took a step back. As if sensing the confrontation, Khalid stopped and turned but made no move to approach. Abdel kept his eyes on the halfling.

"Easy, lass," Montaron said, chuckling. "It's all just business, ain't it?"

"And what business are you in, Montaron?" she asked.

"If ye're talkin' about those purses at the Friendly Arms," he said jovially, "maybe ye should thank me fer gettin' the boy out o' there."

"Getting the boy out o' there?" Khalid asked, his voice nearly lost to the breeze and a squawking crow.

Montaron looked at him and smiled.

"Sure," he said, "an' us all."

"Sleep lightning," Xzar suddenly shouted, "lightning sleep."

Abdel, Montaron, Jaheira, and Khalid all looked in the direction of the babbling mage. Xzar was nearly fifty yards ahead of them now, obviously oblivious to the conversation. Abdel laughed first and Montaron, then Khalid joined him, but a silent Jaheira was the first to march off after Xzar.

"Thank you for that, by the way," Abdel said to Montaron.

"Not at all, kid," Montaron said, "ye'll repay me, I'm sure."

They'd passed through Beregost on their way from the
Friendly Arms, even slept in real beds at an inn Montaron
insisted on paying for. Their stay there seemed all too short,
even for Abdel, who was as used to sleeping under the stars
as inside, and it was a relief for all of them when they
finally entered the mining town of Nashkel.

Abdel didn't know if it was good luck or bad that there
seemed to be some kind of festival going on in a fallow field
outside town. On their way south he'd heard nothing but
bad news from Jaheira and Khalid—even from Montaron—
that made him think Nashkel would have been some kind
of ghost town by the time they got there. The image he'd
formed of it in his mind had been one of desperate miners
begging on the street, shops and other businesses closed,
families loading carts to head for greener pastures, and the
sort of morose drunkenness he'd seen in too many Sword
Coast taverns.

Instead the small town was alive with color. Carts were
set up in every available space, and traveling merchants
were showing their wares. Three men in parti-colored
clothes were juggling flaming torches, a gnome was playing
a rousing tune on what looked like a cross between bag-
pipes and a caravan wagon, and healthy children were running everywhere, apparently no worse for wear. There were
soldiers in the street, dressed in the colors of Amn.

Montaron nudged Abdel and drew the sellsword's attention to a small group of young women the halfling apparently found attractive.

"I'd like to investigate their mines, eh kid?" the halfling
joked, then nearly doubled over laughing.

Abdel was pretty sure he knew what the little thief
meant, but he didn't reply.

Jaheira grunted and said to the halfling, "When this
town is overrun by soldiers, women like that will be very
busy."

"Women like that," Montaron said, "are always busy.

Besides, not many more Amnian soldiers'll waste their time here."

"You sound like you'd be happy to see them march north, halfling," Jaheira said. "Maybe you already know what is wrong here."

Montaron laughed, but the sound had an edge to it that Abdel had been hearing more and more often in the last thirteen days.

"I know nothin', girl," Montaron told her, "less even than ye, if all this talk o' war is true."

"Someone wants blood to spill in Baldur's Gate and Amn," Jaheira said, "that I know."

"An' what if it's an Amnian wantin' it, girl?" Montaron asked, a crafty look curling the side of his mouth. "Will ye be so dead set to stop it then?"

Jaheira inhaled sharply and was about to say something when she stopped abruptly and turned on Abdel. He was trying not to laugh, and it showed.

"This is very serious," she said.

Abdel smiled and nodded.

"We should find an inn," Khalid said, purposefully breaking into the deteriorating conversation. "We can get a good night's sleep and head to the mines in the morning."

Jaheira nodded and followed him into a crowd of festival goers. Abdel watched her walk away, and Montaron noticed him noticing her. The halfling disappeared into the crowd.

"We will go, son of Bhaal," Xzar said, startling Abdel.

The sellsword turned on the wiry mage and said, "Go with Khalid, mage."

Xzar hesitated, and Abdel reached for his arm.

"*Touch* me!" Xzar shrieked. "Don't touch me!"

Two dozen or more people stopped what they were doing and turned to look at Abdel, though it was Xzar who was obviously insane. Abdel sighed, trying to breathe out his desire to kill the twitching mage, then just walked away.

* * * * *

Abdel knew where they all went, but he didn't go with them to the inn. He'd worked and traveled with others before, some of whom he liked and some of whom he didn't. He'd traveled with women before, but none who moved him like Jaheira. He'd met a thousand men like Khalid, he reckoned, quiet, serious types on a mission. Montaron, halfling or otherwise, was a dime a dozen on the Sword Coast; a crafty survivor who knew what was in every pocket and behind every locked door—or would know, eventually. Xzar was a puzzle. He'd met madmen before, too, he figured, but this one was mad and highly intelligent at the same time— delusional and capable of wielding magic.

He wandered the festival grounds and wondered what he was doing there. He'd followed two chance-met strangers—no, four chance-met strangers—on a mission he didn't even understand and certainly wasn't going to be paid for. Montaron seemed to be able to steal enough to keep them at inns and buy an ale or two, but that was not the way Abdel wanted to see the world. He was capable of working for his keep, and he wanted to do just that. Still, there was this problem in the mines—or was there?

At first the festival did a good job of masking the problems that were becoming more obvious to Abdel as he walked on. There were merchant carts, sure, and the people of Nashkel were stopping to look, but almost no one was buying. The men looked nervous and the women serious.

"They're pourin' ale," Montaron said from behind Abdel, "are ye with me?"

Abdel turned, as amused as he was amazed at the halfling's ability to appear and disappear at will in crowds. Abdel would never understand what it was like to be two feet shorter than everyone around him—his problem was just the opposite.

"There is something wrong, isn't there?" Abdel asked.

"If ye mean with the iron mines," Montaron answered, "aye."

"So where is our employer? Who pays us to protect these mines?"

Montaron smiled and shrugged.

"We'll go to the mines tomorrow an' find out. In the meantime," the halfling said, producing a worn leather pouch from a pocket inside his shirt, " 'ere's a bit o' coin. While away this festival a bit, then join me at the inn fer an ale er seven."

"I can't take that money."

"It's been feedin' ye since the Friendly Arms," Montaron reminded him, not expecting Abdel to feel guilty. "Take it an' see what ye can find—fer the common good."

The halfling nodded at a particular merchant's cart, laughed, and disappeared into the crowd once more. Abdel studied the cart and its proprietor. The man was dressed like a Calishite, but his features were decidedly northern. He'd be from Waterdeep, maybe Luskan, Abdel guessed, and was selling a collection of glass and silver vials—perfumes maybe.

The merchant noticed Abdel looking at him and spread a huge, gap-toothed grin across his face in a practiced greeting.

"Potions," the man called, his accent proving Abdel right about his northern heritage, "elixirs, drafts, and ointments for every ill and every eventuality."

Abdel approached, the little purse still in his hand jingling with the weight of coin.

"Ah, my good sir," the merchant said, "I see you have a need."

Abdel was legitimately confused by this and said, "Indeed? And what need have I?"

The merchant laughed, "You fight," he said, then looked Abdel up and down appreciatively, "and fight well, to be sure. You will guard yourself well but still fall victim to the lucky stab or slash here and there, I'm sure. One sip of this" —he lifted a plain silver vial from the collection spread across his cart— "and you'll be feeling no pain."

"Four coppers an ale will do the same."

"Ah," the merchant said, his smile not faltering for a moment, "ah yes indeed, sir, but in the morning the cut is still there—treated only with ale that is—but this beauty will make it all go away. The secret is lost to the ages, but it can be yours, for a price."

"The secret or the draft?"

"Ah, the draft, of course, sir," the merchant said, then glanced at the little pouch in Abdel's big hand, "unless you've a bigger purse elsewhere."

Abdel laughed and came closer still. He asked about some of the other vials and heard tales no sane man would believe. There was something about this act of haggling with some over-cheerful merchant that settled Abdel. He'd been as taut of nerve the last tenday and a half as he'd ever been in his life. Everything had changed abruptly but still seemed to be moving so slowly.

"Acid?" Abdel asked, not understanding the word.

"Aye, good sellsword, aye," the merchant said. "This is a dangerous concoction indeed—like liquid fire it burns—a creation of the mad geniuses of Netheril, for sale today for what an honest man such as yourself can afford."

Exactly what an honest man could afford ended up being a matter of some debate, and it was nearly an hour before Abdel walked back into the crowd with the small leather pouch now containing a small silver vial, a slightly larger glass one, and four coppers.

Chapter Six

"Oh, please, girl," Montaron whined, "I ain't gonna poison ye, fer Urogalan's sake."

Jaheira only grunted in response, but Khalid reached for the wineskin the halfling was offering. He held it gingerly to his nose as if it might explode.

The Amnian sniffed, then shrugged and said, "Smells like ale."

"An' ale it is, my friend," Montaron said. "Go ahead . . . fer luck's sake."

Khalid smiled and looked at both Xzar and Abdel. The mage and the sellsword had each downed sizeable quaffs of Montaron's special ale, and both were still standing, none the worse for wear.

"Khalid—" Jaheira started to say but stopped when Khalid lifted the skin to his lips and drank. He held the liquid in his mouth for a second or two before swallowing, then closed his eyes as it slid down.

When he opened them again, he said, "Go ahead, Jaheira, make the halfling happy. Maybe there is something to rituals like these."

"We're goin' into Oghma only knows what 'ere, girl," Montaron added, "an' a little luck won't 'urt ye."

"Lucky ale," Jaheira scoffed but took the skin and drank from it quickly, just wanting to get it over with.

"Can we go now?" Abdel asked, itching around the collar of his chain mail tunic.

They'd been walking all morning from Nashkel and hadn't made it to the mines yet. Montaron stopped them where a thin strip of brown mud led off from the main path. He claimed it was a shortcut, and that it would get them to the mines in no time. Drinking "lucky ale" was a silly ritual he claimed to have observed whenever his path led toward danger. Abdel drank right after Xzar, giving it no second thought. He'd seen stranger good luck charms in his day. Now he was just anxious to get on to the mines.

Jaheira gave the halfling his wineskin back, and the five of them headed down the path. The coarse grass that bordered the main path gave way to a deep field of black wildflowers. The field was solid with them, and though Abdel never noticed things like flowers, there was something about these that struck him as strange. They were all so alike, and there were so many of them, and there was something about them that just seemed out of place.

"Follow me very carefully, all," Montaron said, his voice low and serious.

"For luck?" Jaheira teased. "Or are you afraid of damaging the pretty flowers."

Abdel leaned down to pick one. He meant to give it to Jaheira, even imagined gently sliding it behind one of her slim, pointed ears, brushing back her jet black hair and—

"This is your garden," Khalid said, breaking into Abdel's thoughts and making him stop, "isn't it Montaron?"

Abdel flushed and straightened, embarrassed, but no one saw.

"There're dangers all about, my Amnian friend," Montaron replied. "Even in a field o' pretty black flowers, though they might be a bit less temptin' in the dark."

The halfling was silent for a moment, walking carefully with his eyes glued to the ground in front of him. He was leading them through the field of flowers in a twisting, nonsensical path. The uniformity of the patch of flowers, the color, and the sighing of the breeze through them had a calming effect on all five of them. Abdel forgot his embarrassment, Xzar didn't swat at unseen bugs or talk to himself, and

Khalid and Jaheira even followed the halfling, saying nothing.

"Damn sun," Montaron said, breaking the silence.

Abdel looked up and saw for the first time that an old, dilapidated farmhouse stood in the center of the field of black flowers. It was a simple structure, paneled in wood that still showed the splintering gray of what was once a bright coat of whitewash. The roof sagged, and moss grew on it. The shutters had come off the windows, maybe years ago, leaving only shadows in the whitewash to mark that they'd been there at all. The windows were just squares of black.

Abdel sighed at the sight of the house. A family's house, he thought, a family once lived there.

"Gods!" Montaron exclaimed and drew up short. The others stopped. Jaheira actually bumped into Abdel's back, and he flinched away from the contact. When he looked back to say something to the woman, he met her husband's eyes instead. Khalid smirked, then looked away, and Abdel flushed again.

"What is it?" the sellsword asked Montaron, hoping to cover his embarrassment.

"A body," Xzar said simply, "a body that is dead."

Abdel squinted and stepped forward, crushing a couple of the flowers. Montaron flinched when he saw that, and Abdel ignored the halfling, who stared at him for the next several minutes as if expecting some change to come over him. Abdel looked down at the body at Montaron's feet. The man had been dead for days, but there was still very little decay. There were no flies, which was what Abdel thought most peculiar. A body laying dead in the open for days tended to attract flies. The dead man was human, dressed in the simple ring mail of an inexperienced mercenary or a common foot soldier. The man's eyes were white, going to gray-green. His tongue was sticking out, swollen and black. There was no blood or obvious wounds.

"What killed this man?" Abdel asked, not really expecting an answer.

"Poison, yes?" Xzar offered, avoiding eye contact with

Abdel, as always.

Abdel nodded, seeing the truth in it. Montaron knelt over the man and started running his hands along the dead soldier's belt.

"Montaron!" Jaheira gasped. "Leave him in peace, can't you?"

"She's right, Montaron," Abdel said. "Leave him."

Montaron ignored them, standing and turning around only when he'd found something.

"Keys?" Abdel asked when he saw what the halfling was holding in his hands. There was a whole set of them, half a dozen big brass keys on a simple iron ring.

"If you can find out where this man lived," Khalid said, sneering, "you'll be a rich man for sure, thief."

Montaron smiled and looked over his shoulder at the collapsing farmhouse.

"Close enough?" he said.

A chill ran down Abdel's spine at the thought of the thief gobbling up what memories might be left in that perfect house, that house he should have grown up in. The sellsword shook his head, trying to shake these odd, weak, melancholy thoughts loose. He caught Xzar's eye and returned the mage's knowing smirk with a curl of his lip.

Abdel snatched the keys violently from Montaron's grip and squeezed them in his big, callused hand until he thought they might puncture his skin.

"Leave it," Abdel said, "and him. We started this trip by heading for the mines, and now we're going to get to those mines."

Abdel turned and walked on, and Montaron let the sellsword lead the way only as long as it took for him to exchange a long, knowing glance with Xzar. The mage nodded and followed.

* * * * *

Abdel had never been in a mine before, but this one was much as he'd expected. The tunnel was simple, square, with a low ceiling held up at intervals of fifteen or twenty feet by large wooden supports. The walls were rough cut into solid rock from the entrance in the side of a deep mine pit. The mining complex was only a couple hours' walk from the field of black flowers.

When they'd emerged from Montaron's shortcut path, they'd stumbled into a group of tired looking miners heading back toward Nashkel with picks and shovels but no cart of ore. The miners gave them only a passing glance, and Abdel's odd little party made their way against a flow of dirty, obviously unhappy men to the edge of the pit. A group of Amnian soldiers didn't so much guard as hang around the steps leading into the mine. A big, sooty, dark-skinned man looked to be in charge of the place. He scowled at the soldiers with obvious irritation, and the youthful Amnian sergeant tried not to notice.

"There is definitely something wrong here," Abdel said later, his voice echoing in the mine tunnel.

"Aye, kid," Montaron's equally resonant voice answered from the gloom behind him, "an' that big fat Emerson fella's willin' to pay to have a stop put to it."

When they had first arrived at the pit, Emerson, the mine boss, had reached into an ore cart and produced a fist-size lump of gray-brown rock. He squeezed it, and it crumbled to dust. The boss cursed loudly and threw the handful of worthless iron dust to the dry ground where it mixed with more of the same. He turned his back on the cart and walked away. The miners who had been standing around the cart looked no happier than their foreman, but their faces were also tainted by the unmistakable look of panic. That dust was once their sole livelihood.

"He doesn't have to pay us for our help, Montaron," Jaheira said. "This mine means life to these people."

"Aye, lass," Montaron chuckled, "an' there're few things as 'spensive as life."

Emerson had eyed them carefully, making note of their features and dress, before he let them into the mine tunnel. The workers had been clearing out over the last several hours, and Emerson held little hope that this hole in the ground, which was once the lifeblood of Nashkel, would ever be mined again.

"You're a true humanitarian Montaron," Khalid said sarcastically. Only Montaron laughed at the comment.

"They'll live," the halfling said, his voice as confident as it was disappointed.

"This way," Xzar said, louder than Abdel had ever heard him say anything. "This way, yes? This way."

Montaron nodded and made to follow Xzar. Abdel took one step to follow them both, but a light touch from Jaheira stopped him. Abdel was secretly happy not to have flinched.

"Why this way?" she asked, glancing meaningfully down the other passage that formed the Y-intersection at which they stood.

"No reason," Montaron said, and shrugged. "One way's as good as any, no?"

"This way," Xzar said, "for sure."

Montaron sighed and looked at his friend.

The mage nodded furiously and said, "This way, Montaron, yes?"

"As good as any?" Jaheira asked, her voice dripping with sarcasm.

"How do you know these tunnels?" Khalid asked, taking a threatening step forward. Abdel looked at Montaron, curious to hear the answer.

"My friend 'ere is a mage," the halfling offered, "an' as such is . . . sensitive to this kind o' thing, eh?"

"What kind of thing?" asked Jaheira. "Poisoning iron mines?"

"Poisoning iron?" Abdel had to ask. "How could such a silly thing be done?"

"Ask your little friend here," Khalid accused.

"If ye'd like to go down the other passage so badly, Amnian," Montaron said, trying with obvious difficulty to remain civil, "then let us go, but not before we ask ye why ye're so set to go that way."

"Accuse us," Jaheira said sternly. "Go ahead, accuse

Amn. This mine supplies—supplied—Amn as well as Baldur's Gate, but I think we all know who's who here, halfling."

Montaron smiled and nodded, "I'm gettin' that idea, young missus."

"This is none of my concern," Abdel said, "and surely of no interest to Gorion, who was no miner or ironmonger or blacksmith. Why are we here at all?"

"To stop a war," Jaheira told Abdel, though her eyes never left the halfling.

Montaron turned and walked several steps down the darkening tunnel with Xzar in tow.

"Bring back the proof," he said, his voice echoing loudly in the confined space, "an' there'll be reward enough in both Baldur's Gate an' Amn."

Xzar muttered something, and a small spot of yellow light appeared above his head, following him as he strode swiftly down the passage. Abdel sighed, watching them walk away, their light making them stand out brightly against the darkness. He waited until Montaron turned to see if they were following before he followed. Jaheira and Khalid made no secret that they came along only under duress.

It didn't take more than a minute for Abdel to catch up, and he was almost in reach of them both when Xzar abruptly stopped. The mage bent at the waist, and the ball of light followed him down, staying only inches over the top of his head the whole way. The flash of reflected light drew Abdel's attention to a small silver vial on the tunnel floor. Xzar took it between thumb and index finger and picked it up slowly, gingerly, as if he were lifting a dead mouse from a trap.

"Amnian," Xzar said, holding the vial out to Abdel, "yes?"

"There it is," Montaron said, "the proof, just sittin' 'ere on the floor fer any fool—no offense, Xzar—to see. Amnian make, fer certain."

"What is this?" Jaheira asked harshly.

"Amnian," Xzar said, shaking and bringing his hands up.

"Nithrik glah—" the mage started to mumble.

Abdel grabbed the mage's hands and said, "Stop it Xzar!" so loudly Montaron and Jaheira both covered their ears.

The mage looked at Abdel with fiery anger in his eyes and shrieked, "Don't *touch* me!"

Montaron drew his sword, and Abdel let the mage's hands fall away and grabbed for his own sword. By the time the big wide blade came out of its sheath Abdel could see that the halfling had drawn not on him but on Jaheira and Khalid. Even before Abdel could make sense of the situation, all four of them were armed, and Xzar seemed ready enough to begin another casting.

"Amnian treachery," Montaron spat, and even Abdel could see the halfling was over selling the point. "Ye saw the vial, Abdel, just like the one ye bought from the vendor in Nash—" and the halfling stopped abruptly and looked at Abdel.

"What vial I bought in Nashkel?" Abdel asked, his fingers tightening on the hilt of his sword.

Xzar twitched, and his hands came up. Abdel reacted fast, but maybe it was something in the unnatural magic light, or the gradual downward slope of the passageway, or the still, dusty air, but he wasn't fast enough. Khalid was coming in with his sword, and just by instinct Abdel batted the blade away and sliced back. He felt his blade sink into the Amnian's midsection, and there was an echoing cry that might have been either Khalid or Jaheira, maybe both. Xzar mumbled something, and Abdel distinctly heard Montaron say, "No!"

Blood splashed in Abdel's face, and he closed his eyes for just a second. His timing was fortunate because at that exact moment Xzar's magical light grew brighter, and Jaheira and Montaron both cursed. Abdel felt Khalid fall. His broadsword was still stuck in the Amnian's side. Abdel let the sword fall but kept his left hand on it. He reached for his dagger with his right hand, but before it came fully out of the sheath he was struck between the legs by something small, hard, and moving fast. The air burst from his lungs, and he stumbled backward. His hand came off the dagger and he heard the clatter of metal on stone. He didn't wait for the echoes to fade before he put his right hand back on his big broadsword and pulled it out of the fallen Amnian.

"After her!" Montaron screamed, and Abdel, blinking to clear his vision from the blood, and the blow to the groin, followed.

As the footsteps of the halfling and the big sellsword faded into the echoing distance of the dark mine, Xzar bent and retrieved the heavy silver dagger. He took a moment to admire the engraving and didn't give chase. He turned in the direction of the entrance and slipped the dagger into his big leather belt pouch.

"Yes," the mage muttered to himself, "yes, so far, yes."

Chapter Seven

Abdel could see that the torchlight bothered Montaron. The halfling protested when he stopped to light it, but they hadn't gone very far from the muttering mage before Abdel couldn't see at all. At the speed Jaheira had fled, Abdel guessed she had enough elf blood in her to be able to see in the dark like one. Montaron was not only able to see in the dark, he very vocally preferred it to any level of illumination.

There were more side tunnels—lots more—than Abdel expected, and he was beginning to realize he would be lucky to find his way back to the entrance, let alone find Jaheira. He was outdistancing Montaron, and Abdel realized he'd have an even worse go of it if he lost the halfling too. He slowed, breathing hard, and eventually stopped all together.

"Forget it . . . kid . . ." Montaron gasped as he came up next to Abdel and stopped, doubling over with his hands on his knees. "She's . . . gone."

Abdel wiped his sweating brow with one strong forearm and nodded, though he hated to admit defeat. The torch sputtered in a sudden draft, and Abdel smelled something that wasn't there before. It was a smell like a wet dog, and there was wet leather . . . sweat maybe.

"Smell that?" he whispered.

Montaron looked up, nodded, and peered into the darkness. Assuming Abdel would follow, the halfling began to creep toward a side passage. Abdel did follow, his broadsword still in his right hand, the torch he'd made from a scrap of dirty cloth and a strip of wood torn from a ceiling support in his left hand. When they came to the corner of the nearest side passage, Montaron peeked around and immediately put out a hand to keep Abdel from going any farther.

"Kobolds," the halfling whispered, and the clatter of stone on stone sounded from the side passage. Assuming the kobolds had heard them, Abdel stepped around the corner and rushed them.

There were three of the filthy little creatures. One was obviously standing guard but wasn't the first to see Abdel come around the corner. Abdel made eye contact with the one who was standing next to a small iron cart. The third kobold was standing on this one's shoulders and was pouring something over the load of ore stacked in a jumble in the cart. The kobold on the bottom yelped—a rich, city-woman's small dog's yelp—and its knees buckled a little in fright or in the beginning of an attempt to run. The guard spun but not at Abdel. Instead the fool looked at its partner, who yelped again when Abdel cut the guard's head off.

This time the kobold on the bottom did run, sending the one on top spilling face first into the cart. There was a jumble of dog noises Abdel didn't wait to hear, and the bottle crashed when it fell from the kobold's hand. The little creature who first noticed Abdel made off down the tunnel at a dead run, and Abdel paused only long enough to rip the throat out of the one in the cart with the tip of his bloody broadsword.

Montaron was next to him by then and held a hand up to stop Abdel from chasing off into the darkness after the fleeing kobold.

"What were they doin'?" Montaron asked.

It took a second or two for Abdel to answer. The blood was rushing through his head again, and he wanted to chase down the other kobold so badly he could taste it.

"I don't know," he answered finally, "pouring something on these rocks."

Abdel motioned in the general direction of the cart and the two dead kobolds but kept his eyes glued on the wall of darkness ahead of him, tuning his ears for any faint echo of the little humanoid's footfalls.

"Filthy beasts, eh kid?" Montaron commented, kicking the severed kobold head lightly so it rolled across the uneven floor, following the downward slope in the direction his comrade had fled. Kobolds were tiny, doglike humanoids with proportionally huge, long-fingered hands, long, curved, pointed ears like a bat's, and short, pointed horns like a lizard's. Their wrinkled skin seemed orange in the torchlight but was probably brown. They were dressed in filthy rags, fashioned into crude vests and loincloths, and they smelled awful.

Montaron squatted next to the headless kobold and flicked at a broken bottle with the tip of a finger.

"What is that?" Abdel asked, glancing at the back of the halfling's head.

"What's what?"

"That bottle," Abdel said, "what were they pouring on those rocks?"

"Ore," Montaron corrected, "not rocks . . . iron ore. I'll assume, if ye don't mind, that whatever it is, it's what's causin' this iron plague."

"Kobolds?" Abdel asked, his voice full of skepticism. He'd heard many stories about kobolds and had run into a few that had dug their way into the basement of an inn in Liam's Hold. These were not creatures who created some Realms-shattering conspiracy to contaminate iron ore and bring about a war between powerful surface nations. Kobolds, as far as Abdel had heard, were cowardly subterranean wretches who hovered at the edge of extinction and whose lack of intelligence was supplemented by a decided lack of ethics.

"Not likely, my friend," Montaron said, laughing, "but paid to do it? Paid by Amnians to brin' 'arm to the people o' Baldur's Gate?"

"And you're certain it's not the other way around," Abdel

said, nodding at the broken earthenware bottle. "The vial I bought in Nashkel—the one I never showed you—was silver and of fine craftsmanship. If you say that is an Amnian vial, well, surely this bottle can't have come from the same place."

Montaron shrugged but didn't turn around. Abdel was still waiting for the halfling to respond when there was the unmistakable shuffle of gravel in the dark passage, and Abdel took two long, fast strides down the tunnel. The torchlight caught the kobold's eyes first, and the two big orange spots shone brightly, widening in surprise and fear. There was a poodle yelp, and the thing turned and ran. Abdel didn't hesitate this time but was off like a shot.

He tried to track the kobold by sound mostly and seemed to do well. As the little creature slipped into one nearly concealed side passage after another, Abdel started to get a feel for running down the rough, gravelly incline in the tricky light of the torch. Eventually he could see the kobold's back as it continued to run for its life. Abdel had to assume that Montaron had been able to keep up and was becoming worried that he wouldn't be able to retrace his steps back to the mine cart without the halfling.

The kobolds came at him from all sides, bursting into the tight radius of his torchlight from the impenetrable darkness beyond. Abdel wasn't stupid enough to try to count how many of them ambushed him, he just started fighting for his life. He used the heavy broadsword in his right hand and the burning torch in his left hand with equal abandon and equal effectiveness. Kobolds died bleeding or burning, and the distinction was irrelevant to Abdel. Occasionally one would get in a lucky cut with a rusted dagger, crude flint axe, or stolen woodworking tool, or make a lucky poke with a spear that wasn't much more than a stick with a sharp rock tied to the end of it. Abdel took maybe a dozen little wounds, none of any consequence, and killed as many kobolds before the few that still lived exhausted their meager supply of courage and slipped back out of Abdel's torchlight.

The fight was a cacophony of yelps and clinks and grunts, and Abdel's ears rang from it, but he was sure the voice he suddenly heard echo through the tunnel was Jaheira's. He couldn't make out a word, but the tone was unmistakable. She was calling for help.

His torch was starting to go out, but Abdel did nothing but follow the sound of Jaheira's pleading voice for what seemed like hours but might have been only minutes. He occasionally heard the scrape and scuffle of kobold feet on gravel in the darkness, and he could still smell the wet dog stench of them all around, but he went on. He needed to find her, even after it occurred to him that she might not want him to find her—someone, surely, but not him. Killing her husband might make any woman feel that way. Abdel put the fact that he hadn't seen Montaron in a very long time out of his mind as well.

He came to a wide intersection where five tunnels all converged in a roughly circular chamber. The ceiling was still just barely tall enough for Abdel to stand at his full height. In the center of the room was what appeared to Abdel's untrained eye to be a natural sinkhole. The floor dropped away abruptly. He heard Jaheira call, "Anybody!" clearly now, and there was no doubt in Abdel's mind that the voice was coming from somewhere down inside the sinkhole.

He rushed to the side and screamed, "Jaheira!" so loudly that the echoes masked the sound of the half a dozen kobolds who rushed him from behind.

The things were no bigger than three feet tall, well under half Abdel's height, and he certainly outweighed each by five or six times, but the six of them together were enough to push him forward that fraction of an inch that made falling into the pit impossible to avoid.

Abdel shouted a curse to his own stupidity on the way down. Two of the kobolds yelped, and a third whimpered. Three of them were either too stupid or too slow to avoid falling in after him. Abdel somehow managed to land on one of them. The scrawny little beast didn't provide much cushion, and when they hit the floor maybe twenty feet down Abdel felt every ounce of the force of the impact, and so did the kobold, judging by the loud, splintering crack.

Abdel didn't get up right away and didn't think to open his eyes. The sounds of the kobolds' dying from the fall were unmistakable. From above the three survivors yelped and barked and cooed in their own primeval language. Abdel was angry and disappointed in himself, but that didn't help him breathe. In the first few seconds after hitting the hard stone floor he could only exhale. Drawing air into his lungs seemed like some kind of lost art.

"Abdel!"

Jaheira's voice sounded closer now, and Abdel pulled in one huge breath at the sound of it. He didn't breathe well right away, but at least he felt like he'd be normal again someday.

This was also when he realized he'd lost his torch in the fall, and it had gone out. Gasping for air, he crawled around the floor at the bottom of the sinkhole in complete darkness until he found the torch. It took him so long to get it lit again, Jaheira finally gave up calling for him, and he still didn't have breath enough to answer her.

When the torch finally caught Abdel saw that he was in an even larger chamber than the one above, and he was not alone.

The smell of the man hit him at the same moment Abdel saw him, and the sellsword nearly gagged. The man was rushing at him with a club fashioned from a heavy tree branch. The attacker's face was not entirely human and had the tell tale snoutlike nose and the nubs of tusks of a half-orc.

The club came down, and the half-orc shouted in incoherent rage. Abdel brought his sword up and easily batted the attack away while shifting his weight and bringing his feet under him to stand. The half-orc recovered so slowly Abdel had time to find his bearings. Confident that the half-orc was too slow to parry a simple slash to the throat, Abdel swung his sword in a fast arc. The blade met resistance and stopped. The half-orc was strong enough to stop the slice, the club was strong enough to remain intact, and the half-orc proved faster than Abdel imagined he'd be.

Abdel took one cautious step back, and the half-orc took five steps back. The look in his porcine eyes was one of mute terror.

The sight of it made Abdel pause and ask, "Who are you?"

"I'm who Tazok sent you to kill!" the half-orc blurted. "You found Mulahey all right!"

The sound of the man's voice made Abdel really want to kill him. It was shrill and dense at the same time and full of panic. The half-orc glanced up at the hole in the ceiling and let loose a series of yelps and growls that sounded just like the kobolds' barking speech. The sounds held the unmistakable weight of an order.

There was another sound that came from the half-orc then, a sound that almost made Abdel laugh, but the smell that followed it was not at all funny.

Mulahey glanced around, and Abdel realized the half-orc was waiting for his kobold reinforcements. The sell-sword decided not to oblige him by waiting too. He came at the half-orc fast and hard and Mulahey put up a defense. The half-orc was strong, but Abdel was smart. He had the fat man backed up into a rough stone wall soon enough and then just started wearing him down. Mulahey was speaking, but Abdel didn't hear him. He was killing the half-orc and whatever the smelly, evil thug had to say just didn't figure into it. Abdel did notice the sound and the smell of Mulahey wetting his roughspun trousers. The wave of nauseous disgust that swelled through Abdel was enough to fuel his sword arm, and the half-orc died bleeding from two dozen wounds.

Chapter Eight

"Open it!" Jaheira almost shrieked. Her voice was quavering with panic and so many other conflicting emotions that Abdel was almost overwhelmed by the sound.

"I'm not sure . . ." he started to say, looking around everywhere for something he could use to pry the stout oaken door open with. The thick wood was banded with heavy iron, and Abdel could see Jaheira's forehead through a tiny barred window, no more than a foot long on a side, cut high into the door. There was an iron lock set into the door, and though Abdel was no locksmith, it looked sturdy enough. Abdel, strong as he was, couldn't pull the door open.

"You'll never get it open, sir," a smooth male voice said.

Abdel stopped and peered through the window. It was dark in the cell, and he couldn't see anything but the shadowy outline of Jaheira's head held close to the door.

"Who is that in there with you?" Abdel asked.

"An elf," she said, obviously irritated with the digression, "but don't worry about that, Abdel, just open the godsforsaken door!"

"I hope he'll stay to feed us and bring us water," the elf said dryly. "If he's killed our jailers and can't get the door open we'll die of thirst before we die of hunger."

"He'll open it," Jaheira said, though there was little hint of confidence in her voice. "Abdel, find the key. There's got to be a key out there somewhere."

Abdel searched the area but found only a few more doors

to some empty cells and a big wooden trunk also bound in iron and shut with a heavy steel lock. The damp floor of the mine was covered in sharp gravel, little mushrooms, and standing water.

"There's no key," he said.

"What about Mulahey?" the elf asked.

"Who?"

"The jailer," Jaheira said, "the half-orc, where is he?"

"I killed that reeking bastard," Abdel reported. "You won't believe what he did right in front of—"

"Where's his body?" Jaheira interrupted. "There must be a key on his body somewhere."

Abdel thought about it for a painfully long second and said, "I'm not sure I remember which way . . . I don't think I could find him."

"Out of the frying pan," the elf said, "and into the fire. This is quite a savior you've set for us, half-breed."

"Shut up, you," Jaheira snapped, her voice growing more and more panicked. "The thief! Where's Montaron?"

"I don't know," Abdel told her as he tried to pull out the bars in the little window. "He didn't keep up with me."

"Not a surprise," she sneered. "What did you find out from Mulahey?"

"What do you mean?" Abdel asked, giving up on trying to pull the bars out. He started to search through his meager possessions for something that might help him open the door.

"When you questioned the half-orc," Jaheira said impatiently, "what did he tell you?"

"I didn't question that evil gasbag," Abdel told her. He was going to say something else but stopped at the sound of metal on metal in his belt pouch.

"You killed Khalid didn't you," she said, her voice very much different, huskier, heavier. "Is he dead?"

Abdel didn't have any idea how to answer. He'd been trying not to think about that. He hadn't wanted to kill Khalid, it was an accident, but he knew he couldn't expect Jaheira to understand that. Abdel sighed at the realization that this was the first time he'd had to contend with the wife of someone he'd killed. It was a curious feeling to suddenly realize that some of those faceless opponents might have someone at home who—

"Sounds like you've mastered the situation here," the elf said dryly, interrupting Abdel's thoughts.

He ignored the other prisoner and held up the ring of keys they'd found on the dead man in the field of flowers. What made him think to even try, he didn't know. It was just blind desperation meeting blind luck. The third key he tried turned, and there was a loud click, and the door hit him in the face hard enough to cause him to drop the keys and fumble dangerously with his torch.

Jaheira pushed the door open and came out of the cell quickly, her legs stiff and tight. Abdel had seen children run away from spiders like that.

"Montaron and Xzar are gone?" she asked, covering her fear.

"Whoever they are," the elf said, "they are wise. My name is Xan."

The elf was just an inch or so shorter than Jaheira and not very solidly built. He had the look of a starving man. His cheeks had gone gaunt, and that only exaggerated the alienness of his big, sharply pointed ears, pronounced even for a full-blooded elf. He didn't smell very good, was unarmed, and his thin frame was swimming in a filthy brown cotehardie and homespun breeches.

Jaheira had been disarmed and was disheveled. There was a bruise on the side of her neck and on her left forearm, but she seemed in good enough shape.

"Take me back to Khalid," she said, her voice softer now, less panicked, but still audibly shaking. "Take me to my husband."

Abdel nodded, wanted to say something, but he thought better of it. He knelt over the trunk and tried four keys before one opened it. Jaheira recognized her possessions, and Abdel stepped aside to let her claim them.

"Where were the keys?" Xan asked.

"On a poisoned corpse near a collapsing farmhouse in the middle of a field of wildflowers," Abdel answered.

The elf huffed and turned away, but there was something in his look . . .

"What?" Jaheira asked, straightening her sword belt.

"The keys Montaron found on the dead man seem to work here," Abdel told her.

"Damn it," she whispered, "Montaron." Then louder, "Which way?"

Abdel picked one tunnel at random and said, "This one, I think."

"Where did this comrade of yours fall?" Xan asked.

Abdel and Jaheira tried their best to describe the mine entrance, and Xan nodded as he listened, then gestured to a passage on the other side of the chamber from the one Abdel had guessed.

Jaheira was suspicious but obviously keen on getting out of the mine, so she followed the elf. Abdel, embarrassed and ashamed, followed the woman.

* * * * *

They didn't encounter a single kobold on their way back out of the mine, but they could occasionally detect a lingering trace of that wet dog smell. It took nearly an hour in torchlit darkness to find Khalid, and when Jaheira first saw the form of her husband, slumped motionless on the cold stone floor of the mine, she sobbed once, hard enough to jingle the sheathed sword and rings that hung from her belt. Abdel turned away, Xan sighed, and there was a fourth sound—a ragged intake of breath—and at first Abdel thought something was wrong with Jaheira.

"Khalid," the woman said, her voice a contradiction of hope, fear, and surprise, "Khalid?"

She ran to him and fell over him, and Khalid moved. Abdel actually gasped—not something the big sellsword did often—and joined Jaheira at her husband's side. He felt a twinge of disappointment that the man, however innocent,

61

still lived. Abdel never fought to wound.

The fallen half-elf couldn't speak, could barely move, though he did manage to flinch away at the sight of Abdel. The sellsword jumped when Jaheira touched his chest to push him away and said, "My darling . . ."

Abdel thought she was saying that to him at first, then blushed when he realized she was talking to Khalid.

"Live," she said, "whatever's come between us, I want you to live."

"At least," Khalid managed to say.

"He's dying," Xan said, and Abdel wanted to slice off the elf's tongue.

"No," the sellsword said. "Give him this." He held out the silver vial he'd bought from the merchant in Nashkel. When his hand brushed the smaller scabbard at his belt Abdel realized his dagger was missing. His heart skipped a beat and sweat broke out on his forehead.

"Poison?" Jaheira asked, though she regretted saying it right away. "I'm sorry. You cannot help your nature."

Abdel had no idea what she meant by that, he just pressed the vial into her hand. It was warm and trembled at his touch, and he let go only very reluctantly. He started searching the ground nearby for his dagger.

"I'm trusting the man who sold it to me," Abdel told her, looking all around, "but there aren't many choices . . . damn that Xzar."

Jaheira nodded and looked down at Khalid who had slipped into unconsciousness. He was breathing but very slowly and very shallowly. She opened his mouth with one gentle finger and gradually poured the contents of the vial—a thick, sweet-smelling liquid—into his mouth. Only seconds later, the Amnian's eyes opened, and he managed a smile.

"Honey," he said, "and orange blossom."

Abdel cursed under his breath, and Xan made a vague, impatient sound. Jaheira turned away, and Abdel noticed a tear on her cheek. Khalid's eyes closed and he whispered, "I'm sorry . . . I told you . . ." before falling into a deep sleep.

His breathing was regular again, and the wound from Abdel's broadsword wasn't bleeding anymore.

"Can we move him?" Xan asked Abdel.

The sellsword shrugged and said, "I guess he'll need to sleep it off, but I can carry him. He's not bleeding anymore." Still looking around for his missing weapon he said, "Looks like that crazy wizard stole my dagger . . . as if I needed another reason to kill him."

"Let's go," Jaheira said. "Let's go back to Nashkel and get Khalid into a real bed."

* * * * *

"You're not planning on going through there, are you?" Xan asked, though he knew full well they were.

Abdel stopped, Khalid slung limply over one shoulder, and asked, "Why not?"

"We came this way," Jaheira said, only reluctantly stopping herself.

In the early evening gloom the edge of the field of black flowers seemed to glow with a soft gray light. Xan was being very obvious about trying to keep his distance and was already walking slowly along the wider, more often-used path back to Nashkel.

"I'm not sure how you survived that, exactly," Xan said, "but it's death to walk through that patch of flowers. Those are black lotus flowers—powerful poison planted here by the Zhentarim."

Abdel turned on the elf and took a menacing step forward. Xan's eyes widened, and he continued to back away.

"Zhentarim?" the sellsword asked.

"Montaron," Jaheira breathed. "How could I have been so blind? Only the Zhentarim could be responsible for such an abomination."

Abdel looked at her and sighed.

"If your missing friend was a Zhent," Xan said, "he might have had some kind of—"

"Lucky ale," Jaheira finished.

Abdel wanted to spit. He wanted to kill the halfling. He wanted to punch somebody in the face, but there was no one to hit.

"I don't work with Zhents," he said through clenched teeth, realizing he had done just that for the last tenday and a half.

"They planted those flowers there to block the path to the mine," Xan explained. "They tried to charge a toll for passing through or around them, but it didn't take long for the mining bosses to hire some . . . I believe they called themselves 'adventurers' . . . to drive the Zhentarim off. That took care of the tolls, but no one's been able to get rid of those damnable black flowers."

"Montaron . . ." Jaheira whispered.

"I'm going to kill him," Abdel said, not turning to look at her. "That halfling is going to die, and it will not be a pretty sight."

Abdel looked at Jaheira when she started to babble what was apparently a string of meaningless syllables. She was holding her hands in front of her face, fingertips touching, palm-to-palm, and her eyes were tightly closed. Abdel thought he recognized one word, a name he'd heard before maybe? Jaheira spread her hands to her sides and opened her eyes.

"We have to get Khalid back to Nashkel," Jaheira said, motioning Abdel and Xan closer to her, "stay within two paces of me, and the flowers will not harm you."

"Khalid is breathing well enough," Abdel said. "It'll be a long carry, but I'd rather not walk through poison—"

"You serve . . . ?" Xan asked Jaheira, ignoring Abdel.

"Mielikki," she answered simply. It was the name Abdel thought he'd recognized in her strange chant. Mielikki was some kind of nature goddess Abdel had had little interest in . . . until now.

Xan nodded and shrugged, walking quickly to stand beside the half-elf. Jaheira locked eyes with Abdel and looked like she was going to say something.

The look made Abdel cringe, but he turned and followed

Xan saying, "Half a month later and I find out you're a druid. Anything else you need to tell me?"

He didn't expect an answer and didn't get one as they passed through the poison flowers, protected by Jaheira's magic.

Chapter Nine

Montaron flinched at the first drop of blood that hit his face, and the second, but realized after the third that there'd be more so he managed to steady himself. The girl was surprisingly strong, and though Montaron had resisted her hold on him he'd been unable to break it.

"Xzar," the halfling said, looking up in horror and disgust.

The mage was hanging upside down from a long chain that hung from the high ceiling somewhere in the darkness of the cavernous chamber. The light coming from the half-dozen tall floor-standing candelabras was dim, flickering, and unsure, but Montaron could see Xzar's tattooed face well enough. The mage's lifeless eyes bulged, and the blood that dripped on Montaron's face came from the mage's mouth. One of his ears was missing, and his arms and one of his legs were hanging from other chains in farther corners of the room. There was a glass jar on a little table nearby that held—Montaron almost retched when he realized what it was. A big steel hook protruded from Xzar's bellybutton, and his other leg was nowhere to be seen.

"Congratulations on a job well done my stubby friend."

"Sarevok," Montaron said, his voice cheerful in a terrified sort of way. "Th-thank ye, uh, sire."

Sarevok was wearing armor of black metal and silver, full of vicious, unnecessary, terrifying spikes. The man was enormous and his eyes glowed an unnatural yellow. His voice sent chills down Montaron's spine, and it was all the halfling could do to hold his bladder.

"I was being ironic," Sarevok said, and Tamoko kicked Montaron's legs out from under him. There was a loud snap, and Montaron heard a reedy, girlish shriek then realized as he slumped to the ground that it was him shrieking.

"I did what ye asked," Montaron screamed, stupid enough to think there might be some mercy coming his way.

He didn't hear or see Sarevok close the distance between them, the huge armored man was just suddenly there. He was holding a dagger Montaron recognized—wide, silver blade, engraved—the one Abdel had used to kill the drunk in the Friendly Arms.

" 'E 'as the keys," Montaron whimpered. " 'E 'as the keys, an' I set 'im in the—in the direction of Mul-Mulahey. 'E was goin' the right way, si—"

The rest of that word comprised Montaron's last, gurgling breath on this plane of existence. Sarevok traced a red line across the halfling's throat with Abdel's dagger; then he held his finger out to playfully deflect the blood that fountained from the severed artery.

* * * * *

"Everyone who's ever repeated that name to me has had a different idea about what they want exactly," Xan said as he walked slowly in the direction of Nashkel. The elf looked tired, and he fumbled with the laces on the high collar of his cotehardie.

Abdel was breathing just as heavily—though he'd been carrying the sleeping Khalid.

"We should rest," Jaheira said.

Abdel and Xan needed no further encouragement. The sellsword leaned the unconscious half-elf against a tree on the side of the path and stretched. Whatever protection Mielikki had sent through Jaheira's prayer had gotten them through the field of poisonous black flowers no worse for wear. Xan sat heavily in the rough brown grass at the wider path's edge. Jaheira knelt next to her husband and touched his face lightly. She didn't look worried, but guilty somehow. She noticed Abdel looking at her and turned quickly to Xan.

"The Iron . . . ?" she asked.

"Throne," the elf answered. "The Iron Throne."

"So they're a splinter group of the Zhentarim," Jaheira concluded, "trying to control the iron mines—like with the poisonous flowers."

Xan shrugged and said, "Maybe. I wouldn't put it past the bastards, but there's something . . . different about this. Controlling iron mines is one thing, rendering the iron useless so it snaps when forged, rusts in a day, is weaker than plaster . . . and then there's the Amnian problem."

"War," Jaheira said, "war with Baldur's Gate."

"How would the Zhentarim benefit from that?" Xan asked.

"There are many ways to profit from a war," Abdel offered. "I've made a decent living at it my—"

He stopped when Xan suddenly straightened and looked off to his left. Abdel was smart enough not to ask what was wrong, he just drew his sword and listened. A bird called, there was the buzzing of a bee or a big fly, and the whisper of the breeze moving through the leaves of the scattered trees. Tall brush obscured most of Abdel's view of the south side of the path, the side Xan was still looking at.

The elf stood slowly, silently, and whispered, "We're being tracked."

Xan nodded in a more specific direction, and Abdel concentrated his attention there but still heard nothing. The elf took two silent steps backward and knelt next to Khalid and Jaheira. Abdel heard the breath of a whisper. He could see Xan's lips form the word "Sword," and Jaheira gave him Khalid's. Xan stepped over the sleeping half-elf and began to climb the tree.

Abdel heard something in the bushes then, but it may have just been a bird or an animal. Xan made it to the first layer of stout boughs and kept going. Abdel could see the elf's leg muscles twitching from exhaustion and dehydration. His stay in Mulahey's "care" had obviously taken its toll.

Abdel jumped at the loud swish of brush and put both hands on his sword. The sound startled Xan, and Jaheira gasped when he fell from the tree.

The elf didn't hit the ground. A figure came out of the bushes and caught him, holding Xan like a baby and maybe saving his life. The elf's savior was immediately followed by a wave of reeking stench. Jaheira put a hand to her mouth and succumbed to a rather unladylike gag. Her chin tucked itself into her neck, and her spine seemed to pop out of her back and shimmy.

Abdel grunted and turned his face away. Xan said something loudly in Elvish and leaped from his savior's arms.

Abdel looked back to see Xan vomit on the edge of the path.

"Well," a gravelly, resonating voice said, "pleased to make your a-a-acquain—to meet you, too."

"Get away from me, freak," Xan spat and scuttled away from the speaker, bringing Khalid's sword to the ready.

The man—if you could call him a man—who saved Xan's life was a short, stocky figure in rags. The skin of the creature's face was an ashy white with small specks of black. Gray hair clung to its blotchy scalp in patches. Its eyes were sunken orbs of pale yellow shot with a spider's web of tiny red threads. The eye sockets were swollen and seeping black, infected blood.

"Gods," Abdel said, keeping his sword in a defensive posture, "that's worse than the half-orc."

"Korak," the creature said. "My name is Korak. Do I look that different?"

"Korak?" Abdel asked, his voice seeming to spin in time with his head. He knew this . . . man. "By all the gods, I was at your funeral."

"Didn't quite take," the creature replied, grinning to show gums crawling with maggots.

Xan backed up even more, his legs shaking even worse.

"Leave us alone," he said. "Go away, or we'll kill you."
Xan looked to Abdel for support on this last point, and the
sellsword's reply was a confused shrug.

"I join you," Korak said. "I'll join with you walking!"

"I don't—" Jaheira started to say, then gagged again. She
obviously wanted to back away but opted to stay with her
husband.

"I don't think so, Korak," Abdel finished for her. "You're
not quite . . ." Abdel let the thought trail away since he
couldn't think of a single diplomatic way to finish it.

"I help you," Korak persisted, taking a step forward, "like
when we were kids."

Xan flinched and stood up straight, taking a step in with
his sword out.

"Come no closer, ghoul!" the elf called.

"Ghoul?" Abdel asked, surprised.

"You know this thing?" Xan asked Abdel.

"It was a long time ago," Abdel answered, "in Candlekeep, when we were kids. He died three years ago."

"Ghouls don't—" Jaheira stopped at the sight of Korak's
long, thin, pointed, inhuman tongue. The thing lashed out
like a snake to lick at the pestilence under the creature's
right eye.

"Gods," the woman whispered.

Abdel felt more pity for the creature than the loathing so
obvious on Xan's face or the horror reflected in Jaheira's
gaze.

"Go on now, Korak," the sellsword said, "back into the
brush with you."

"I help you," Korak persisted, though he came no closer.
"I help you on the road—the dangerous road."

"Abdel," Xan said, "help me kill the thing!"

"No, no," Abdel replied. "Korak is going to go on his way
now, aren't you Korak?"

"I help—" Abdel burst forward, and the ghoul fell backward, then scrabbled into the tall brush.

"Stay in there, Korak," Abdel said. "You can't go where
we're going."

"We'll kill you if you follow us," Xan added, his voice shaking from fear and exhaustion.

The ghoul backed away, but not too far.

Chapter Ten

The man was too short to really head-butt Abdel properly, so the sellsword took it on the chin. The mason's skull was hard, and his neck was strong, so it hurt.

Abdel spat a curse and punched the bricklayer across the jaw. There was a resounding smack, and Abdel thought he saw the man hit the floor but couldn't wait to be sure. He had to dodge the stool that someone threw at his head. He took a step forward, planting a foot on the fallen mason's stomach and grabbed for the man who'd thrown the stool. The little, chubby commoner thought he could get away, was so confident, in fact, that he was smiling as he turned to bolt. Abdel took half a yard of the faded fabric that made up the man's shirt in his left hand and punched him in the throat with his right hand. The stool-thrower went down gurgling.

"Get off me!" the mason yelled from the floor. He was about to say something else, but when Abdel kicked him in the head he shut up.

"Abdel!" Jaheira called, and the sellsword ducked another stool. He looked up to see Jaheira knee one of the barroom toughs between the legs. The man's breath shot out of him, and he identified Jaheira as a female dog as he crumpled to the floor in a most undignified fashion.

Abdel laughed at the sight but stopped abruptly when another stool shattered across the back of his head.

"One more chair," Abdel growled, then spun on the man

behind him. The assailant was the youngest of the ruffians and the tallest, though he still looked diminutive next to Abdel. There was no fear in the young tough's eyes, and Abdel took offense to that.

The kid tried to punch him, but Abdel grabbed the younger man's fist. The young blond man screamed in a decidedly girlish fashion as Abdel crushed the bones in his hand.

"One more chair hits me in the head, and I'm going to start cutting off *heads!*"

The last word came out so loudly that glassware behind the mildewed bar tinkled in response. The fear Abdel wanted to see flashed brightly in the kid's eyes.

Jaheira called, "Don't kill him, Abdel, we don't have anyone to plant evidence on this one."

The young tough began to cry and said, "He hires s-sellswords—sellswords for the Iron Throne."

"Tazok?" Abdel asked. They'd returned to Nashkel with only one bit of information: a name. When they'd inquired at the inn, after putting both Khalid and the exhausted Xan safely to bed, they'd been met with violence.

"T-Tazok," the young man answered. Abdel still had a tight hold of his hand, and the kid whimpered through another short series of distinct cracking sounds. "He hires humanoids too—orcs and the gods only know what else. He doesn't care who—who w-works for him."

"Where do we find this man?" Jaheira asked, stepping over the man she'd recently emasculated.

"Beregost," the boy whimpered. "Tazok's a—a—he's an ogre—works out of Beregost. . . ."

* * * * *

"Damn Zhent pigs," Abdel muttered. "I hate those thrice-bedamned—"

"So why are they doing this?" Khalid interrupted. Abdel looked at him vacantly.

"To manipulate people," he said, "like they teased me up

73

and down the Coast Way, killed the only father I ever knew—"

Abdel stopped himself this time by putting his fist through the thin plaster wall of the room Jaheira and Khalid were sharing. He heard someone in the room next door say, "Hey—" but didn't respond. He pulled his fist free and looked at the others. All three of them looked like they were ready for him to burst into flames, or just kill them all right there. He turned away, and Khalid cleared his throat nervously.

"This 'Iron Throne' is obviously a Zhentarim splinter group of some kind set up to disrupt the iron trade and foment a war between Amn and Baldur's Gate. The why of it concerns me less than finding a way to stop it," the nervous half-elf explained.

"That is why we were sent—" Jaheira said, stopping herself at a quick, warning look from Khalid. Abdel let it pass, but Xan did not.

"Sent where?" the elf asked, "by whom?"

Xan was looking better. Color had returned to his face though he still moved slowly, stiffly, and the occasional crack and creak sounded when he walked. He'd slept a long time and looked like he should sleep some more, but he would live. Khalid looked a bit better. The magic from the potion and a long rest on his own had made him a new man. Abdel looked at him and tried to think of a way to apologize to Khalid for almost killing him.

"My father knew something, didn't he?" Abdel asked Jaheira. "He was meeting you. . . ."

"Yes," Jaheira said, "but we don't know what it was. He had someone—or something—who could—that could . . . help us."

She was lying. Abdel had been around lying enough to see that. These two had their own secrets, just like Montaron and Xzar.

"Who are you working for?" Xan asked again. Khalid and Jaheira avoided the question skillfully enough that the elf finally let them keep their secret.

"We could all use a decent night's sleep," Jaheira said, looking pointedly at Xan. "Then we should be off to Beregost. If this Tazok is there, we should speak with him."

* * * * *

The inn in Nashkel was old and smelled bad, but it was good enough for Abdel, who'd slept in worse. He couldn't remember the name of it—the Bloody Hen, or the Bloody Mess. The Bloody something. Among the many amenities it lacked were well oiled hinges. This failure in basic maintenance was something Abdel actually appreciated, since the long creaking of the door was enough to wake him. Someone was coming into his room.

He didn't open his eyes or move. He wasn't expecting any late night visitors, and he wanted whoever this was to get closer to him. Abdel counted footsteps and tracked the distance the intruder was from him by hearing alone. He hoped suddenly it was Montaron. He wanted the little Zhent to come back to try to kill him or rob him. He wanted to see that little bastard just one more time.

His broadsword was under the straw bed. He could get to it, but it would be obvious he was going for a weapon and would take time. If it was Montaron, Abdel had no doubt that the wily thief could stab him in the back before he could bring the sword to bear. Abdel was sleeping in his sweaty bliaut, his chain mail tunic under the bed next to his sword. A dagger could slide through cotton easily enough.

Abdel didn't clench his fist, still not wanting to betray to the intruder that he was awake. Two more steps, Abdel figured. He counted them: one—two—and he was up. He swung his hand around behind him and spun on his rump, bringing his feet to the floor and standing as he sliced his left hand up, grabbed soft material with a lot of slack in it, then swung in with his right. He pulled the punch a little. He was trying to heed Jaheira's advice. After he killed Mulahey she'd lectured him about something she called "interrogation," which was some kind of new practice of asking questions of an enemy before killing him.

The punch connected with skin that was surprisingly soft. There was no scrape of stubble, and Abdel realized he'd hit a woman. He relaxed a little, and the woman pulled back, but he didn't let go. He'd met women who could kill him as easily as any man. His eyes were starting to adjust to the light, and he could see the outline of the intruder's face. Her jaw was strong, and her face wide and her nose—it was Jaheira.

"Abdel," she whispered huskily, "don't."

"Jaheira?" he said, also whispering, though he hadn't made a conscious decision to.

He let go of her, his hands suddenly starting to sweat. The fabric was silk, soft and expensive. He crossed on shaking knees to the little table in the corner and lit the rusted lamp that was the room's only accessory. The room was bathed in an orange glow, and he could see Jaheira close the door, her back to him. She put a hand to her face and turned around slowly, not making eye contact. Abdel could see that her nose was bleeding.

"Jaheira," he said, surprised by the gentle embarrassment in his voice. He cleared his throat and felt ridiculous.

"It's all right," she whispered. "I'm all right."

"What are you doing here?"

She met his eyes then and looked at him as if she thought he ought to know the answer to that question.

"Khalid and I—" she started to say, then turned back to the door and mumbled, "I'm sorry. Go back to sleep."

He watched her body slide under the silk nightgown, and the sight of it almost made him gasp. She slipped out the door, and he let her go. He blew out the lamp and went back to bed, but didn't sleep.

Chapter Eleven

Morning came damp and gray to the slowly dying town of Nashkel. The inn was busy even less than an hour after dawn. Guests were settling their accounts, removing their horses from the stable, and taking to the suddenly more crowded Coast Way. With mile upon mile of humanoid-infested wilderness to the east and the rocky, unforgiving surf of the Sword Coast on the other side of the Cloud Peaks to the west, there were only two choices for those not willing to tough it out in Nashkel. Some headed for Amn, hoping to find something there before they headed farther south to Tethyr and Calimshan. Others, like Abdel and his three companions, went north past Cragmyr Keep to Beregost. Abdel figured most of the refugees would continue north to Baldur's Gate, maybe settling as far north as Waterdeep.

Abdel, tired of walking, had tried to find horses before the others woke but had no luck. There were horses for sale, but with the iron plague-fueled exodus only beginning, the going price for a decent steed was easily ten times what Abdel thought the four of them might muster. He had nothing left, though he thought about trading the acid he still hadn't found a use for. Xan was penniless, didn't even have a sword, and Abdel had no idea how much gold Jaheira and Khalid were carrying, but he couldn't imagine it would be enough.

He returned to the inn on foot, already tired and weary of

a road that now just seemed pointless. He saw Xan first, the elf was still limping a bit but was otherwise fit for the road.

Abdel returned his new friend's warm smile and asked, "The others?"

"Here," Khalid said from behind him. Xan peered around Abdel's hulking frame and a look of stern disapproval crossed his face. Abdel turned and there, both clad once more in their well-worn armor, were Khalid and Jaheira. The woman's beautiful round face was marred by a purplish bruise, and there was a decided swelling to her otherwise strong nose. She'd washed, but there was still a trace of dried blood around one nostril.

Xan sighed and said to Abdel, "I cannot ride with a man who beats his woman."

Abdel flushed, wondering how Xan could have known, then he was ashamed.

"Xan, no," Jaheira said, her voice sounded as embarrassed as Abdel felt. "It's not—"

"It is," Xan said, his leaden gaze shifting to Khalid, "what it is. Isn't that right, breed?"

Abdel shook his head and held up a hand. He'd heard half-elves called "breed" before and a fight always followed—always.

Khalid, though, actually smiled. "Easy, my friend, you've made a mistake."

Xan stood straight and said, "I cannot ride with this Amnian half-breed."

"Why are you riding with us anyway, elf?" Khalid shot back.

"That's enough," Jaheira said. "Xan, Khalid did not strike me. He never has, and he knows well enough not to try."—the two shared a knowing glance—"My nose is as the rest of me—my own business."

Xan heard her and understood as much as he was able. "As you wish," he conceded. "We should ride."

"Actually," Abdel said, "we're walking."

"To Beregost?" the elf asked. "Are you mad? It'll take a tenday!"

"A bit less maybe," Khalid said, "but we may be able to—"

"No," Abdel cut in, "we're walking." He looked at Jaheira and nodded, hoping the gesture would say, "good morning," "I'm sorry," and "why did you come into my room in the middle of the night in the first place?" all at once. From the look he got back from the woman, he figured it did.

"So we're off," she said, and they set off onto the north-bound Coast Way.

"Why *are* you coming with us, anyway?" Abdel asked Xan as they fell into step behind Jaheira and Khalid. Abdel was hoping to fill an uncomfortable moment as the married couple whispered heatedly between themselves.

"This Tazok," the elf answered, "this ogre . . . whoever he is, was keeping me in a cave, closed in like a veal calf, to work as slave labor for this Iron Throne of his. Why wouldn't I come with you to help kill him?"

"I didn't say I meant to kill him."

Xan actually laughed at this. "As you wish, my friend, but—"

"Don't *tell me* you care!" Jaheira shouted at Khalid, loudly, and practically ran ahead. Khalid paused, letting her go. The half-elf didn't turn around, but the back of his neck blushed. When she'd passed him by a dozen paces or so he continued on behind her.

"Well," Xan muttered so only Abdel could hear, "this is going to be an even longer walk than I thought."

* * * * *

"Beregost," Abdel said, nine days later, as they crossed into the dusty, crowded, vile-smelling town. "What a hole."

"Indeed," Xan agreed. "Precisely the sort of hole in which one might find an ogre hiring kobolds to sabotage an iron mine."

Abdel returned the elf's smile and said, "Two days, Xan, no more."

"I understand, Abdel," Xan replied. "It will take at least that long for me to find gold enough for a decent sword, longer maybe to find a sword worth that gold—human swords, to think . . ."

"And it will take us that long to find Tazok," Jaheira added. She seemed sad, maybe even frightened that Abdel was taking leave of them, but she didn't try to stop him.

"Don't kill him," Abdel told her, then turned his gaze to include the two men, "until I get back."

* * * * *

The wide-bladed broadsword came out of Abdel's back sheath with a metallic ring that echoed across the flat plains north of the Way of the Lion. He'd come to Gorion's grave to finally return the corpse to Candlekeep where breath would once again be breathed into his father by the grace of Oghma, or where the old monk would lie in peace forever. What he found would have made him retch if it hadn't made him so angry. Maybe anger wasn't even the right word. He was angry—he hated, he was consumed with hate.

He'd expected to find Gorion's holy symbol gone, even cursed himself for being so rash—so distraught—that he'd left it there in the first place. Instead he found the grave not merely desecrated, but completely exhumed. Gorion's body was nowhere to be found. There was blood, strips of viscera that might have been flesh or tendon, and was that part of a ribcage in the hole there next to one of the ghouls?

Abdel's mind went completely away, and he succumbed, as he'd done too many times in his life, to red, murderous fury. Any other man on the face of Toril might have at least hesitated before jumping into an open grave with two reeking, putrescent, flesh-gorged ghouls. Abdel not only didn't hesitate but grew frustrated with the unhurried pull of gravity on the way down.

One of the ghouls let out a little girl's shriek at the sight of this completely dedicated young man, nearly seven feet tall and rippling with muscle, practically flying at them with a huge broadsword swinging back then up and down then in.

One of the ghouls lost an arm. It went spiraling away and caught the lip of the grave, falling back in and was itself cut in half by another slash of Abdel's blade. The sellsword let out an inhuman scream of rage and went at the rapidly back-stepping ghoul again. The blade ripped through the undead thing's chest, and it screamed and flailed its blood-crusted claws at him. Abdel was aware of the stench of his father's rotted flesh on the ghoul's breath, and his scream became a shriek. The ghoul echoed the cry but with an edge of cowardice and panic not at all present in Abdel's. The thing got in a lucky swipe with a claw, and Abdel's left hand came off his sword and popped up, though the sellsword kept hold of his weapon with his right hand. The ghoul grabbed Abdel's left wrist with speed born of mortal terror. This thing didn't want to die again.

Abdel spun his sword through his fingertips, whirling it back behind him. He was too close, and he knew it. The ghoul brought his left hand to its mouth and bit down hard. Abdel could feel the pain and the cold of the bite, and he roared again in rage. He passed his blade in front of him hard and fast and opened the ghoul's belly. One of Gorion's eyes rolled out with the meat and guts, and Abdel screamed from hatred of these ghouls and horror at the sight of his dead father's body parts. The ghoul went down without twitching, its twisted face serene and begging for some mercy it would never find in whatever hell it went back to.

Abdel's muscles started to stiffen right away, and though it only took him a few seconds to climb out of the open grave, it seemed to take hours. The other ghoul had run off, and when Abdel's eyes finally crested the muddy lip of the grave he could see its receding back. It was fleeing to the north, away from the road, toward a clump of trees that spread out in the direction of Gorion's grave like a tendril thrown off from the distant Cloak Wood.

Abdel followed but each step was harder to place than the last and he stumbled twice, following still, working his cramping legs as best he could. Still blinded with rage he didn't stop to ponder his sudden paralysis. He kept after the fleeing ghoul one painful step at time. He staggered again, stumbled, and fell, his chin hitting the coarse, wet grass hard. A fly or a bee buzzed in his ear, and he grunted at the effort of pulling his arm in and under him. He cut himself—not seriously—on his sword when he tried to stand, and the pain sent a burst of energy through him like he'd been splashed with cold water. He stood and, one step at a time, gave chase.

Abdel took no more than half a dozen steps before falling again. This time he had to stop and think. He couldn't move at all.

He lay there for what seemed like forever, just wanting to get up and run after that hideous stinking piece of undead garbage that had done this unspeakable thing. The horrid creature had eaten Gorion's body. Gorion—a man who had led a life in the service of Torm at the monastery of Candlekeep, raised an orphan child for no apparent reason other than that it was the right thing to do for that child—was now food for useless carrion eaters, two members of a leech species that should be eradicated—burned—from the face of Toril.

Abdel became a paralyzed mass of white-hot indignation, and he screamed loud enough to scare birds from trees miles away. A child in Candlekeep started to cry, and his parents didn't know why. A whale swimming past the rocky edge of the Sword Coast took note of the sound and formed a rumbling response that gave the sahuagin communities pause. A god, then another glanced down, but it was by sheer force of will that Abdel made himself stand.

A scream—less forceful, more terrified, weaker—came from a thick clump of trees almost big enough to be called a forest several yards in front of him. Dragging his feet like they were booted in lead, Abdel followed the still echoing sound into the trees. It was dark in there, and he blinked his eyes trying to get them to adjust, but like his feet they reacted slowly. He was holding his sword—too tight, but he couldn't relax. He doubted he could fight, but he might be able to kill, and the way he was feeling now, might be was good enough.

He tripped over something wet and heavy that smelled so bad he actually started to vomit before his face hit the ground. He made himself roll, and it took long enough that some of the meal he'd eaten that morning splashed back into his face. He grunted in anger and disgust, but not at himself. He'd tripped over the ghoul, and a wave of disappointment washed over him. The thing was already dead.

"I told them," a strangely familiar, inhuman voice came from above. "I told them not to eat that one—not that one."

"Korak," Abdel grunted more than spoke the ghoul's name. He managed to get to his feet again, and when he wiped the vomit from his face he could smell the ghoul and actually regretted wiping the vomit away.

"Korak, yes, that's me," the ghoul said. It was sitting in a tree above him, and Abdel brought his sword up, sure the ghoul was going to try to drop on him.

"Bastard," Abdel breathed, "you bastard . . ."

"Not me," the ghoul said indignantly. "No, not me! I knew! I knew not to eat that one. I told them not to eat that one. I killed one for you."

"What?" Abdel muttered. "Who killed . . . ?" He put a hand stiffly to his head and staggered. He wanted to fall down and sleep—fall down and die—but he knew he had to remain standing. Like always, what seemed like every day of his life now, he had to take vengeance. He had to settle a score. He had to kill. Abdel was tired.

"I killed this one that ate my old teacher, your father, though I can't remember his name—your father's," the ghoul explained.

Abdel shook his head and walked away.

"I did," Korak pressed.

"I know, I know," Abdel said.

"Come with you, yes?" Korak babbled. "You go to Cloak Wood. I know Cloak Wood."

"I'm not going into the Cloak Wood."

"I know Cloak Wood. I take you there. I come with you."

"No," Abdel said. "No, ghoul. I'll kill you if you follow me. You're lucky I don't kill you now, whether you took out that other thing or not. I should kill every last one of you. I should make it my life's work."

"Just eating," Korak tried to explain, "that's what we do, like you and cows, you and pigs. We eat."

Abdel wanted to laugh at that, thought he might cry, but did neither.

"If you follow me," he said again, "I'll kill you."

Korak sat in the tree for a while and watched Abdel go. The big sellsword didn't turn around, and when Korak thought it was safe he reached around to the other side of the tree and brought out the arm he was saving. He bit into the rotting flesh, and the taste made him smile.

"Just eating," he mumbled as Abdel disappeared from sight. The ghoul's grin widened as he munched on Gorion's rotting arm.

Chapter Twelve

The fact that Tazok actually struggled amused Sarevok to no end. The ogre huffed and wriggled and squirmed in the leather restraints and even tried to slide around the descending blades. It took Sarevok several hours to kill the ogre, and Tazok felt every stab and slice. The wide-open metallic "pear" that had broken the ogre's jaw prevented him from speaking. Sarevok didn't care what Tazok might have to say. He wasn't interrogating the ogre, he was committing murder, pure zealous murder in the name of Sarevok's father and in the cause of the Iron Throne.

"Very good," Sarevok said, looking up from his victim at an identical ogre—Tazok in every way but for the bleeding cuts and oozing wounds—standing over the table.

The other Tazok smiled, then seemed to blur. Sarevok didn't feel the need to blink, like most people who saw a doppelganger transform often did. He went back to work killing the real Tazok and looked up again only when the creature had fully reverted to its gray, smooth, wide-eyed, thin, and freakish form. Sarevok didn't remember this one's name, though he recognized a small scar on its forehead and knew this one had been useful to him in the past. The other doppelgangers, who had been looking on from the shadows of the torture chamber, took a step forward into the warm orange light of a glowing brazier. Sarevok's eyes flashed yellow in appreciation, and he smiled at his secret army.

"You have done well," the son of Bhaal said, "Beregost is turning. I will not require so many of you there now. You will have new missions, all of you, new . . . selves to take on, closer to home this time. Go now, revel in the city for a night, then come back here for your . . ."

Sarevok stopped and looked down. Tazok, eyes wide, let his last blood-reeking breath slip through the open steel pear.

Sarevok smiled and continued, ". . . instructions in the morning. Your rewards will be waiting for you at the door."

The doppelgangers bowed in unison and turned to leave. Some of them began to transform even as they walked. They'd be drinking side-by-side with the common citizens of the city this night. The thought of that amused Sarevok, though not as much as the sight of the dead ogre.

The doppelganger who had taken Tazok's place turned to leave as well, and Sarevok held up a hand to stop him.

"Not you," he said.

The doppelganger turned and bowed slightly, saying nothing.

"You will return to Beregost in the *other* form you learned today."

The doppelganger bowed again, and its skin seemed to grow furry, though it wasn't hair but a trick of the light over its magically shifting form. Sarevok laughed a little at the grotesque sight. When it was done, a short but powerfully built human stood over the table across from Sarevok. The man was handsome, in a rugged, hard way. Scars crisscrossed his face, and his clothes were pure Sword Coast sellsword—hardened leather and patches of steel plate. The man smiled, showing crooked yellow teeth and a malevolent glint in his dark brown eyes. Red stubble covered his otherwise smooth head.

"Extraordinary," Sarevok breathed in admiration. "Tamoko."

The doppelganger jumped when the slight woman appeared from the shadows. She'd been there all along, watching Sarevok's back, growing ever more sickened by the tortured death of the ogre, and none of the doppel-gangers had seen her. Sarevok could see the one who now took the form of this stocky sellsword take note of that.

Tamoko bowed deeply, never looking at the doppel-ganger or the dead ogre.

"Bring Tranzig from his cell," Sarevok told her. "He can meet his double before I kill him."

* * * * *

"If it's over, it's over," Khalid said, "but I won't be made a cuckold while—"

"Stop it, Khalid," Jaheira interrupted. "There's nothing . . . Abdel . . ."

"Spare me, Jaheira," the half-elf countered, "you've made your feelings plain to us all."

Jaheira's eyes flashed angrily in the dim light of the nearly empty tavern. They'd been in Beregost almost three days and had discovered little of value about the Iron Throne, but both of them had had a chance to think.

"I'm not—" she started to say but stopped when she realized she had no idea how to finish that sentence.

"Do you love him?"

"Did you love Charessa?" she spat. Khalid sighed, closed his eyes, and shook his head.

"That was a long time ago."

"That was three months ago, Khalid," Jaheira argued, "and more before that."

"I like—" It was Khalid's turn to start something he couldn't finish.

"She's a Harper, Khalid," Jaheira said, though he certainly already knew that. "You can't even find your . . . your . . ."

"Dalliances?" he provided, smirking with a combination of humor and guilt.

Jaheira wasn't at all amused, or at all forgiving. "We worked with her," she said.

"I'm not proud of that, my wife—" Khalid started.

87

"Don't call me that."

"It's true, isn't it?" Khalid asked. "At least for now?"

"For now, maybe."

Khalid's face grew serious, and he leaned over the table holding her eyes with his gaze.

"Abdel is a freak, Jaheira," he said quietly. "He is the son of the Lord of Murder."

"I know that," she whispered, ripping her eyes away to stare at the pewter wine goblet on the table in front of her. She wanted to drink, but her hands were shaking, and she didn't want Khalid to see that. Her husband sat back, his gaze softening a bit.

"Can I blame the Harpers?" he asked. Jaheira shook her head in response. "We were happy before we joined."

"We were happy when you were faithful," Jaheira said simply, then looked him in the eye again.

"Very well," Khalid said, his voice carrying a note of finality.

"Maybe . . ." Jaheira whispered. Khalid sat forward again to hear her. "Maybe it is the Harpers. We've been using Abdel, you know? How am I not supposed to feel sorry for him?"

"Pity isn't driving you to him, Jaheira," Khalid accused.

"No, perhaps not," she agreed, "but are we any better than the Zhentarim—manipulating this simple man into . . . into the gods only know what?"

"We all have a destiny," Khalid said, shrugging. "Abdel's is just more . . . intense than most."

Jaheira allowed herself a little laugh at the understatement. "He doesn't even know."

"Would it help him any if he did?"

"He has that right, doesn't he?" she asked, really wanting an answer.

"Yes," Khalid said, "and no. I ask again: Would it help him any? Has it helped any of the children of Bhaal?"

"I don't know about any of the others," Jaheira replied, "but Abdel has good in him. Maybe it was his mother—whoever she was—or Gorion—certainly Gorion—but there's a .

. . a struggle in him. He kills easily, yes . . . the man in the Friendly Arms . . . but he trusts easily too. How else would we have been able to manipulate him—"

She stopped to sob, then quickly pulled herself together. She sniffed and looked away.

"We should have had children," Khalid said, "you and I. It would have changed things. You would be a good mother. You have been—to Abdel."

* * * * *

Xan rubbed his aching forearm. Letting the orc beat him at arm wrestling was as painful as it had been productive. He was in the process of buying the orc a drink, but the ugly creature who called himself Forik was already talking.

"Tazok's a punk," Forik growled, "who still owes me seventeen copper pieces."

"Indeed," Xan said, "then you'll help me find him?"

The orc grunted and said, "If I knew where 'e was I'd'a beat da copper outta 'im by now, elf."

"He's recruiting men and humano—orcs, and other . . . warriors. He's got to have some kind of—"

"Nah, nah," the orc interrupted, "Tazok ain't in town dat long when 'e's 'ere. 'E's gotta guy, though, over at da Red Sheaf."

"The inn?" Xan asked.

"Wha'd'ya think?" the orc growled. The big humanoid looked Xan up and down, taking stock of the gaunt elf. "I 'ate elves."

Xan shook his head and asked, "You what?"

"I 'ate elves," Forik repeated, then smiled and added, "but yer awright."

"For my sake," Xan said, returning the creature's ugly grin, "I hope you're dropping the 'h' off the front of 'hate.' "

This made the orc laugh. "Yeah, yer awright."

"So Tazok stays at the Red Sheaf?"

"Nah," the orc said, " 'E's gotta guy in Beregost—calls 'imself Tranzing, er Tazing, er somethin' like that. Tanzazing stays at da Red Sheaf—works fer Tazok."

"Have you tried to get your copper out of this . . . Tranzing?" Xan asked.

The orc looked away and shrugged, trying not to look scared. " 'E don't owe me."

* * * * *

"How long are we going to just sit back," the burly old miner shouted to the slowly assembling crowd in the center of Beregost's quiet marketplace, "and let Amn do as she pleases with us? How long are we going to watch our brothers be thrown out of work—our mines spoiled, our livelihoods destroyed? I'm not moving to Waterdeep! Waterdeep has nothing for me! This is my home—I mine iron—and Amn isn't going take that away from me, or my sons!"

Xan touched Khalid lightly on the shoulder, and the half-elf and his wife turned and greeted him.

"Getting testy?" the elf asked, nodding at the speechmaker.

"He'll call for war next," Jaheira predicted, and the burly miner reciprocated in kind.

"If I have to take my pick to an Amnian head before I take it to a vein of good iron—so be it!"

There was a spattering of applause in the growing crowd, and someone shouted, "Let's march!"

A man in Amnian attire slowly backed out of the marketplace, knowing when to make himself scarce.

"Tazok has an associate," Xan reported, "a man named Tranzing, or Tanzing, staying at the Red Sheaf."

"That makes sense," Khalid said, nodding.

"We've heard that Tazok has worked out of that inn before," Jaheira added, "and that people—strangers—from the south have visited there looking for him and his right-hand man. We hadn't heard this name Tanzing."

"Are we going to let Amn *strangle* us?" the miner shrieked, and the crowd, now over a hundred strong, roared back. Fists flew up into the air.

"We should get out of here," Xan said, eyeing the crowd and his companions' Amnian features.

Khalid nodded, took a flinching Jaheira by the arm, and followed Xan back to the inn. When they entered the front doors, passing another crowd of travelers preparing to head north, the innkeeper stopped them with a frantic wave.

"Sirs and madam!" the innkeepers called. He was a stout, bald man with bad skin and no teeth. "Your large friend is back. He asked me to ask you to ask that he . . . he asked that I ask . . ."

"Easy, there," Xan said, placing a condescending hand on the flustered little man's shoulder.

"He's waiting for you in his room."

Xan smiled, and the innkeeper said, "Everybody's checking out!" as if that were some explanation.

"As will we, I'm afraid," Xan said. The crestfallen innkeeper nodded and turned away.

* * * * *

"Come in," Abdel said in answer to the light rap at his door. The old door squeaked open just enough for Jaheira to slip through. He nodded and looked back down at the washbasin on the little table in front of him. She had taken the time to change. A soft green silk blouse and a simple cotton skirt made her look less like the warrior he knew her to be. He didn't want to look at Jaheira the woman— Jaheira the wife. She moved toward him slowly but didn't come too close.

"We have some . . . we know more," she said quietly. "Are you all right?"

Abdel tried to smile but couldn't. He'd been trying to wash the grime of the road and the ghouls off him for hours, dipping an old rag in a basin of cool water over and over again. His shirt was off, and he could feel Jaheira's eyes on him. Her gaze made his skin feel hot.

"Tazok has a man in Beregost," she said, recognizing his unwillingness to talk about his visit to Gorion's grave.

"There's a man living in one of the inns here named Tranzig who helps Tazok recruit sellswords and humanoids for the Iron Throne. Xan has gone to try to find him, to keep an eye on him. Khalid will come to tell us if he leaves the Red Sheaf."

Abdel nodded, though he'd only barely heard what she had to say.

"I'm . . ." he said.

She stepped closer in response. He reached out a hand and touched the soft fabric of her skirt, felt the firm warmth of her thigh beneath it. She stepped into him, and without consciously willing himself to do so he began to kiss her taut stomach through the silk of her blouse. His skin tingled, and he drew in a sharp breath and heard Jaheira do the same thing. There was something about the feel of her that was just perfect—and perfectly wrong.

He pushed her away gently, and Jaheira sighed.

"Khalid and I . . ." she started to say, but stopped when he shook his head.

"I can feel . . ." Abdel said quietly. He stopped to clear his throat and continued, "There are two voices to my thoughts, I think. One that wants to kill, that loves to kill, and another that wants . . . I don't know what it wants, I hear it so infrequently. The voice that wants to kill also wants you."

A tear rolled down Jaheira's sun-browned cheek, and she put a hand on Abdel's head, in his hair. He put one big hand over hers, held it and drew it away from his head. When he let go, she left him alone.

Chapter Thirteen

"We have horses," Khalid said, "thanks to Abdel."

"Arm wrestling," the big man said. "What an odd pastime."

Khalid smiled and looked pointedly at Jaheira, who was admiring Abdel's powerful arm. She caught her husband's eye and blushed, shooting him a look that clearly said, "Say nothing!"

"Good," replied Xan, "we'll need them right now." The elf pointed at a short, stocky fighter whose stubbly red hair shined in the feeble morning sunlight. It was Tranzig, and he was mounting a fast-looking horse on the street outside the still-sleeping Red Sheaf inn.

The four companions stood casually, assuming that Tranzig had no idea who they were or that they'd been watching him. The red-headed man rode off at an easy pace, taking the dirt road out of Beregost to the north toward Baldur's Gate.

"Here we go," Abdel said as he climbed on his new horse, a sturdy brown stallion.

Tranzig left Beregost early enough that they weren't caught in the refugee press northward, and they let him get out of sight before they followed. Xan and Abdel could easily make out the hoofprints left in the muddy road by their quarry's horse. They left Beregost, and Abdel was happy to see it behind them, for a number of reasons. He looked at the road, his horse, the trees here and there, and a hawk flying overhead—anywhere but at Jaheira. She didn't look at him either. They rode in silence for over an hour before they saw anyone else.

They were just dots far ahead on the open plain when Xan spotted them and drew the others' attention to the figures. Six people on foot, crossing the ragged grass, were moving slowly toward the road.

"We'll meet them on the road," Abdel observed, feeling uneasy about the encounter.

Xan shrugged and said, "Fellow travelers."

"Perhaps," Abdel answered, "but I've seen things on this road . . . we should be ready anyway."

"I'd say they're making for that building, there," Khalid offered. He pointed to a crumbling structure in the far distance. Made of white stone, the dilapidated structure was overgrown with weeds, ivy, and brambles. A thin line of mud showed where a path once led from the road to the columned structure that might have once been a temple.

"If we can avoid them," Jaheira said, "we should. We can't let Tranzig get too far away. Remember, we're here to find this Iron Throne, and with any luck Tranzig will lead us there. If some pilgrims have come to this ruined temple to pray, let them."

Abdel nodded at the simple, safe logic of what Jaheira said, but he didn't hold out much hope for the outcome.

* * * * *

Abdel's horse took the first hit and went down screaming. Jumping out of the way of the animal's falling bulk, Abdel rolled on the ground and got to his feet with his sword in front of him. Jaheira's horse reared and threw her. She exhaled sharply when she hit the ground and fumbled a bit in drawing her sword but was otherwise unharmed. Xan slid from his horse and slapped it on the rump to keep it out of the way of the things that were attacking them.

Abdel had no name for these hideous man-shaped creatures. They were covered in—seemed to be made of—some kind of transparent olive-green semiliquid. There were six of them, the would-be pilgrims. Abdel could see their skeletons through the slime. He couldn't see any guts. It was as if these men had somehow jellied, then hung on their bones to kill in mute mockery of life. They coordinated their attacks on the party like wild dogs, and Abdel didn't doubt that one of his friends might be taken down. Xan slashed at one, sending a trail of olive slime shooting out over the road. The creature staggered but kept fighting. The monsters came at them with hands held high and apart as if they meant to embrace their victims. Abdel had no idea what effect the touch of this oozing, algae-reeking goo might have on the living, but he had no intention of finding out the hard way. As if recognizing his superior strength, three of them came at Abdel, and he defended himself with wild abandon. He hacked into the inhuman things, taking more care not to let any of the slime splash on him than in fighting with any finesse.

Jaheira held her own opponent back, as did Xan, but Abdel spared a glance at Khalid long enough to know that the half-elf was hard pressed. Khalid was backing into his own panicking horse.

Abdel took the head off one, and the thing collapsed. It wasn't like a man falling over, this thing literally splashed onto the ground as if the bones had just disappeared. Indeed, Abdel could no longer see the dark gray outline of the creature's skeleton. One of the two still trying to touch him finally succeeded, and Abdel flinched fast and hard, whipping his right forearm out and sideways. Some of the creature's slimy substance had stuck to Abdel's chain mail sleeve, and the sellsword took three big, fast steps backward as he continued to flick the ooze off. It hit the ground, and Abdel could swear he saw it move back toward the amorphous feet of the slime creature. There wasn't any left on his sleeve, but there was a shiny patch, and Abdel watched it for signs that it might burn through to his skin.

He could only look for a second, but that was enough for him to decide that the creatures weren't acidic. Still, they were trying awfully hard to get that slime onto him, and Abdel couldn't imagine it would be to his benefit.

Jaheira shrieked, more in anger than in fear, but Abdel couldn't turn to look at her. He was busy with the two slime creatures who were pawing at him desperately. Another went down, and Abdel realized his sword was covered in the viscous, foul stuff, the blade feeling noticeably heavier. Abdel adjusted his stance and grip accordingly to account for the new weight and went back at his remaining opponent. This one seemed to have learned from the death of his two companions. It was dodging back out of Abdel's reach now and trying to come in low, grabbing for Abdel's legs.

"Khalid!" Jaheira screamed. Abdel heard footsteps—heavy, fast, but irregular—in the grass to his right. He had to keep his eyes on the creature still swiping at his knees. He heard a thick, bubbly splash and knew that one of the others had taken a creature down.

"Khalid!" Xan shouted. There was a ring of desperation in the elf's voice that Abdel didn't like at all.

Abdel, knowing something was wrong with Khalid, spun his sword up and over his head to make a downward slash into the creature's head. The monster saw its opening, dropped down on what sufficed for a rump, and went to kick out at Abdel's shin. Abdel was waiting for the attack, though, and nimbly hopped over the slimy legs, twisting in the air to fall backward. He slid his sword behind him, along his right side, and landed directly next to the creature—too close he realized only after it was too late to stop his fall. The sword pierced the slime creature's "skin," and the thing's bones went limp. Abdel gasped and whirled out of the way, leaving his sword in the growing pile of ooze. He stood and without thinking checked his body for any of the slime.

"Khalid," Jaheira yelled again, "Abdel—"

The sellsword jumped but not at the sound of Jaheira's voice. The puddle of viscous slime was moving and moving at him. Tendrils of syrup licked out of the mass of stuff, whipping at all of them like snake's tongues. Abdel raised his hands as he stepped backward but hesitated. His sword was still stuck in it, and though he would have felt better if he was armed, he wasn't sure it would help. It was as if striking them with a blade only dropped them out of their humanoid form but made them no less capable of attacking. In what must have been their native form, could they be cut at all?

Jaheira began a mumbling chant, and both Abdel and Xan backed off quickly at the sound of it. The pool of slime still advancing on Abdel formed a thick tentacle and drew it back as if to strike. Abdel held up his fists, still not sure how to defend himself against this thing, and then Jaheira stopped speaking, and the slime stopped moving at the same time.

"They are plants," she said. "I thought they smelled like plants."

"What did you do?" Abdel asked her.

"By Mielikki's grace," she said, "they won't be able to move for a few minutes."

Abdel bent and retrieved his sword, having to pull hard to free it from the sticky grip of the inert substance.

"Khalid," Jaheira said, "where's Khalid?"

Abdel looked all around and saw only Xan's retreating back. "This way!" the elf called.

* * * * *

"Elves made this," Xan said, examining faded carvings in the stone of the crumbing temple, "a very long time ago."

"*Khalid!*" Jaheira screamed again. She was crying, and though she'd been embarrassed about it at first, now she just didn't care.

Abdel heard a rustle of leaves on the other side of a broken wall and stopped wiping the slime from his sword long enough to determine that it was only a squirrel. The oblivious rodent scurried up the side of a pillar and disappeared into a fold of ivy vines.

"Why did he run?" Xan asked, not expecting an answer.

"It got on him," Jaheira said, her voice quivering. "That . . . stuff, that slime got on him. What was that? What were those things?"

Abdel shook his head, not sure what to say. Seeing Jaheira like this, in an emotional panic, made him feel like he did the right thing in pushing her away, but that made it no less painful for him.

"Khalid!" Abdel called out, covering his emotions with the task at hand.

There was another rustle of leaves, and Abdel sighed. "Damned squirrels," he muttered and stepped forward and up onto a crooked paving stone. The stone collapsed at the same instant that Khalid—or what *was* Khalid—burst through the vegetation and lunged at him.

Abdel bent at the waist, instinctively flinching from the attack as he fell, and this was just enough to make him fall backward, away from Khalid and down six inches to the rest of the crumbling stones. Jaheira screamed. It was a painful, desperate, horrified, purely female sound, and it made Abdel's heart flip in his chest.

Khalid was changing. There was no doubt that he was becoming one of those things. Already Abdel could see through what was left of the half-elf's skin. He could see the shadowy traces of ribs. Internal organs were shrinking fast enough that Abdel could see their progress. Khalid's left eye was gone, his right was dissolving rapidly after having slid into the mass of slimy material that was once his head. There was no trace of brain in there, and Abdel knew his friend was dead.

Xan uttered some curse in Elvish but gagged on the end. Jaheira was whispering the word "no" over and over and over again.

The thing that had been Khalid lunged at Abdel again, its dissolved feet making a sickly slurping sound on the uneven stones. Abdel didn't think, he just reacted, bringing his sword up and in front of him. It slid through one of Khalid's arms slowly, easily, and the arm came off and splashed on the stones next to Abdel. The sellsword had to roll backward and stand to avoid putting his hand down in the slop that was Khalid's arm.

"Abdel—" Jaheira coughed, her voice pleading, but Abdel had no idea what she wanted him to do. Khalid kept coming at him, and Abdel kept backing up. He was fending off the creature's groping attacks and trying not to kill it, though it certainly couldn't be Khalid any more. He made little cuts in the thing, hoping it would panic and run, but it didn't seem to feel pain.

"Abdel, for the love of all the gods . . ." Xan said.

Abdel closed his eyes and thrust his sword out and through Khalid's body. He could feel the mass collapse and opened his eyes again.

Jaheira barked out a strangled "No!"

Khalid collapsed into a pile of dissolving bone. The finger joints of one hand worked in the quivering pile of soupy stuff, twitching as if trying to grab on to, or hold on to something.

"Oh for—" Xan started to say but instead just turned around and staggered a couple steps away before sitting hard on the ground. The elf covered his eyes, and Abdel looked at Jaheira. Her eyes locked onto his. Her face was a mask of pain. Her beautiful, refined features were twisted and ugly. He never wanted to see that look on her face again. She looked back at what was left of her husband and screamed into the overcast sky.

Abdel dug into his pouch with one shaking hand and brought out the vial he'd purchased in Nashkel. He threw his sword away, and as it clattered along the paving stones he uncorked the vial, wax trailing off to drop silently in his lap. He threw the contents of the vial onto the puddle of quivering ooze that was even now moving to embrace him. He looked away, holding his breath.

"Oh," Jaheira groaned, "oh no, Khalid . . ."

The slime sizzled away, sending acrid smoke into the air of the crumbling temple. Abdel sat there with his eyes closed, just listening to Jaheira cry.

"How did you know that would work?" Xan asked him

99

after a time. "The acid, I mean."

Abdel shrugged, sighed heavily, and didn't look the elf in the eye when he said, "I know how to kill people. I always know how to kill people."

Chapter Fourteen

The tracks of Tranzig's horse left the muddy road less than a mile north of the ruined temple. Abdel had searched in vain for his horse, remembered it had been infected with the olive slime, and took Khalid's instead. They'd mounted and rode on in complete silence. The cool breeze hissed through the dry grass. Birds and bees and mosquitoes made the only living noises. Even Jaheira had stopped crying. Abdel looked at her occasionally, confused by her livid emotions. Her eyes were red, and the skin of her face both puffy and taut. He was afraid she might explode. She looked like she might explode.

They rode hard and fast, knowing they'd lost time with the costly attack from the creatures. Tranzig must be miles ahead of them by now, and it was getting dark. Far off to the west the sun was just touching the black line that was the distant Cloak Wood forest.

Tranzig's tracks picked up a small, rough, muddy animal trail that wound around low hills, making it difficult for Abdel, riding in the lead, to see more than a few yards ahead. He kept the pace brisk anyway. All three of them were as intent on leaving the horror of that afternoon behind them as they were on catching up to Tranzig.

Abdel hoped he'd never have to face that kind of sick, demented, impossible death again. That wasn't a way for a man to die, reduced to jelly then burned away with acid poured on him from his wife's—what? Not lover, but

101

something. She was something to him. The kind of relationship they had might have had a name in the civilized courts of someplace like Waterdeep, but in Abdel's experience they were only—

His thoughts piled into each other and burst apart as he pulled his horse to a sudden, bone-jarring stop. The others followed suit; a preoccupied Jaheira passed Abdel before she got her animal under control. One of the horses—Abdel thought it might have been Xan's—snorted loudly, and Abdel hushed it. He slid from his horse, put his finger to his lips, and began to climb a short, bowl-shaped hill.

Xan looked like he wanted to say something but knew enough to heed Abdel's warning to be quiet. The elf and Jaheira slid from their horses and followed Abdel up the hill. At the top they crouched behind a small, thorny bush, and Abdel pointed to a lone figure standing next to a well-rested horse on the edge of the little trail. Tranzig had one of the horse's hind legs in his hands and was working at clearing something from the animal's shoe.

"We almost rode right over him," Xan whispered. Abdel nodded, and Jaheira sighed almost silently. She looked down on Tranzig with a face that was a mask of hate, a mask that hid the pain underneath, but not too well.

They watched Tranzig for a few minutes, then they heard one of their own horses shuffle in the weeds on the other side of the hill. Tranzig looked up sharply in that direction, and Xan cursed quietly in Elvish.

Tranzig paused a moment, then casually remounted his horse and followed the animal trail away from them at an easy pace. Abdel looked up, hoping to take advantage of the height of the hill to get some sense of where Tranzig was heading. He saw three thin tendrils of smoke drifting up into the air on the other side of a set of four higher, rounded-topped hills.

"Cook fires," he whispered.

He followed his friends' gazes back to the smoke and saw a star break through a gap in the relentless clouds. Night was coming fast, so Abdel fixed the site of the cook fires in his mind as best he could and led Jaheira and Xan down the hill to camp.

* * * * *

Jaheira was shivering, and Abdel wanted to put his arm around her. He thought about how that would feel and sighed when his mind wandered in a direction that embarrassed him. He let her hug her knees to her chin and shiver the cold away herself. He'd killed her husband that day, and the thought that either she or the ever-watchful and sarcastic Xan might think he was trying to move in sickened him. The night was turning decidedly colder with every increased gust of damp wind. Stars twinkled in patches in the sky, patches that were quickly obliterated by fast-moving clouds. They hadn't built a fire on Xan's urging. He was afraid the Iron Throne camp, into which Tranzig had ridden, might have outriders who would be attracted to a campfire so close to their secret lair.

"So they're Zhents," Abdel said, his words barely squeezing through a jaw held tight to keep his teeth from chattering.

"We think," Xan said. "I want to find out for sure."

"Not by yourself," Jaheira said, her voice scratchy from screaming and crying, then hours of trying not to.

"We can all go," Abdel said. "The three of us, with the element of surprise . . ."

". . . would be swarmed by hundreds of Zhentarim men-at-arms," Xan finished for him. "Not me, thank you."

"How do you know that?" Abdel asked. "It could be this Tranzig and three or four of his smelly orc toughs back there. We've killed a lot of these Iron Thrones, you know, including the kobolds."

"We don't know," Jaheira said. "That's all Xan's trying to say. There could be hundreds of them—a bandit army massing to bring down the mines . . . I don't know."

"They're trying to start a war," Abdel said. "If they have an army, why would they be sneaking around pouring potions on iron ore?"

"I can go there," Xan offered, "in the dark, quietly, look around, and find out."

"And get yourself killed," Jaheira said quietly, "or worse."

"I've been a prisoner of the Iron Throne before," the elf said.

"That's what I'm afraid of," Abdel said. "No offense, Xan, you're an excellent swordsman and a good man, but . . ."

"But what?"

"We need you," Jaheira answered for Abdel. "Now more than ever."

Xan smiled sympathetically and caught Jaheira's exhausted, red-eyed gaze.

"I'm an elf," he said simply.

Abdel sighed, then shrugged. "You're a madman."

Jaheira moved slowly, stiffly, sliding a gold bracelet from her left wrist. She reached out, offering the jewelry to Xan.

"For luck," she said.

"Has it brought you luck?" the elf asked with a wry smile.

"It used to," she answered in a husky voice.

Xan smiled and took the bracelet. The elf examined the piece with obvious admiration. A delicate engraving of twisting vines curved around the thin gold band. He looked at Abdel, touched the bracelet to his forehead in salute, stood, and disappeared into the darkness. Abdel heard only the first three steps, then nothing.

"He's good," Abdel said, "and I've seen enough to know. He'll be fine."

Jaheira nodded, not believing him, but not believing there was any choice.

"I'm cold," she said after long, silent minutes had passed.

"We were ill prepared to travel," Abdel said. His voice sounded loud and cumbersome. He cleared his throat and said more quietly, "Xan was right not to build a fire."

"Put your arm around me," she said quickly, like she wanted to get it out all at once. "Sit next to me, Abdel. Sit with me." She started to cry, and Abdel moved next to her.

She seemed tiny in his huge embrace.

She didn't cry very long, and Abdel just sat there with her in his arms and was surprised that it felt so familiar, like he was supposed to hold her like that.

"We've lied to you," she whispered.

"I know," he said, though he hadn't thought about it at all.

"All of us."

"I know," he whispered, and she cried some more.

* * * * *

Abdel opened his eyes onto the first blue sky he'd seen in quite some time. He was immediately aware of the warm pressure of Jaheira at his side. Her head was resting on his right arm, and though she was far from heavy, the warmth and weight of her made Abdel feel like he was being embraced by the whole world. Her tears had dried on his shoulder, and the rough blanket she'd spread over them that night had slipped away. The loose blouse she wore under the hardened leather armor had slipped too, revealing the gentle, smooth curve of her right shoulder. Her breathing was deep, regular, and as relaxed as it was relaxing. Abdel closed his eyes and just lay there, soaking in the feel of her and the soft whisper of her breath against his rough stubbled cheek.

Still asleep, she shifted, bending her right knee so that it slid up the length of Abdel's leg. His body reacted, and his eyes came open. He cleared his throat and shifted, waking her. She seemed startled by the proximity, and he gently drew away just as she did. She was blushing. She was beautiful.

"Where's Xan?" she asked, her voice as soft as her skin.

"I—" Abdel started to say that he didn't know and then a rush of chill gooseflesh rippled across his body, and though the clear morning was cold he began to sweat. "Torm take me," he breathed. "Didn't he come back?"

Jaheira, still not fully awake, shook her head and said,

"I thought he—" then she stopped as she too realized "—he never came back?"

"By the gods and their cousins," Abdel cursed, casting about for his sword. "I fell asleep. I can't believe I fell asleep while he was out there."

"We both did," Jaheira told him, though neither found any comfort in that fact. "He should be back by now."

Abdel collected his sword and struggled into his chain mail tunic too quickly and ended up getting fouled in it when some links locked together.

"Damn it all!" he shouted, too loud so close to the Iron Throne encampment.

"Abdel," Jaheira whispered huskily, "let me help you."

He felt her hands on his, cool and soft, and she guided the tunic down.

"I'll find him," Abdel told her. "I'll find him if I have to—"

"—kill everyone on Toril?" Xan finished for him.

Abdel and Jaheira jumped at the sound of his voice. Abdel's relieved and irritated exhale sounded like a hurricane in the still morning. Birds chirped in response. "Or kiss Umberlee's—"

"Xan!" Jaheira stopped him. "Where were you?"

"Sleeping peacefully with a beautiful woman rubbing up against me," the elf joked. "Oh no, that wasn't me, that was—"

"Xan," Abdel interrupted, "what did you find?"

The elf laughed, and Jaheira turned away to assemble her armor and weapons. She whistled quietly for the horses, and one of the animals responded with a snort.

"What did I find, indeed," Xan said, pulling from his back the small leather rucksack Khalid had bought for him in Beregost. He looked inside first, as if reluctant to merely stick his hand in there. "I don't think this is the Zhentarim we're following. They look more like bandits to me—cutthroats and toughs—nobodies, but they're organized, and there are indeed too many for the three of us to hack through . . . sorry, my friend."

Abdel blushed a little at Xan's grin.

"I managed to get inside and poke around a bit, though," the elf continued, "and I found these." He pulled two items from his rucksack: a neatly folded sheet of parchment and a rather impressive book. It was the book that caught Abdel's eye first. He held out one big hand to the elf, who gently placed the book in his grip. It felt odd—like leather but smoother, somehow more dry. It was a strange, gray-green color, and the touch of it set off some of the same responses in Abdel as Jaheira's touch often did. He remembered the feel of her leg on his and took a deep breath. On the cover was a symbol that Abdel recognized but couldn't exactly place. It was a carved relief that actually looked like a human skull, split in half and somehow bonded to the center of a circle in which tear drops—or drops of blood—were sprinkled. The binding was two long, surprisingly delicate steel hinges. He opened the book and found it a neatly ordered, skillfully illuminated text in a language he couldn't readily identify. He turned a page, and there was a line drawing of a woman tied to a wooden ring and—

Abdel closed the book with a loud thud and straightened his elbow sharply like he was throwing it away, but his hand didn't open. He didn't want to let go of it, but he didn't want to see any more.

"Are you all right?" Jaheira asked him. When he didn't respond she said, "Abdel?"

"I'm fine," he said. "Where did you find this book?"

Xan looked confused, surprised by the question. "It was on a stand in one of the tents. It seemed important, expensive, I don't know. No one was around, so I took it. What is it?"

"Evil," Abdel said simply. Jaheira and Xan exchanged a confused look. "It's—it should go somewhere safe. I should bring it to Candlekeep."

"Fine," Xan agreed quickly. "Are you sure you're—"

"Yes," Abdel said, tucking the book safely into his backpack.

"Well," the elf said, "I do have some bad news. I'm afraid

the bracelet you gave me slipped off, Jaheira. I lost it."

Xan held up a thin wrist as if to point out that he hadn't gained back much weight yet.

Jaheira smiled and said, "Just as well, I don't think it—"

Abdel burst into movement, and at the same time the thick bushes a few yards from their camp site exploded into a loud rustle. Something big moved through the brush away from them, and Abdel was following fast, his broadsword in his hand.

Abdel hit the wall of thorny growth fast and hard enough to break it down, and he found the other's path in less than a second. He took big, almost careless strides and was on the man in less than three heartbeats. Abdel didn't stop to look who it was, he thrust his sword hard through the man's retreating shoulders, and the blade came up and out of the man's mouth. The fleeing man didn't have time to scream. His last breath was a gout of bright red blood. Abdel walked over him as he fell and came to a stop half a step past the man's head.

Jaheira and Xan burst through the brush behind him, and Jaheira took a quick step back at the sight of the grisly scene.

Abdel waited for the rush to come over him as it always did when he killed so quickly, so without hesitation or remorse. He'd come to know the feeling as his reward for following his instinct to kill. It was a guilty pleasure, but his only pleasure for a long time. This time, though, it didn't come. He looked up and met Jaheira's gaze.

"He was headed for the camp," Abdel said, not sure why he thought he needed to explain.

Xan crouched next to the body and grunted, pushing the corpse over onto its back.

"It's one of the bandits," he said.

"We should go," Jaheira said. "There'll be more."

"The map shows our next step, I think," Xan said.

"The map?" Abdel asked.

"While you were reading that book," Jaheira said, "Xan was showing me the map he found . . . the parchment?"

Abdel nodded.

"It shows the location of a mining camp," Xan told him, "an Iron Throne mining camp deep in the Cloak Wood."

"So they're mining their own iron," Abdel said, "to sell at a higher price when the Nashkel mines go bust. Sounds like the Zhentarim to me."

"They're hoarding iron in the camp here," Xan said, "I saw cart after cart of ore there."

"All this," Jaheira said, "for gold."

"Men have done worse," Xan said, "for less."

Abdel, knowing he was right, nodded.

"I'm not looking forward to going into the Cloak Wood," Jaheira said, "I've heard stories . . ."

"Me too," Abdel said, "but if we had a guide . . ."

"A guide?" Xan asked, confused.

"Help me lift this body," Abdel said. "It's coming with us."

Chapter Fifteen

"There are so many things that are wrong with this," Jaheira said, "I have no idea how to begin to—"

She stopped when Abdel put a finger to his lips and tipped his head to one side. She knew they should be quiet—they were trying to hide after all. It had been two days since they'd left the hills and the bandit camp behind, and she'd had no luck trying to talk Abdel out of this insane plan. Xan had been more vocal about his distaste for the enterprise. He complained and refused to pull the makeshift travois they'd used to carry the dead bandit to this little off-shoot of the deeper Cloak Wood forest.

The dead bandit hung, stinking, from a tree where Abdel had left him, and he, Jaheira, and Xan waited behind the also rotting hulk of a fallen tree.

"Abdel," she tried again, whispering this time. "Let's just bury—"

She stopped when Abdel whipped his head to one side, eyes wide and searching in the gloomy forest light. She heard the footfalls as well, whoever it was wasn't trying to be quiet. Xan bit his lip, and when he made eye contact with Jaheira he shook his head slowly. She closed her eyes and sighed, hoping the elf would realize that he'd just have to understand.

"Oh, my, yes," Korak said, emerging from the underbrush and considering the dead bandit hungrily. "Yes, this will do fine."

Jaheira could see Abdel let out a silent breath. She tried not to breathe through her nose. The ghoul was downwind, but she could still detect traces of his moldering flesh stink. She put a hand over her mouth to calm the gag reflex.

"How did you get yourself up there?" the ghoul asked the silent body.

"I helped him," Abdel said. Korak yelped, leaped backward awkwardly, and fell into a prickly bush. "Come on out, Korak, I've changed my mind."

"That you?" the ghoul asked, only the top of his gray, dead head showing from behind the bush.

"Come on out," Abdel said, standing, sword in hand, behind the fallen tree. Xan breathed some Elvish curse but otherwise stayed out of it. Jaheira had no interest in standing, either, still afraid of the full force of the ghoul's reek and not too fond of its appearance at that.

"You won't kill me?" the ghoul asked hopefully. "I come with you?"

"We need a guide," Abdel said. "We need a guide in the Cloak Wood."

"I knew it," Korak answered. "Follow me."

* * * * *

The spider was brown with irregular blotches of black and white spattered across its spherical body and eight armored legs. It was about as big around as Jaheira's thumb—not the biggest spider in Faerûn, but it felt like it to Jaheira. She let out an embarrassingly impish yelp as the thing dropped on her shoulder. She jumped, and that served only to startle the spider, which proceeded toward the closest dark shelter it could find—Jaheira's modest but well-rounded cleavage.

She patted at her hardened leather bustier and said, "Oh for Mielikki's sake," in a shrill, scared voice. "Damn it . . . damn it."

Abdel turned around and flinched away from a slender branch that almost caught him in the eye. The brush and trees were thick. He couldn't see Jaheira's face but could see her swatting at something. The half-elf woman took a step backward and yipped again.

Abdel shouldered his way through the vegetation to her and asked, "What is it?"

Jaheira didn't answer him at first. She just proceeded to remove her leather armor.

"What are you doing?" Abdel asked again, dumbfounded.

Jaheira managed to say "Spider," and sort of hop-stepped in place as she got her bustier off. Her undershirt was loose, and she started to shake it. She made a rather convincing Calishite dancing girl. Abdel smiled in spite of his worry, still not sure what was going on.

"Are you all right back there?" Xan called from somewhere in the thick vegetation.

"I think Jaheira's run afoul of a—" Abdel started, then was interrupted by a pained yelp from Jaheira.

"Oh gods," she cried, "it bit me—it's biting me!"

A tear burst from her eye, and Abdel stopped smiling. She was trying to pull her blouse off, and he helped her. The fabric tore away with an echoing sound, and Abdel swatted the spider from between Jaheira's exposed breasts before either of them realized what he was doing. The spider jumped nimbly onto Abdel's right hand, and the sellsword slapped it with his left, leaving only a crinkling of legs in a brown spot.

"It went right—" Jaheira started to say. Abdel looked up at her, naked from the waist up, and his mouth came open. He'd never seen anything so—

She clapped her hands across her chest and turned away. Even through her shoulder—length hair Abdel could see her neck blush bright red.

"I'm sorry," he said.

"It's—"

"What's going on back there?" Xan asked. Abdel heard the elf approaching. Even Xan couldn't be quiet in this trailless mass of weed and tree.

"It's all right," Jaheira called, and the footfalls stopped.

Abdel realized he was still holding Jaheira's torn blouse. He held it out to her bashfully. She paused, turning her head slightly toward him, but he couldn't see her eyes.

"Keep up please," Xan remarked testily, and though Abdel still couldn't see the elf, he heard Xan turn and walk away, in the direction the ghoul was leading them.

Jaheira waited a few seconds, also listening to Xan's receding footfalls, then she turned and reached for the blouse. Her hands came away from her body, and her eyes met Abdel's. They stood there for what seemed like a lifetime, their fingers intertwined with each other's in the smooth silk of the torn blouse. Jaheira let go first, reluctantly, and Abdel, maybe more reluctantly, turned and walked on, leaving her to dress alone.

"Xan," he called, "watch for spiders."

"Yes," Korak said, his voice loud, too close to Abdel. "Spiders, for certain."

Abdel turned, and the ghoul was there. The horrid reek didn't seem as bad. He never would have believed he'd be able to get used to it, but maybe he had. The ghoul turned in the direction of Jaheira, and the thing's hideous tongue came out to lick at a puss-dripping boil on its sunken cheek. Abdel took two steps forward and grabbed the ghoul by the tattered shirt.

"You're here as a guide, ghoul," Abdel said, his voice heavy and threatening, "so guide from the front, or spiders will be the least of your problems."

Korak grunted and scurried off into the thick vegetation ahead. Abdel felt something tickle the back of his neck and brushed away a bug of some kind. "Torm," he breathed, looking up into a daylight sky darkened by a thick canopy of trees. He could see the sparkle of spider webs above him.

He glanced back at Jaheira, who was already following the rest of the party as she finished fastening her bustier. He didn't say anything but felt a sudden burning desire to rip the dead guts out of the ghoul Korak. How much had the thing seen? Those dead eyes didn't deserve to see what Abdel had seen, and Abdel was surprised by the next thought: no man did. He'd killed her husband only two days before, but already Abdel was feeling like he and Jaheira—

He pushed those guilty thoughts from his mind and took his frustrations out on the twisted brambles that blocked his way.

They walked for another hour or more through nearly impassable undergrowth, and Xan finally emerged from the curtaining bushes to walk, as best he could, at Abdel's side. Jaheira was only a few steps behind them. Abdel picked at the thin webs that tickled his face and fouled in a growing beard. Abdel was as used to living outside as in but found himself fantasizing about an inn, a warm hearthfire, a flagon of ale, and Jaheira—

"Admitting that a plan has failed," Xan said, breaking Abdel's reverie, "is a lesser sin than continuing down a course that can only lead to disaster."

"For Torm's sake, Xan," Abdel shot back testily, "I'll kill the reeking son of a slug with my bare hands if it'll shut you up, but it won't get us out of this godsforsaken forest any faster."

"This Korak of yours," Xan said, "is an undead *thing*, Abdel. How could you possibly trust it?"

"I don't," the sellsword answered. "I never trusted him when he was alive, but I'm not sure I have much choi—*damn* it!"

Abdel stopped short. The spider was nearly the size of one of Jaheira's small hands, and it was sitting in the middle of an elaborate web not more than an inch from Abdel's nose. The spider remained motionless while Abdel took a step back and drew his broadsword. The blade scraped against a tree branch behind him, and Abdel heard Xan say, "Wait!" but he didn't hesitate to split the big arachnid in half with a single well-placed slice. The spider's chitinous body broke open, and hundreds—maybe thousands—of tiny baby spiders burst out of the otherwise empty shell and scattered in the undergrowth and along the web.

"Oh for Torm's sake . . ." Abdel breathed.

Jaheira shuddered visibly and said, "Let's get out of

here. Let's just get out of here."

"Not long now," Korak muttered, his head just visible over the bulk of a huge fallen tree.

Jaheira spun on the ghoul and said, "You'll not eat me, ghoul, you'll not live to taste—" she stopped to flick away one of the baby spiders. She screamed loud and long out of frustration, anger, and revulsion. She put her hands in her hair and ruffled it violently, her finger sticking in a tangle. At least one spider shot out of her hair. Abdel drew in a breath when Jaheira looked up at him, her strong face framed by her now wild hair. Abdel reacted physically to her appearance and turned quickly when he saw Jaheira notice. A spider landed on his left cheek, and he brushed it off hard enough to kill it and smear guts across his face.

"Mielikki has turned away from this wood," Jaheira said, as much to herself as to the others.

"Spiders are just . . . spiders," Abdel offered feebly.

"Yes, they are," Jaheira replied, "as much a part of the order of nature as anything, but I'd prefer they didn't . . . order on my . . . nature."

Abdel smiled, and so did Jaheira, just a little.

"If you're leading us into some kind of ambush," Xan said to Korak, obviously not noticing the scene between his two living companions, "I will gladly die as soon as I make you suffer through a second death."

"Threatening me all the time," Korak said, his yellowed eyes looking the elf up and down with obvious disdain, "will get us to your mine no faster."

"That's it," Xan said, pulling his sword, "I've had e—"

Abdel pushed Xan back hard, and the elf almost fell on his rump.

"We're going," the sellsword said to Xan, then turned to the ghoul and said, "Get us there. Now."

The ghoul nodded and turned to continue on its way. Xan, breathing heavily, only watched Abdel and Jaheira avoid the crawling web and continue after the ghoul. The elf stood there for a while, brushing away the occasional spider, then followed.

"That's it," Abdel said sternly, "we're going back."

Korak stopped and turned to look at the sellsword. "Back?"

"That's it," Abdel said simply.

"You're leading us into some sort of spider . . . spider . . ." Xan stammered, searching for the right word, ". . . spider hell."

"Let's just go," Jaheira said, her voice weak and quivering. She was beginning to twitch, and Abdel couldn't help but be reminded of the Zhentarim mage Xzar when he looked at her. That feeling was a large part of why he wanted to get her, and the rest of them, out of the Cloak Wood. From the moment the spider climbed into Jaheira's armor and bit her between her breasts, the number and size of the spiders they encountered quickly increased. It was already dark in the thick forest, but it was obvious that the sun was going down. The shadows were getting deeper and could conceal ever more, ever larger arachnids. Jaheira itched at her chest and tussled her hair again. She constantly scratched at something on the back of her neck.

"Let's just go," she said again.

"Not much farther," the ghoul objected. "I'm guiding you. I'm guiding you."

"You're dragging us through a sea of spiders," Xan countered, "toward what? What are you bringing us to?"

"The mine," Korak pressed. "I'm taking you to the mine. Follow . . . follow . . ."

The ghoul made quick hand gestures, beckoning them forward. Abdel had had enough, though, and didn't move. He spat like he'd done a hundred times in the last hour, to clear a thin strand of spider web from his lips.

"No more, Korak," Abdel said. "Get us out of here, or I'll kill you, and we can take our chances on our own."

"As you wish," the ghoul said, bowing showily. "As you wish, good sir." Korak turned and continued in the same direction as before.

Xan sighed loudly and said, "Let me. Please, Abdel? Let me kill him."

Jaheira marched off behind the ghoul and said, "Let's just go."

Xan took a breath to sigh again, then stopped, letting the breath ease silently out of him.

"There's something out there," he whispered in a voice just barely audible.

Abdel had already begun to follow Korak and Jaheira who were loudly thrashing through the spider-infested wood. The big sellsword turned slowly and put his right hand on his broadsword.

"Where?" he whispered to Xan.

"Behind us," the elf returned, "and to the sides—both sides."

"How many?"

"Enough," the elf said, quickly falling in behind Jaheira. "Let's go."

Abdel hesitated, wanting to stand and fight.

"Abdel," Xan said in a loud, clear voice. The elf must have felt that whatever was following them knew exactly where they were. Abdel followed but walked backward as much as forward.

"Can you see them?" he asked Xan quietly.

"What is it?" Jaheira asked. "Are we being—"

"—hunted?" Xan finished for her. "Yes, we are. Keep going."

"We should split out," Abdel whispered to the elf, "try to circle back."

"They smell bad," the elf said, and Abdel realized the elf was very much afraid. "I don't know what they are, Abdel, but they're not human or elf. I don't want to split up."

"They're herding us?" Jaheira asked.

"Yes," Xan answered. "Following us into wherever—whatever—that ghoul is leading us into."

"I may admit that mistake soon enough, Xan," Abdel said, forcing a grim smile.

"It can be a difficult thing," the elf retorted, "being right all the—*there!*"

Abdel stopped and followed the elf's finger. He saw just a sliver of the rust-brown side of the thing. It was furry, but the fur was coarse.

"Like a spider," Jaheira said, finishing Abel's thought.

"Spiders die," Abdel said, hoping to reassure her, "just like everything else."

"Keep moving," Xan said. The elf was beginning to sweat profusely, and he drew his sword. "We need to just keep moving. If they get overconfident . . ."

"They'll come in close enough to—*ack!*" Abdel spat the spider out of his mouth and grabbed at his face with both hands to clear the web.

"You walked right into it," Jaheira said, as if Abdel had to be told.

There was a loud rustle in the undergrowth behind them, and Jaheira took hold of Abdel's arm and screamed, "Come on!"

Abdel didn't bother to resist. He picked away the last sticky bits of web and followed Jaheira, who had gone after Xan and Korak at a dead run. The rustle subsided behind them, the creature, whatever it was, didn't attack.

Abdel got his face clear just in time to see Xan's still back and stop before he ran the elf over.

"What's wrong?" Abdel said, then looked up, heard Jaheira stifle a scream, and nearly screamed himself.

The trees gave way to a clearing, a clearing full of webs of all sizes, shapes, and levels of complexity, from simple strands hanging from one twisted branch to another, to enormous ropy constructions resembling tales Abdel had heard of the cities of Evermeet. Things that looked like nests crawled with tiny spiders, and in one enormous web, with strands easily thicker than the stoutest rope Abdel had ever seen, was a spider the size of a cow. Its bulbous, black body was stippled with red. Smoking green venom was dripping from its twitching mandibles.

Jaheira just stood there with her mouth open and her eyes bulging. She'd gone past panic, past the ability to scream. Xan mumbled something in Elvish that was certainly a prayer, and a single tear tracked through the grime of his right cheek.

Korak shuffled his feet, trying to decide which direction to run away in, and said, "Oops."

In the center of the clearing was what Abdel could only describe as a building.

Chapter Sixteen

The giant spider looked up and screamed. The sound was echoed by a shrill, mindless shriek from Jaheira. Abdel almost screamed himself as his flesh crawled over the muscles of his arms and shoulders, down his back, and into his tightening groin. He looked at Jaheira and almost screamed again. She was losing her mind.

The ettercaps—the bristle-furred humanoids—chose that moment to attack, or maybe the giant spider's scream had been an order. When they came out of the spider-infested undergrowth Abdel quickly slid his sword out of its back sheath and met their charge with his usual grim determination. This set the ettercaps off balance, and the first one to him had to make its opening attack alone.

The things were shorter than Abdel but taller than Jaheira and Xan. They moved no faster than an average man, but their thin—yes, spidery—limbs flailed wildly and made them appear fast. The one that charged Abdel opened a fang-lined mouth, and Abdel almost gagged at the smell of its venom. He swiped at the thing with his sword, but the blade sliced across too high and only clipped off the tip of one of its long, pointed ears.

The ettercap yelped but pressed its attack. Abdel heard Xan move in to attack another one that had burst from the growth near him. A long-fingered hand raked sharp claws across Abdel's left arm, drawing blood and a string of curses from the sellsword. It was at this moment that

Abdel stopped thinking about the world around him, and even forgot about Jaheira, who he'd last seen in a state of horrified paralysis. He was fighting now, and that was all.

He took the ettercap's hand off, and the thing let out a long, whistling shriek and backed two quick steps away to be replaced by two more of its kind. Abdel stabbed one in the eye while the other managed to tear into his right leg with those awful, needlelike claws. Abdel grunted, lifted his left leg and kicked out at the thing, hitting it squarely in one sagging breast. The stubbly fur crinkled under the blow, and the creature let out a stinking breath all at once and fell to its knees. Abdel brought his sword around and up, then sliced down hard into the kneeling monster's right shoulder. It didn't make a sound, but Abdel must have hit an artery. Blood came out of it fast and pulsing with the thing's rapid, but rapidly decreasing heartbeat. It put one spindly hand to the wound, and its lifeless gray eyes rolled in its round, bulldog skull.

There was another raking pain in Abdel's left shoulder, and he jumped back one step—just in time. The only unwounded ettercap scratched him again, but Abdel had avoided a venom-dripping bite. He stabbed fast and hard with both hands, and the tip of his bloody broadsword pierced flesh, clicked off bone, and came out of the ettercap's back with a pronounced popping noise.

Abdel had to kick it off his sword with one foot, and before it hit the ground, Abdel whirled at the sound of a scream behind him.

Jaheira called, "*Khalid,*" and Abdel winced at both the name she chose as her possible savior and the woman's most dire predicament. She was wrapped tightly in what looked like a net made from thick, strong strands of spider silk. Two of the hulking humanoid spider things were dragging her harshly through prickly underbrush and nest after nest of tiny crawling spiders. Jaheira was gasping for air, gasping to scream and scream again.

Abdel took one step forward, ignoring Xan fighting for his own life, then the big sellsword was tripped. His ankle was tangled quickly in a thick, adhesive rope. An ettercap moved in at him as Abdel flipped over onto his rump and slashed out at the strand. Trying to avoid cutting off his own foot, Abdel reached out far, and his sword came down into the ettercap's distended belly instead of along the length of the web. The silk strand was coming out of the ettercap's abdomen, and the web mixed with blood and lost its cohesion when the thing died shrieking. Hot blood and liquid spider silk splashed on Abdel's legs, and he kicked the sticky substance, almost getting it off his leg before more, thicker, stickier strands of the stuff fell on him from above. His sword arm was pinned, so he risked tossing the heavy blade to his other hand. Once it was in his free hand, he spun again on his rump and brought the blade up to protect his face.

The giant spider they'd first seen sitting in the middle of its enormous web was coming down the face of a bark-stripped tree, coming fast and hard at Abdel, poison oozing from between its sideways jaws.

"Torm save me," Abdel called and sliced his sword back to his left, then right. The spider paused, and Abdel rolled all the way over to one side, hoping to escape the web. Hair was pulled painfully from his arm, and a strand of web stuck to his neck. He was a fly now, a meal for this eight-legged predator, and like a fly, his desperate struggles only served to cement his captivity in the sticky web.

"Hold still," the spider said, and Abdel flinched at the sound of its voice. It was a sound like glass being drawn across steel, and it set Abdel's hair on end as much from the sound of it as from the horror that such a creature had the power of speech at all. "Hold still, human, and let Kriiya drain you. Let Kriiya drain you dry."

Abdel screamed and lunged upward. He feinted once, and the spider fell for it, twitching quickly to one side. Abdel fed the thing his sword, and the blade went into the spider's mouth over a foot before meeting resistance. Blood and poison gushed from the dying thing's mouth, and it convulsed so hard that Abdel nearly lost his grip on his sword. Its legs curled up under it with a loud crinkling sound that masked Jaheira's scream enough so that Abdel only thought she screamed, "Daddy!" but couldn't be sure.

The thing was falling right at him, and Abdel, eyes and mouth closed tightly to avoid the horrid poison, pulled as hard as he could and shifted the thing's weight—and it was easily a ton—off the tree in a slow semicircle. It hit the undergrowth, and the thing's shell cracked, sending a gushing wave of slime, poison, and stomach acids sizzling through the webs and vegetation.

"*Jaheira!*" Abdel screamed, but there was no answer. From down on the ground it was hard for Abdel to see, so he tried to stand, but couldn't. He was still stuck in the strands of thick spider web, and his range of motion was severely limited. He still held his gore-soaked sword in his left hand and after some struggling and some cutting managed to sit up. He could hear Xan fighting, the elf was breathing heavily but steadily and footfalls were hard to mask in the tangled underbrush. When Abdel could finally see the elf, he was immediately impressed with Xan's swordsmanship. They'd been traveling together for some time, but Abdel hadn't had much opportunity to see Xan in action. Typically, when Xan was fighting, so was Abdel, and when Abdel was fighting he rarely had an eye for much else. The elf's sword was a bright blur in front of him, and to Abdel the blade resembled some kind of magical shield more than a sword, but there was no magic about it, the elf was good.

There were two ettercaps on the ground in front of the elf, and Xan was busy wearing down the last. The thing was bleeding from dozens of cuts, and its gray eyes showed a look of obvious desperation, but it didn't hesitate. It kept at the elf, and Abdel, not daring to shout encouragement for fear of distracting the elf, could only look on and hope. It didn't take long, though, before Xan managed one more cut, then another, then—gurgling on its own blood—the thing went down.

"Xan!" Abdel called. The elf looked at him sharply, still on his guard. Abdel could see a coin-sized spider skitter across the elf's chest just as he felt one cross his own leg. "Xan, get me out of this! We have to help—"

The huge spider jumped on Xan's back. It just came out of nowhere, and Abdel grunted in surprise along with the elf, who was pushed roughly forward and to his knees. Xan made eye contact with Abdel and looked confused. Abdel pulled at the web on his ankle and the skin started to tear. The sellsword screamed as he continued to pull away, leaving his skin behind. The spider on Xan's back opened its sideways jaws around the elf's neck, and Xan, still looking at Abdel, realized what was about to happen.

"Xan!" Abdel screamed, still pulling himself off the web. "*No!*"

The spider's jaws came together, and the elf's head came off with a loud, crackling pop.

"No!" Abdel screamed again, and his right arm came free, trailing blood and strands of spider silk. He screamed again and stood.

The spider leaped at him, and Abdel cut it in two in midair. This spider's blood was so hot it actually burned Abdel where it splashed on him. It twitched and rolled violently in the undergrowth, and Abdel turned away from it.

"Jaheira," he said, "I'm coming."

"She's in there," Korak said. Abdel looked up with a start. He'd forgotten about the ghoul. "They dragged the lady into there." Korak pointed, and Abdel made to charge him. The ghoul ran away, and Abdel, panting, soaked in blood and venom, burning and bleeding and shaking, let him go. He turned in the direction the ghoul had pointed, to the center of the hellish clearing.

It was a building.

It looked like a domed hut but of massive size, as big a building as Abdel had seen on the Sword Coast. It was a mass of brilliant white and pale gray, smooth in places, but irregular. It was made of spider silk, but there was something else Abdel couldn't make out clearly until he got closer. The thing was constructed from bodies—human bodies, mostly—drained of blood and guts, desiccated and cocooned in spider silk to act as buttresses for this inhuman domicile.

Abdel didn't have time to be sickened by the sight any more than he had time to be impressed with its construction. Jaheira had been pulled inside there, Xan was dead, and the ghoul had run off. She needed him, and he knew he couldn't go on without her. Under any other conditions he might have paused to consider that revelation, maybe even argue with the feeling. He was in love with her. She was in there, and Mad Cyric alone could imagine what might be happening to her. If he couldn't save her, he wanted to die trying. He knew he didn't want to live without her.

* * * * *

Spiders and what could only be baby ettercaps scattered when Abdel burst into the chamber. The two adult ettercaps who had dragged Jaheira into the dome spun on him and attacked without pausing to think. Abdel went at them like a wild animal and actually laughed when he brought the second one down. Both of the things lay at his feet, their death spasms subsiding, and Abdel looked up.

What he saw there made him take two steps back. His knees shook, then gave out on him. He knelt on the uneven floor of the ghastly chamber and heaved once, then again, before he noticed that even the floor of the place was made from the desiccated husks of dead humans. He vomited into the gaping, screaming face of a mummified woman, and his hair stood up on end, and he scurried away repeating "Torm, Torm, Torm," under his breath.

Jaheira whimpered, and Abdel stood up so fast he nearly went all the way over onto his butt. She was alive, he saw then, wrapped in the sticky net she'd been dragged in. Her back was too him. She was breathing, and her back and side quivered.

Directly over Jaheira's prone, web-wrapped form was what Abdel might only have described as "the queen." Webs hung in loose strands, draped from the dead-body walls.

Suspended in the center of the open space was a thing that once must have been a woman, maybe a human woman. It was tremendously, unnaturally fat, bloated and purple. Fold after fold of pale flesh dripped off the massive form, and it was dark enough in there that Abdel couldn't see clearly what it was that moved in and out of those folds of flesh—spiders, certainly, and there were humanoid forms, small and furry. Abdel realized the spiders and their humanoid cousins were using this woman to breed, using her like a nursery, like an incubator, and Abdel retched again.

"Am I so hideous?" the woman asked, with a voice like a pig rooting in slop. "Yes, I suppose I must be."

Jaheira screamed and said, "No, oh no."

Sections of the woman's pale, bloated flesh had been stripped away, eaten by her thousand crawling charges. Her face was a bruised, purple, venom-soaked mockery of the human form. One roll of flab actually fell across her forehead, blocking one eye. They were keeping her alive in here, alive but immobile, paralyzing her maybe with their poisons just to use her as a breeding ground. Abdel didn't have anything left in him to vomit out, and thought his guts might come next. He couldn't imagine the Abyss being any worse and wondered if maybe they had followed the ghoul off of Toril itself and into some nightmare dimension. What had Xan called it? Spider Hell.

"Jaheira," Abdel said, ripping his mind free of the horror.

"Abdel," she gasped, "Abdel, help me . . ."

He crossed to her, glancing at the bloated woman whose one porcine eye followed his path.

"I'm here," he told her, and those two words seemed to relax her. She was wrapped tightly in the sticky webs, and Abdel didn't have any idea how he was going to get her out.

"Fire," the bloated woman said. "Take fire to the webs, and you can free her."

"What are you?" Abdel asked, not looking the thing in the face.

"A victim," she answered. "My name is Centeol."

"What have you done?" Abdel asked her. "What could you possibly have done to deserve this?"

"I fell in love," she said sadly, "and that was enough."

Abdel felt himself sob. It might have been the first time in his life he'd ever done that.

"Do I have to beg?" Centeol asked.

"What?"

"Kill me," she said.

Abdel stood and blinked tears from his eyes. Jaheira passed out. Her breathing echoed loudly and smoothly in the big chamber. Abdel held his sword in both hands, reached up as high as he could, and pierced the cursed woman's flesh with a single powerful stroke. Centeol grunted and died as her bloated abdomen ripped open. A torrent of blood, spent venom, spiders of a thousand species, and unborn ettercaps poured over Abdel. There was so much of it, it knocked him off his feet. He kept his eyes and mouth closed, but some of it got in his nose. Crawling through a pile of viscous gore, Abdel managed to slide more than walk to Jaheira. She was heavy, dead weight, and he was exhausted and demented enough to have to strain to lift her. The webs stuck to him and actually helped him hold her.

He walked out of that evil dome, and when he got into the tree line he started running. Branches and thorns poked and ripped at both of them, but he didn't care. He kept running until he got to a fast-running stream. It must have been several miles from the spider wood. It was dark and cold.

He set Jaheira down and pulled himself painfully away from the web. He tore a scrap of cloth from his thick trousers and wrapped it around a sturdy branch, forming a simple torch. It took him a while to find his flint and steel by touch alone, but he eventually had the torch lit. He never stopped to think in the hours it took to carefully burn the webs away from the still unconscious Jaheira. He wiped blood and drying venom from his eyes as he worked. The sun was coming up when he finally had her free. She opened her eyes and looked at him, then closed them again and cried. He removed her clothes slowly, carefully, then removed his own and carried her into the surprisingly warm water of the stream. He lay down next to her, letting the water wash them both clean. She cried for a long time, and he held her there and cried too.

After a time, they climbed out of the water, and Abdel tried not to look at her as he started to wash his clothes. She left her own filthy garments where they lay and just stood there, staring at his back, knowing, like he did, that they would never be apart again.

Chapter Seventeen

"One missing guard doesn't frighten me, fool," Sarevok growled into the empty picture frame. He paused, waiting for or listening to an answer Tamoko couldn't hear.

She stared at her lover's back and tried with no luck to center herself. Here she was again, in Sarevok's bed, watching him peer into, then talk into, then shout into, then threaten into that accursed frame. He was nervous, Tamoko could see that. Things weren't going against him. Sarevok wasn't the type of man, if man he was, who would tolerate that. If some part of his plan was going awry, he would have gone out himself to fix it rather than sit and issue commands from afar. He trusted no one, including Tamoko, and suffered fools and lackeys with only a modicum of patience. Still, he was intent on something. Something was coming to a head, and she didn't know what it was, but she could feel it out there, in the winds.

She ran a hand down her smooth, strong arm and concentrated on the feeling of that simple touch. Sarevok had touched her like that but not recently. As whatever was happening gained its momentum, his interest in her had waned. She missed him, missed his touch, and every day she grew more afraid. She wasn't afraid of Sarevok, though she'd seen that he was capable of extraordinary cruelty. She was afraid *for* him. She saw the potential in this commanding individual, and she couldn't help thinking he was wasting his potential. This man who had an air of supernatural strength

to him—mental strength as much as physical strength—
was serving some master even as he planned a rise in his
own power. He was wasting his many gifts on a grab for—
what? Power? Gold? He could have Tamoko, a trained assassin who gave herself freely to no one before. He commanded
unnatural creatures—doppelgangers the least of them. Men
trembled at the sound of his voice, the burning of his stare.
Tamoko knew this man could be king of the world, but he
seemed interested only in mines, and ore, and bandits. He
employed bandits.

She wanted to say something, convince him that he
could have more, that he could *be* more, but she held her
tongue. She was afraid even thinking these thoughts in
front of him, was sure he knew what she was thinking and
was only biding his time, waiting for her to outlive her use-
fulness.

He will kill me then, she thought, kill me slowly like the
others. Could he really touch me the way he has, kiss me
the way he has, and kill me like that, like a traitor, scorned
and dishonored?

The fact that he could, that she knew he could, made her
shudder.

"What do you mean you can't find the book?" Sarevok
said, his voice as heavy as the world itself. "He wasn't supposed to see the book."

* * * * *

"There are men, and elves," Jaheira reported quietly,
"and a large number of dwarves. They're in chains."

"Slaves," Abdel agreed.

Jaheira twitched, brushed away a spider that wasn't
there, then shivered in the cool air. She wasn't comfortable
in the tree. She kept looking at it like it might come to life
and grab her, grab her and drag her off. Abdel had been
watching her for a day and a half, very closely, and though
at first she was uncomfortably like Xzar, eventually her
twitches and panicked brushings of her neck and shoulders,

the ruffling of her hair, started to go away. Abdel couldn't blame her. It would be a long time before he'd look at a spider the same way he used to. Jaheira believed the little spider that had bitten her had carried some mind-altering poison she was still feeling the effects of.

"There're too many," Jaheira said, nodding at a cluster of guards. The men were obviously sellswords, dressed in piecemeal armor. There were no uniforms or heraldry of any kind evident in the mining camp, at least not on the edge of it, which was all Abdel and Jaheira's vantage point allowed them to see.

They'd found the mining camp almost by accident. After escaping the spiders they had wandered the Cloak Wood in more or less complete silence, each trying to get past the experience. They'd heard voices first, of guards and slaves, then the sound of whips and the clatter of chains. The camp was set up in a clearing at least as broad as the one occupied by the spiders. In the center of this clearing, though, was a low hill. Cut into the side of the hill was a wide, square opening propped up with stout wood planks. Iron tracks led into the mine, and there were a number of functional hand carts, some filled with the dull rocks Abdel had come to know as iron ore.

"So what do we do?" Abdel asked, eyeing the cluster of guards with murderous intent.

"We can't just rush in there and attack, Abdel," she answered. "These people must be expecting someone to wander past here, even in the middle of the Cloak Wood. They must have a trail somewhere to get that ore from here to the bandit camp. Xan . . ." she paused after saying his name but didn't cry. Abdel thought she might have cried herself out. "Xan said they were hoarding ore there."

"With the Nashkel mines closed up," Abdel said, "they'll be able to get a good price for these rocks in Baldur's Gate."

"They won't sell it there yet, though. They'll wait until the war starts or maybe until the war is finished."

Abdel eyed her closely and asked, "You're still convinced that someone wants to start a war, that someone wants

Amn and Baldur's Gate to rip each others' throats out?"

She looked at him sadly and said, "I don't have any idea what I believe anymore, Abdel, I really don't. I was sent—I came here to find out . . ."

Abdel let her think he wanted her to go on. She had her secrets, of course, but Abdel had no idea how to tell her he just didn't care. Whatever she wanted, whatever she was doing—preventing a war, starting one, protecting some rich Amnian's interests—he didn't care.

"We can't sit in this tree forever," Jaheira said, biting her bottom lip.

"Oy, you boys there!" a gruff voice called out. Abdel thought they might have been discovered and put a hand on his sword just in case. "Get that cart loaded onto the wagon as soon as it stops. I want it on its way to Beregost by highsun."

The speaker was a round but well muscled man with a shaved head. At first Abdel thought the man was another half-orc, but he was just ugly. He was wearing simple peasant clothes but swaggered and spoke with the confidence of command. The guards turned when he spoke but not to the leader. They looked at a group of dwarves—half a dozen of them—all chained together. The dwarves spared mute glances at the guards and shambled reluctantly over to the round man. One of the dwarves said something, but Abdel was too far away to hear.

The round man spoke next, but his loud voice was drowned out by the clattering rumble of an approaching wagon. It was a stout, well-built vehicle pulled by two strong, wide-hoofed horses and driven by a short man in chain mail. The driver brought the wagon to a stop and quickly jumped down from his seat. He approached the leader with a limp, and the dwarves started to slowly transfer big chunks of iron ore from one of the steel mining carts to the wagon. The leader held up a hand to silence the driver and motioned to one of the guards. The sellsword stepped up and took his whip to one of the dwarves. Jaheira turned her head from the sight of the torture. The lashing had its intended effect, though. The dwarves started loading faster.

"They seem to be concentrating their guards on this side of the camp," Abdel said.

"It's the only path—the only way in," Jaheira offered.

"They don't expect anyone to get through the spiders," Abdel said, "and whatever else this cursed wood might have in store for wandering do-gooders."

"So?"

"So," Abdel said, "we go around the back."

* * * * *

At first, the slaves Abdel freed refused to even run away. They looked at him suspiciously, didn't even want to speak at first.

"Go!" Abdel whispered harshly, his voice echoing with a disturbingly distinct metallic clang.

One man, dirty, weak, sweating, and coughing with every other breath, said, "I know . . . my place, master. Please don't . . . test me."

Abdel exhaled sharply and just turned away, pressing his back against the rough stone wall of the mine. He looked back at the five men now standing in a pile of broken chains. Two of them looked at each other, then at Abdel, and one of them smiled. Abdel nodded in response and slipped into the side passage.

"Abdel," Jaheira whispered, and he took three long, quiet strides into the dark tunnel, stopping so close at her side their arms touched. "They won't all run, will they?"

"They think I'm one of the guards, testing their loyalty."

"They'll get the idea," Jaheira said. "We can't carry them out."

"This way," Abdel said. He didn't wait for her to acknowledge, just went off deeper into the tunnel.

The mine was lit periodically by oil lanterns hung from hooks driven into the stone ceiling. Some of the slaves were elves, most were dwarves, so they could see in the dark. The humans tended to work only pushing the heavy carts on their tracks, so they didn't need much light to work. Abdel had a difficult time navigating the tunnels, so he relinquished the lead and put his faith in Jaheira's superior eyesight and attention to detail.

"Here," she whispered and ducked into a side passage almost too quickly for Abdel to see where she'd gone.

He followed her and came into the short passage. Jaheira was whispering to a group of dwarves who were sitting on the floor. Their picks were leaning on the wall, and they were slothfully munching some kind of jerky, and one of them had a big canteen.

"You have got to be kidding," one of the dwarves said in heavily accented common.

"We can break your chains," Jaheira told him, "but you'll have to take it from there."

"How many have you freed?" the dwarf, whose beard was long even for a dwarf and going gray in patches, asked.

"Almost two dozen so far," Abdel told him quietly, "including you five."

"How many *dwarves*, lad?" the dwarf asked pointedly.

"You five make twelve," Jaheira answered.

The dwarf grinned, showing gray, yellow, and broken teeth. His voice was slow, dull, like the life had been lashed out of it. He scratched at the iron manacle around his left ankle that trailed a thick chain to the left ankle of the next dwarf in line. They were fastened together that way, in series, all five of them.

"A dozen dwarves'll do ya, lass," the dwarf said, making his four companions grin. "The name's Yeslick. Looks like we got a revolt on our hands."

* * * * *

The Iron Throne slaver died screaming, and Abdel thought the man was just pitiful. He glanced over at Yeslick, who had just finished beating the last guard to death with a length of chain, and said, "Looks like you're free, my friend."

The dwarf grinned, then winced. A huge purple-black bruise blossomed on Yeslick's forehead, making any sort of facial movement painful.

"Thanks to you two," he said, slowly, his voice muffled by his own throat.

At first Abdel thought the dwarf must be as slow of mind as he was of speech. Hours later, when the Iron Throne slavers were dead or scattered into the forest, he realized that Yeslick was anything but stupid. The dwarf fought with foresight and experience, and a calm certainty that he was smarter than his opponents. The Iron Throne had scraped the bottom of the barrel for recruits at this camp, though. Abdel lost count of how many inexperienced mercenaries he killed—at least eight—and he had barely broken a sweat, though he did have one nasty cut on his left forearm from some bumbling fool's lucky slice with a short sword.

"How did you come here, Yeslick?" Abdel asked, hoping he wouldn't insult the steady dwarf by asking. "How did these fools manage to get a dwarf like you in chains?"

Yeslick laughed and sat heavily on a loose rock. "If it was these fools who chained me," he said, tossing the chain away to let it clatter and shed drips of the guard's blood on the uneven floor, "I would have to kill myself for the shame of it. It was Reiltar himself who done me in."

"Reiltar?"

The dwarf looked up at Abdel and squinted at him in the dim light. "Come to the surface with me, lad," the dwarf said, "and I'll tell you my story."

* * * * *

"This doesn't sound right, Yeslick," Turmod of Clan Orothiar said, his gravelly voice echoing in the tight mine shaft. "Hear?"

Turmod took his heavy iron pick to the wall again, and there was—at least to the assembled dwarves—a noticeable change in the tenor of the ring. Yeslick was in charge of this cutting party, and he'd been charged with thirty feet a day, and he was going to keep that goal. The engineers had sent them here, pointed them in the right direction, and gone off to another part of the mine as soon as Yeslick and his crew of fifty had started digging. Dwarf engineers had made mistakes before, but not Orothiar engineers. When they decided a tunnel should go in one direction, it always headed straight for whatever ore they were looking for. This time they were after iron, and odd clang aside, Yeslick felt confident there was iron in the direction in which they were digging.

"Keep going," Yeslick told his crew.

"You heard it—" Turmod started. Yeslick interrupted by holding up one rough hand.

"At least send for one of the engineers, Yeslick," Turmod offered.

Yeslick felt a wave of relief wash over him. If he got an engineer out here he'd only appear cautious, not cowardly. He wouldn't have actually made a decision, so he wouldn't ever have to back it up. Yeslick knew he was too young to lead a mining detail and so did the miners who followed him. He was a smith by trade and by training, but every dwarf in clan Orothiar took a turn in the mines, and this was Yeslick's. He'd "earned" the leadership of the crew by impressing one of the mine masters. He'd impressed the master with his smithery, of course, not his digging, but it didn't matter to that particular mine master. The engineers would point them in the right direction, all Yeslick really had to do was occasionally remind his crew to pause for the occasional sip of water or taste of jerked rothé. Dwarves liked to work, liked to dig, so he wouldn't have to force them to dig, or beg to keep them on task. He did have to stop to make periodic measurements, though, to make sure they were digging in the right direction, but that wasn't too difficult.

"Jomer," Yeslick said, and a young dwarf he'd gone to reading classes with dropped his pick and looked over at him, "go fetch the engineers. They should be down the

thirty-third shaft by now. Tell them we've run into something . . . or are about to."

Jomer nodded and scurried off into the darkness.

Yeslick looked at a smiling Turmod and said, "Well, don't
just stand there grinning. We can keep digging till they get
here. Whatever's in that rock is still a ways away."

Turmod, apparently content that the engineer would be
on his way, turned around and began banging away at the
rough stone at the end of the tunnel, oblivious to the danger
that hid only a few feet beyond.

As the years turned into decades, Yeslick would think
back to that moment time and time again. He always found
it difficult to believe that the strange sound of the picks
clanging off stone was the only signal. He couldn't believe
there wouldn't have been a trickle first, even a spot of wetness or a spurt or something. The stone wasn't even wet,
didn't even absorb any of the water behind it. He was a
good smith and a bad miner, but he was a dwarf, and he
should have been able to tell that there was a lake of freez-
ing-cold water only a few inches away. He blamed himself
for what happened next, but as the years dragged on, he
came to accept the truth. It was the engineers—the infal-
lible Orothiar engineers—who had pointed them in the
wrong direction. It wasn't his fault.

The water came out all at once. They were working,
Yeslick, Turmod, and the others, banging away at rock and
then, just all at once, they were underwater. There was a
loud sound right away, then an eerie silence. Yeslick held
his breath, closed his eyes, prayed to Moradin, and was
tossed like a cork in hurricane seas for what seemed like
forever. He'd timed himself, years later, and never made it
past about a hundred and fifty heartbeats, but he could
swear that day he had held his breath for hours.

Eyes closed, right hand tight over his nose and mouth,
his left arm flopping free to strike rocks and the bodies of his
crew at hard, slamming, random intervals, Yeslick rode a
backwash out the top of the tunnel and into a natural cave
system he never knew existed. He came to the surface a few

times and gasped for air reflexively, though he didn't have any clear, conscious thought for his own life then. He came up for air maybe half a dozen times before he finally passed out.

He woke up coughing, some impossible to determine length of time later—days? He lived—along with two members of his crew, including Turmod and a handful of others who had found ways out—by sheer luck. What was left of clan Orothiar wanted nothing to do with them. They dug in the wrong place, the elders said. Turmod killed himself. It was his pick that made the final strike that let in the water that destroyed the mine. Yeslick went away, just started walking, and ended up in Sembia. He got work doing the one thing he could always get work doing. He was a good smith, and as the years passed, creeping ever closer to a century away from the mines of the Orothiar, he let himself forget.

And then he met Reiltar.

* * * * *

"Reiltar took an interest in my work," Yeslick told Abdel. "I'm a good smith, and many a man in Urmlaspyr—all of Sembia—had heard my name. I did some work for him, some specialty stuff that looking back . . . well, it gives me the heebie-jeebies, I can tell you that much."

Abdel nodded, not sure what the "heebie-jeebies" were, but content that it was some kind of dwarf thing.

"Damn me for the gnome-kissing dolt I must be," the dwarf continued, "but I counted that lanky, elitist bastard a friend. I hired on with him eventually, did some work—some weaponsmithing even—for this trade group of his. He never explained to me what the Iron Throne was, and I never asked. Frankly, I didn't care.

"I used to live here, in these very tunnels—well, these are new, but tunnels near here. Before we hit that lake other crews hit iron, and lots of it. Reiltar, he got me drunk, got me talking about the old times, got me crying about the old times. I let him in on a strike, the way he saw it. He brought me back here in chains to work it for him, afraid I'd claim it for my own, maybe, or in the name of a clan that's long moved on, without me, to the Bloodstone Lands. I'd have given that piece of rothé dung the mine, he could have had every nugget of iron in the place. I was in Sembia, and though I didn't like it much, I sure as a gnome's curious didn't want to come back here."

"This Reiltar," Abdel asked finally, "he leads the Iron Throne?"

"What are you here for, son, if you don't know that?"

"He runs this gang of his from Sembia?"

The dwarf didn't answer, just smiled.

"Abdel!" Jaheira called. He looked up and saw her running toward them out of the light at the end of the tunnel. "There you are."

"Jaheira," he said, smiling, happy to see her as well. They'd split up when the fighting got heavy, and he trusted her safety to a pack of dwarves who turned out to take somewhat better care of her than she'd enjoyed the last tenday or so with him.

"I may have something," she said. "I saw a sigil on the crates of supplies and tools, and on one of the wagons. All this stuff is coming from the Seven Suns, a trading coster we've had our suspicions about."

"We?" Yeslick asked. Abdel only smiled when Jaheira blushed.

"They're from Baldur's Gate," Jaheira added.

Abdel sighed and said, "Close enough to look into, but our new friend Yeslick here tells me we're looking for a man named Reiltar—and he's in Sembia, not Baldur's Gate."

"Oh, no," Yeslick said, "Reiltar's never been out here. He has a man—I don't know his name—in Baldur's Gate."

Chapter Eighteen

Baldur's Gate.

Abdel and Jaheira picked up a rickety ferry on the south bank of the River Chionthar. Abdel had never thought to ask if Jaheira had ever been as far north as this, but when she first caught sight of the city, sprawled over the north bank of the mile-wide river, she could do little but stare in awe. There was something about the look on the beautiful half-elf's face that warmed Abdel's heart. He saw the little girl in her.

They'd been on the road for four and a half days and in that time had never been as close as they had been in the water, when they clung to each other as much to stave off the cold and madness as simply to touch. Jaheira was mourning her husband and to a surprisingly equal degree, Xan. Abdel had never traveled with anyone for very long. He'd known Jaheira now almost as long as he'd known anyone. He'd fought alongside men who'd died before—died close enough to spill some of their blood on him—and he never found it in him to mourn. Gorion's death had changed all that. The sellsword used to revel in death, in killing, more than as a symbol of victory or a simple turning of the great wheel of life. Now, he saw the pain in it, and he hoped he could kill as easily when he needed to, and thought maybe he wouldn't kill so easily when he didn't.

When Abdel finally turned his attention to the city across the gray water, he felt a fresh sense of wonder. Certainly it wasn't the most beautiful city in the world. He'd never been to Waterdeep, but Abdel knew this was no City of Splendors. It was no Myth Drannor, no Karsus, paled in comparison to even Suzail and Calimport, but after nearly two months of the backwater towns of the Sword Coast, well . . . Baldur's Gate was no Waterdeep, but it sure beat Nashkel.

The ferry rocked violently in the cold water, and Abdel grunted at the queasy feeling already beginning to take hold in his otherwise iron stomach. The rocking came more from the incompetence of the ferryman than the currents or wind.

"Ferryman!" Abdel called to the hopelessly frail old man manning the tiller.

Six younger men worked at oars and refused to look up for anything. There were a few other passengers, including a rather unpleasant smelling ox. The ferryman made no move to indicate that he'd heard Abdel, so the sellsword approached him, zigzagging across the pitching deck.

"Ferryman," he said again, and this time the old man shot him an annoyed look.

"We'll get there, we'll get there," he croaked. "What d'ya think we are, a bunch of golems?"

"Do you need a hand, old man?" Abdel offered.

"I'm fine, kid," the old man spat out. "I'm just old, my knee 'urts, and I don't give a shite no more."

Abdel laughed, and the old man looked offended for a heartbeat or two, then laughed along with Abdel. Ending in a spasm of phlegmy coughs. the ferryman stepped aside and let Abdel take the tiller.

"Steer 'er if you want to, son," he said, sitting stiffly on an old barrel that had been nailed to the deck, "I'll take what I can get."

Abdel had never actually steered a ferryboat before and was surprised at the strength he had to expend to keep the boat on course, let alone steady, and wondered that the old man could do it at all. Jaheira stood next to him and ran her fingers through her hair, letting it flow freely in the chill breeze.

"It's amazing" she said, and Abdel nodded before she could say, "that anyone could live in such a midden pit."

This took Abdel by surprise, and he said, "You don't find it . . ."

"Rank?" she finished. "I'll say, and look at that harbor. What in Umberlee's name were they thinking? How could they possibly defend this city?"

"This river makes a convincing wall," Abdel said weakly. He'd never actually considered Baldur's Gate from a tactical point of view.

The city sat at a point in the wide river where the water took a sudden bend to the north before continuing on to the Sea of Swords. Once they'd crossed the bulk of the width of the river, the old ferryman kept nudging Abdel, so he'd keep the ferry close, but not too close, to the rocky river bank now on their right side as they approached the busy harbor. The bend in the river made a sort of bay, and the city proper bent around that bay in a roughly horseshoe shape. Most of the city was surrounded by a high curtain wall that never ceased to impress Abdel. The number of stonemasons that must have been required, the time, the resources, all of it made Abdel marvel at the power behind the city's rulers. Rulers who, like him, were mercenaries, or had once been.

Few of the buildings in the city were taller than two stories, most of them shops with apartments above. There were houses, and cramped row houses. The air over the city was thick with smoke from countless fireplaces. Years of smoke had stained the once pale waddle and daub a dark gray. The sea of squat structures was occasionally punctuated by the odd unusual edifice. Even though it sat far back in the city's northernmost district, Abdel could see the tops of three of the seven towers of the High Hall, the city's ducal palace. The steeply arched roof of the temple of Gond—the so-called High House of Wonders—blocked the other four towers. To the west, jutting out on a brick-lined island and connected to the city by a strong stone bridge was the Seatower of Balduran, a fortress of five tall, round towers linked by a high wall, crinkled with battlements. Here the city's protectors, a mercenary company called the Flaming Fist, kept watch over the busy harbor.

And busy it was. Abdel counted thirty big merchant vessels tethered to piers or at anchor in the deep water before he gave up counting altogether. Two ships were leaving, slowly slipping through the traffic of smaller boats with only a small portion of their sails up. At least one massive ship was slowly making its way in.

The ferry passed the southernmost tower, and Jaheira appraised it ambivalently as they passed by. Two soldiers peered over the side at them, their faces only pale dots against the gray sky. Abdel made out the hair-thin line of a spear.

The sight of the first close buildings along the waterfront made Abdel's heart race. After what they'd been through—way beyond his already considerable experience as a sellsword—Abdel longed for the sense of normalcy a city like this could provide. He'd find a bath here, and a bed, and a flagon of ale, and an actual meal of seasoned meat and roasted vegetables. Abdel's mouth watered at the thought of it.

"Which is the Seven Suns?" Jaheira asked the old ferryman. Abdel had almost forgotten why they'd come to Baldur's Gate.

"The Seven Suns?" the ferryman asked. "Yeah, I 'eard of them. Which what's there's?"

"Warehouse?" Jaheira asked. "Or maybe they have a pier to themselves?"

"I think they do," the old man answered gravelly. "See that first big pier—the one with all the little piers sticking out of it?"

Jaheira nodded.

"Well, it ain't that one."

Jaheira turned on the old man, and her smile was disturbingly unamused. "It was a simple enough question, ferryman."

"I'm not a tour guide, missy," the ferryman spat back, then turned to Abdel and said. "Steer us to that first pier,

143

son, and let me get the womenfolk on their way."

Jaheira sighed and surveyed the city silently for the next half an hour as Abdel helped the old man and his crew maneuver the wide boat to the edge of the pier. A set of crumbling stone steps led up to the quay, and when Abdel made to disembark the old man put up a hand to hold him back—a comic sight in itself.

"Easy there, big fella," he said, "I want that fart-smelling cow off here first."

Jaheira looked at the old man like she was going to kill him, then blushed when she realized he was talking about the ox.

* * * * *

Someone spat on Jaheira as they walked through the crowded streets from the ferry landing to the Elfsong Tavern. The culprit was fast enough and knew the streets well enough to slip away before Abdel could kill him—and Abdel would have killed him. Jaheira took it in stride, though, and this surprised and, on some level, disappointed Abdel.

"It's because I am Amnian," Jaheira tried to explain. "The Iron Throne is getting their way, if slowly."

The looks on the faces of the crowd made it clear that if there were sides to be taken, the spitter would have plenty of locals on his side. Abdel took her smooth elbow in one hand and led her more quickly through the streets. He breathed a sigh of relief when they finally crossed the threshold of the big, venerable tavern Abdel had visited so many times before.

The Elfsong was an institution in Baldur's Gate, a place where people like Abdel could find work, and people who hired people like Abdel could find people like Abdel. Adventurers and treasure seekers came here for information, thieves came here to lie low and spend their takes, information was exchanged, pacts made, hearts broken, and noses bloodied. Abdel stood in the entryway and just breathed in the smell of it, savoring the tangible sense of community and familiarity until he noticed that Jaheira was looking at him strangely.

"It's good to be here," he told her, "you'll see."

She shrugged, not wanting to believe him. Abdel noticed the dark circles under her eyes. She hadn't been sleeping, and though the exhaustion hardly marred her beauty, Abdel feared she'd pass out on her feet.

"We need to eat," he said. "I'll send for my friend, and we can wait for him over stew, fresh baked bread, and the best ale on the Sword Coast—well, the second best." There was the Friendly Arms, after all.

Jaheira forced a smile and squeezed his hand with a casual familiarity that made Abdel's heart race and ache at the same time. He returned her smile and saw her to a table, then crossed the crowded but not too noisy room to the long bar. He paid the bartender a gold piece—nearly the rest of the coin he'd made arm wrestling miners and Amnian soldiers—to get his message sent, ordered drinks and food, then rejoined Jaheira.

"This friend of yours," Jaheira said, "he knows the Seven Suns?"

"If this trading coster operates in the Gate—if they wander past on occasion—Scar'll know them." He assured her.

" 'The Gate'?" she asked.

Abdel laughed and said, "It's what the locals call the city. You should use it, and maybe do something about your clothes, if being from Amn will get you spit on in the street."

"I don't hide who I am," she said, not managing to sound appropriately offended.

Abdel grinned and asked, "No?"

"Abdel, I . . ." Jaheira blushed, and when Abdel put the back of his hand gently to her cheek she leaned in to the touch and smiled. "Khalid and I are . . . were—"

She stopped when Abdel put a hand to her mouth. She stopped more from surprise than anything, then she realized the general tenor of the place had changed. It was almost dead quiet, save for the rattling of a shutter in the wind, and a woman's singing. Jaheira gently drew Abdel's hand from her mouth and held it. She scanned the room for the source of the ethereal voice, but no woman stood among the quiet, suddenly thoughtful patrons.

"Who—?" she started to ask, and Abdel's hand was on her mouth again. She furrowed her eyebrows at him this time, but when he smiled gently and glanced up at the featureless wooden ceiling of the place, she realized what was happening.

The voice was the most beautiful sound Jaheira had ever heard. It was a lone woman, singing a tune that played not with notes and sound but with the rhythms of heart and soul. The language was Elvish, but a dialect Jaheira couldn't identify if she tried, and she didn't try. There was a sense that putting words to this song, grounding this perfect play of tone and quaver, into the base, brutal bludgeoning of spoken language would be nothing short of a crime.

Surely this unseen woman—ghost, if that's what she was—couldn't know Jaheira, but the song had Khalid in it, the way he looked at her when they'd first met, the words he'd spoken to her on their wedding night, and the sad times too, the affairs and the lies and the subtle humiliations. A tear ran down Jaheira's cheek, then another, and Abdel wiped each away in turn with a big, gentle, callused fingertip.

The song evaporated into the nothingness from which it came, and Jaheira sagged in her chair. Conversation started to spatter through the room, and by the time the tavern had returned to as close to normal as it ever would, the bartender stood at their table with a fine silver wineglass.

He offered the glass to Jaheira with a knowing smile, glanced pointedly at her ears and said, "A tallglass of elverquisst, on the house."

Abdel nodded to the bartender, and Jaheira just reached out and took hold of the glass. She looked at it, letting the tears come as they may.

"It's a tradition," Abdel said, "when an elf hears the lady sing for the first time."

"I'm only—" she said, stopping herself with a loud sniff.

"It doesn't matter," Abdel told her as she sipped the sweet elven wine.

* * * * *

Abdel was frankly amazed at how quickly Scar made it to the Elfsong. It was as if his friend had been expecting him.

It didn't take a seasoned warrior to see that Scar was just that. Everything about the strong man showed that he had many a battle, and many a command, under his belt. He and Abdel embraced, and though when he entered Jaheira thought Scar was an enormous, imposing man, next to Abdel, he was merely a man. Scar seemed happy to see Abdel, happy and relieved.

"Abdel, you old pirate," the man said, "where have you been?"

Abdel's smile faded quickly, and he said, "I buried Gorion."

Scar's own smile faded. "I'm sorry to hear that, my friend. Gorion was . . . well . . ." Jaheira was amazed that a shrug from Scar seemed to make Abdel feel better.

"Sit," Abdel said, motioning Scar to a chair at their table, now cluttered with empty stew bowls, wineglasses, and pewter flagons.

"Been travelling long?" Scar asked facetiously, eyeing the mess instead of sitting.

"A lifetime," Abdel answered. "Jaheira, this is my good friend, who goes by the name Scar. If he asks you if you want to see what gave him that name, please refuse, or he won't be my friend anymore." It was Abdel's ham-handed way of telling Scar that Jaheira was more than a travelling companion or fellow soldier.

"Scar," Jaheira said. She wanted to stand, knew it would

147

be impolite not to, but she just couldn't. She was exhausted. "Please join us."

"Actually, I thought we might go upstairs," Scar said, turning to Abdel.

"Will a candle do it?" Abdel asked, referring to the Elfsong's policy of renting their private upstairs rooms by the length of time it took for one candle to burn down.

"I've made the arrangements," Scar said, motioning them to one of the dark, twisted staircases Jaheira had mistaken for pillars. Abdel helped her stand, and they followed Scar up the tight, treacherous steps. They sat at a small table surrounded by a richly embroidered curtain. A small oil lamp sat in the center of the table, casting a dim red glow that made Jaheira look a bit less pale. Scar grew serious the moment he sat down.

"Your message said you needed information, and my help."

Abdel, sensing it was time for straight, serious talk said, "We need to know about a trading coster that we think is operating out of the Gate. They call themselves the Seven Suns."

Scar just stared at his friend, saying nothing for the longest time. When Abdel crinkled his brow to urge his friend on, Scar sighed and asked, "Why?"

"We think they're involved with some group—maybe a splinter of the Zhentarim," Jaheira broke in, "maybe some merchant cabal from Sembia—that calls itself the Iron Throne."

"This Iron Throne," Abdel picked up, "is sabotaging the iron mines at Nashkel and other places, and Jaheira and the Harpers think they mean to start a war."

Jaheira looked at him sharply, and he returned her look with a confident smile. He'd been around awhile and knew a Harper when he fell in love with one.

"By Torm's hairy—" Scar said. He rubbed his face with his hands, his expression at least as worn as Jaheira's. "The Seven Suns is not just some merchant troupe that "might" work out of the Gate. They're a serious force in the power structure here. This is the first I've heard of this Iron Throne of yours, but I've been worried about the Seven Suns—very worried—over the last tenday."

"What have you heard?" Abdel asked.

"The Seven Suns are the same as any merchant company either of us has ever been hired to guard, my friend. They're in it—whatever it might be today—for the gold. That doesn't make them terribly altruistic, but it certainly makes them predictable. Over the last . . . well, I'm not really sure how long . . . they've been neglecting too many of their usual trade ventures—routes that always gave them steady profits. We've asked them, through proper channels and all very up front, if anything's wrong. Jhasso—that's the man behind the Seven Suns and a well known local—told us, in no uncertain terms, to mind our own business."

"But the business of the Gate is your business, no?" Abdel asked.

"Indeed," Scar agreed, "but try telling that to Jhasso. It's like the man has lost his ability to play the game—you know the game we hate so much?"

"Politics," Abdel answered with a sigh.

"Well," Scar continued, "I've learned that the dreaded 'P' word does have its place, but in this case it's getting in the way. I can't find anything that Jhasso's doing that's openly contrary to the interests of the dukes, or the Flaming Fist, or the citizens of the Gate. My hands are tied. I can't launch an official investigation . . . unless you two have brought proof of this sabotaging of the mines?"

The warrior looked at them both hopefully, and Jaheira had to look away. Abdel sighed, then pounded his fist loudly on the tabletop.

"Well," Scar said, understanding the answer to his question, "there are always alternatives."

"Just tell me where they are," Abdel said, a crafty smile spreading across his lips.

"Wait, wait," Jaheira said weakly, holding up a hand, "I didn't come here to end up in somebody's dungeon. If this

Jhasso is as connected as you say, sneaking around looking for . . . whatever we might go looking for, well, if we can't prove it now, who's to say we won't end up behind bars?"

Abdel laughed, and Scar just looked embarrassed.

"The Flaming Fist," Abdel said to Jaheira, "is a mercenary company with a long and well-respected history. They've taken on the role of . . . well, everything in the Gate: city watch, army . . . jailers."

"And?" Jaheira prompted.

"And," Abdel said, gesturing to Scar, "meet their second-in-command."

Chapter Nineteen

"That's it," Jaheira said, "the sigil I recognized on the crates and wagons."

Abdel nodded and looked carefully at the big warehouse in the rapidly dimming light. Scar told them where to find the place, and they waited across the busy street as the crowds diminished with the setting sun. Their conversation, their planning, consisted mostly of Jaheira trying to talk Abdel out of simply storming the place.

"Your friend Scar wanted information," she said, "information he can use to bring the Iron Throne down. I don't think he wanted dead bodies all over this beautiful city of his."

Abdel grunted and touched her arm, then pointed to a side door of the warehouse, visible from where they stood. A small group of sweaty teamsters emerged from the building, talking and laughing amongst themselves. They stayed together, probably on their way to one of the many dockside taverns, and eventually wandered out of sight.

The Seven Suns warehouse was built onto a long, wide stone pier and was only one of a dozen similar buildings, though by all accounts it was the biggest. The mark Jaheira recognized was emblazoned in red paint on the short end of the roughly rectangular brick structure. The sigil was eight feet tall, and Abdel couldn't help being a bit embarrassed that they'd had to ask Scar where to find the place. The Iron Throne may have been some kind of secret organization, but the Seven Suns trading coster certainly wasn't.

Other than the one warped wooden door, Abdel and Jaheira could see a handful of large windows, all of which were protected by heavy iron bars.

"It won't be easy to get in," Jaheira said.

Abdel grunted again and nodded. He was anxious to be on with it, but he knew he needed the sun to set.

"I've never actually done this before," Jaheira told him. He looked at her, confused, and she said, "I mean, I've never broken into a building before. This is burglary, right? We're thieves now."

Abdel smiled and shrugged. "We're spies," he said.

"What do you think we'll find in there?" she asked.

"Carts and crates full of iron ore," he offered. "Maybe some of that iron-weakening potion . . ."

Jaheira allowed herself her first real laugh in days and said, "Yes, with huge labels that say: Iron-Weakening Potion, Made in Baldur's Gate by the Iron Throne . . ."

". . . for all your iron-weakening needs," Abdel finished, and they shared a laugh.

"How did you know I was a Harper?" she asked, breaking the mood for the space of a heartbeat before Abdel started to laugh again.

"No," she pressed, "I'm serious. I could get into trouble if . . . well, you weren't supposed to know."

"Please, Jaheira," he said, "you're not the only Harper I've ever met. You people are about as secret as . . . well, you're not as secret as the Iron Throne, let's put it that way."

She looked at him sharply, going from surprised to offended to horrified and back to amused in a fraction of a second. She smiled and said, "I thought I—I thought we were being so coy."

"You were on a mission, you said," Abdel explained. "The rest of us were just looking for work."

Jaheira gasped at that last statement and actually hit him lightly on his powerful arm with her small fist. "That insane mage and that halfling were Zhentarim agents," she reminded him. "They were on a mission too, I can assure you."

"True enough," he agreed, then seemed somehow wistful, "and the mage still has my dagger. Gorion gave me that dagger. I do intend to kill those two."

"I'm sure you do," she said "I won't try to stop you, if that's what you mean."

Abdel forced a smile. He couldn't help feeling disappointed. He was starting to depend on Jaheira to do just that.

* * * * *

Night came to Baldur's Gate, and no light was visible through the barred windows of the big building.

"No one's there," Abdel said. "It looks empty."

"We should go."

Abdel followed Jaheira across the street. They walked arm in arm to allay suspicion, just two young lovers out for an evening stroll along the riverfront. They got to the side door, and Jaheira tested the rusting iron handle.

"Locked," she whispered.

Abdel brushed her aside lightly and took hold of the handle. He leaned sharply into the door, and it opened inward with a disturbingly loud crack. He smiled at Jaheira, who could see his white teeth in the darkness and said, "Abdel Adrian, Master Thief."

He almost laughed, but froze instead. She used that name: Abdel Adrian. The only other time he'd heard that was when he met Khalid in the Friendly Arms, what seemed like a lifetime ago. He hadn't thought anything of it then, but hearing it again now, after all that had happened, for some reason filled him with a nameless, undefined dread, like his heart was suddenly mired in mud.

He couldn't see her face clearly in the dark, but she tipped her head to one side. He shook his head slowly and forced a smile. He'd just opened the door into what might be no less than the Iron Throne's secret enclave. Now wasn't the time for conversation. Determined to ask her about that name as soon as they were finished here, he gently pushed the door open.

Inside there was only impenetrable darkness. Jaheira touched his shoulder, her touch warm and familiar. He bent down to let her get her lips as close to his ear as possible so she could whisper, "I can see."

Abdel nodded. Jaheira was a half-elf and had inherited her elf parent's extraordinary night vision. It made Abdel feel a bit better that at least one of them could see, but he still felt at a decided disadvantage. Fumbling around in the dark he was as likely to hurt—or even kill—Jaheira with a misplaced sword thrust as he was to take out a member of the Iron Throne. He shut his eyes tightly, then blinked, hoping his eyes would adjust, and he'd be able to see. It helped a little, but he was worried still.

Jaheira brushed past him and crept lightly into the expansive space. The whole building must have been one single room. Abdel followed closely, and she reached out a hand and grasped his. Abdel didn't like that they were so close together and without both hands at the ready. He tried to pull away, but she held on tight. He returned her grasp nervously, forcing himself to trust her.

She led him through the building slowly, making a number of zigzagging turns to avoid stacks of big wooden crates that were just enormous black mounds to Abdel's human eyes. For all he knew, there were a hundred men with crossbows encircling them in the darkness even now, just waiting for a clear head shot. That stack of crates in one corner could as easily be a manticore, stalking them. Abdel wanted to pull his sword and just start swinging it. He had to consciously will his hands away from the pommel, and he tightened his grip on Jaheira's hand to help. She squeezed back.

She stopped abruptly and uttered a barely audible shush. Abdel wasn't making any noise, so he knew she wasn't trying to tell him to be quiet. She was alerting him to something. Abdel opened his eyes as wide as he could, hoping to drink in any spare scrap of light, hoping just to be able to see anything at all. Jaheira didn't move and out of pure frustration Abdel closed his eyes. When he did, he heard the noise. It was so faint at first he'd assumed it was coming from outside, from the nearly empty street. Voices, deep and resonant male voices, muffled by some intervening structure, echoed in the darkness.

He leaned in close to Jaheira's ear and didn't stop until the tip of his nose brushed her fragrant hair.

"Where?" he whispered.

Jaheira didn't answer but started moving again. Still holding Abdel's hand, she led him to what even Abdel could see was a wall. At first Abdel thought his light-starved eyes were playing tricks on him, but there it was: a thin strip of flickering orange light. The voices were louder now but still muddy and undefined. The speakers were trying to keep their voices down. Jaheira shifted her weight, moving enough to reveal another source of dim light. From the size and distance from the floor, Abdel assumed it was a keyhole. Jaheira gently tugged him down, and he realized she wanted him to look through it. He obliged, holding the sheath of his sword with his other hand to keep it from rattling on either his own chain mail or the floor.

He blinked once and squinted through the keyhole. From this rather limited perspective he could make out much of the room beyond. There was a wood floor, same as the big warehouse room. Something moved, and the movement startled him. It was a man, maybe an elf—humanoid at least. The figure was in silhouette. He could hear what he thought were two voices. The light must have been coming from a torch or maybe a fireplace. Abdel could feel the heat on his eye.

The two figures conversed a bit more, and Abdel still couldn't tell what they were saying. The side of the figure he saw blurred, and Abdel blinked. The strain of peering through the little keyhole was obviously affecting his eyesight. When he pulled away he heard the scuffle of feet, and Jaheira put a hand on his shoulder, and he could feel her tense next to him. He didn't stand, though he desperately wanted to, for fear of making any noise. The footsteps were receding, and there was something about the pattern Abdel couldn't quite put his finger on.

"Steps," Jaheira whispered in his ear. The sound of the receding footsteps quickly faded away. Abdel could see nothing through the keyhole now but the wood floor and the orange firelight.

He stood slowly and put one hand on the middle of Jaheira's back. He drew her in to whisper into her ear, but her head wasn't turned to the side as he'd expected it to be and their noses touched. She gasped and leaned a minute fraction of an inch toward him, and he forgot where he was, what he was doing, and kissed her.

Her lips were warm and soft and welcoming, and lights danced behind Abdel's closed eyelids. He felt her hand on his chest, and he held her tighter, and her mouth opened just a little more—

—and a bright light blazed in the darkness, and a gruff voice grunted, "Pretty."

Abdel pushed Jaheira away and drew his sword in the space of time it took the half-elf woman to blink once and close her mouth. Abdel's eyes burned, and he could only imagine what Jaheira's more sensitive eyes must feel like.

"Alive!" the voice commanded, and there was the loud stomping of men rushing at him. Abdel, still blinded, holding his stinging, dripping eyes tightly closed against the light, just stabbed out at the sound.

One man went down with a wet thud, and Abdel tried to open his eyes. The light was still too bright, but he could see the outline of a small man in front of him—too close. Abdel couldn't get a swing in before the figure pushed into him.

"Move!" Jaheira shouted, and Abdel realized it was she who had pushed him. He took three quick steps back and felt the weak wooden door pop open behind him. When they passed through the doorway, Abdel's eyes cleared enough to see two men—wharf rats, all torn blouses and bandanas, and bad tattoos—coming at him with wooden cudgels. He pushed Jaheira to one side of the doorway and hefted his sword, looking to cut both attackers' heads off with one slice.

Instead, the door slammed shut in his face, knocking the tip of his sword to one side. Jaheira pressed her back against the door and set both feet. The men outside started pounding on the door.

Jaheira, tears streaming out of eyes now bloodshot and aching, said, "Wedge it closed, we're going downstairs."

Abdel only shrugged. The little room held only a crude stone fireplace—the crackling fire slowly dying—and a thin wooden stairway leading into darkness below. He didn't have anything to wedge a door shut with at hand.

Jaheira sighed, then began mumbling the words to another prayer. Abdel stared at her, feeling the pressure of each second as they passed by like hours. The men outside pounded, then leaned against the door trying to push it in. Jaheira looked concerned, but continued her chanting, then closed her eyes. Abdel could hear a creaking noise, faint at first, then a loud cry of warping wood.

"They're pushing through!" Abdel warned her. "Move aside!"

"Wait," Jaheira said, "that was me . . ."

The leader of the wharf rats clearly said the word "crossbows," and Jaheira jumped away from the door and into Abdel's arms. The tips of two crossbow bolts appeared in the middle of the door where the back of Jaheira's head had been only seconds before. Those two were followed by a third, and Jaheira didn't wait for the fourth. Taking hold of Abdel's hand she ran down the stairs, and he followed.

"I warped the door closed, but—" Jaheira started to say when they ran right into a strange humanoid creature that was so unnaturally featureless, with smooth gray skin and big, dead eyes, the woman screamed at the sight of it. The creature hissed and as Abdel brought his sword up, having to slide it past his own bulk in the thin stairway, the creature blurred, bulged, and started to transform. Steel plates appeared from nothing, and its eyes shrank to human size, the dark-gray whitening quickly, and the center popping into a medium blue color. Abdel's sword came down and clanged on a metal plate, sending a spark flying. The thing grunted and fell backward.

Abdel swung his sword around, and Jaheira dodged away, trying to give the big sellsword the room he'd require in the confined space. She wasn't fast enough, and Abdel had to hesitate. The creature regained its balance, fully transformed now, and it was a man, in plate armor and tabard emblazoned with the heraldry of the Flaming Fist, who then ran away from them into the darkness. Abdel took one step to follow and paused when he heard the crash of the door upstairs breaking free of its hinges. Feet scuffled on the wood floor above.

Jaheira said, "Let's go!" and tore off after the transformed creature.

Abdel hesitated again. The wharf rats were coming down the stairs, and Abdel turned and put one foot on the bottom step. He met the eyes of the first man down. The thug stopped short, surprised to see Abdel so close to him, sword out in front and ready for the charge. The wharf rat's comrade couldn't stop quite as fast, not having seen Abdel, and he inadvertently pushed his friend from behind. The first wharf rat fell onto Abdel's sword and let out a thin, gurgling whimper as he slid down the length of the blade, stopping only at the polished brass hand guard. Blood poured over Abdel's hands, and he pushed forward to try to clear his blade.

"Abdel!" Jaheira shouted from down the corridor. "There's too many of them!"

Abdel didn't care how many there were, he just wanted to get this one off of his sword. He tried pushing him off, but the press of thugs on the stairs kept pushing their dead friend back onto Abdel's blade. He couldn't move sideways in either direction, so he opted for backward. He took only one and a half steps before his back touched the stone wall.

"Abdel!" Jaheira shouted sharply. He still couldn't free his blade.

One of the wharf rats fired a crossbow bolt, and Abdel was lucky. The steel quarrel clanged harmlessly off the wall next to his right ear.

"Alive, I said!" the gruff voice called out angrily.

Abdel was still trying to clear his blade when another of the featureless gray creatures appeared out of the darkness to his right. This one lifted a thin, gray-skinned hand, and Abdel saw the flash of gold—it was wearing a ring—and the thing touched its cold fingertips to Abdel's temple. The sellsword distinctly heard the creature whisper a single word: "Sizzle."

A pain like Abdel had never felt before exploded in his head, and he was conscious of his elbows jerking up with sufficient force to rip the dead wharf rat from gut to shoulder blade, and then there was only darkness, the scuffle of feet, echoing voices, and hands all over him.

* * * * *

The act of simply opening his eyes sent such a wave of pain through Abdel's head that he quickly regretted having awakened and shut his eyes again. That action was followed quickly by another wave of pain, then a third at the sound of Jaheira's voice, muffled as it was, saying, "—ake up, for Mielikki's sake. Abdel!"

He tried to answer her but opening his mouth was pure agony, and all he was able to produce was a quavering groan.

"Abdel," Jaheira called from wherever she was, "you're alive." The relief in her voice was apparent.

"Who are you people?" a strange voice, as distant as Jaheira's, asked.

"Who are you?" Jaheira answered.

Abdel opened his eyes, and this time the pain was less intense. He'd felt this way before, after long nights of ale and other spirits, but this was worse. Much worse. There was light coming in through a tiny window, a square maybe a foot on a side, so Abdel had enough light to survey his surroundings.

Philip Athans

"Damn," he breathed when he realized he was in a cell. He was locked up like an animal.

"I asked you first," the strange man replied suspiciously.

Abdel had no idea how long he'd been on the floor of the cell. His sword was gone, and so was his chain mail tunic. He could smell himself, and his throat was burning with thirst. There was a bucket, but the contents of it were unspeakable. There was no water, just a bit of hay and a stout wooden door reinforced with iron bands. Iron bars protected the little window.

"Abdel," Jaheira called, apparently from another cell, "say something."

"I'm thirsty," he said loudly, and the strange man laughed.

"Tell me about it," he said, "these doppelgangers are lousy hosts."

"Doppelgangers?" Jaheira asked.

Abdel had heard of these vile, shapeshifting beasts. From what he'd heard, the city of Waterdeep was all but ruled by them. Some were convinced that nearly every city and realm on Faerûn had at least one doppelganger in its political structure. Abdel had always laughed those stories off, though. He knew people could be evil enough on their own without having to have been replaced by monsters.

"If you are doppelgangers," the stranger said, "I'm not telling you anything new. If you aren't, you might be able to help me get out of this."

"Who are you?" Abdel asked.

"The name's Jhasso. I used to run this place."

Chapter Twenty

Harold Loggerson of Bowshot cut himself playing with his father's best axe at the age of nine. He couldn't sit down for the three weeks it took the cut to heal, and it left a long, ragged scar, a scar that few had ever seen, but that gave him a name more fitting for a leader of mercenaries than Harold.

In the years since that cut—and the harsh words that followed from his father, even as his mother stitched the cut with quilting thread—Scar had avoided axes. He wasn't afraid of them so much as embarrassed by the sight of them. Two years ago, he killed a Zhentarim soldier while protecting a caravan bringing apples (and raw gold mined in the Serpent Hills hidden under the fruit) from Soubar to Baldur's Gate. The Zhent attacked him with a solid, heavy mithral axe decorated with gold that flew farther, straighter, and faster when thrown than any weapon Scar had ever seen. It took him a long time to kill the Zhent, and he almost died trying, but in the end Scar took the axe.

He'd only shown it to one other man and never worn it into battle or on the streets of Baldur's Gate. He practiced with it only rarely, and only when he was alone, and only at night. The rest of the time he kept it locked in a dwarven-work iron box slid under his bed.

Scar hefted the axe and felt its weight, then spun it in his hand, his left palm cupped around the end of the steel handle. When he sliced it through the air it seemed to sing,

161

or was that the air itself screaming at being cut? Scar smiled at the sound, but the smile was tinged with sadness. His father had fallen to heartstop long before he could have seen this wonderful axe in his son's hand. His father had been more confused than disappointed by young Harold's desire to enter the soldiery, and they'd spoken only once in his father's last eight years of life. His father was a good man, but a simple one, with simple needs and simple desires. His father lived to be almost fifty years old, and had never been more than half a day's walk from the two-mule hamlet of Bowshot. Harold—or Scar, as the two were really different people—had been to Waterdeep, had lain with an elf maiden in the High Forest, climbed the Star Mounts, sailed to the Moonshaes, skinned a dozen wolves in the Wood of Sharp Teeth, and been lashed by the burning sands of Anauroch.

"I should go to Bowshot," he whispered to himself, then chuckled at his sudden, silly sentimentality. "Away with you, now," he said to the axe and laid it gently into the velvet-lined box.

There was a knock at the door, heavy and urgent, and Scar jumped at the sound. He closed the lid quickly and clicked the dwarven padlock into place.

"Who is it?" he called gruffly, though not unaccustomed to being roused at all hours by urgent news and duties.

"Abdel," a familiar voice said from the other side of the door. "I have Jaheira with me. We need to talk."

"Coming," Scar said, then slid the iron box under his bed, replaced the hanging edge of the quilt his mother had given him years before, and stood. He crossed the room quickly and pulled back the heavy steel bolt. He opened the door to see Abdel, clean and no worse for wear. The young sellsword's face was expectant, almost nervous.

"Come in, lad," Scar said. "I didn't expect to see you until morning."

Abdel nodded once and stepped in. Jaheira followed him, taking careful stock of Scar's chamber. It was a simple room, for a man with needs that had become nearly as simple as his father's. A crackling fire provided warmth and light. There was a wide bed, a stout table with three chairs where—before that game of dice he was still trying to live down—there had been four. A shield bearing the distinctive heraldry of the Flaming Fist hung over the mantel. The shield was dented and scratched from years of use.

Scar motioned them to the chairs, but neither sat.

"We've been to the Seven Suns," Abdel said.

"Indeed," Scar replied, "let's have it. Did you see Jhasso?"

"Yes," Jaheira's voice came from behind him. He hadn't noticed her circling him. "Yes, we did."

Scar's eyes narrowed, and he turned to follow Jaheira as she continued to wander slowly around the room on stiff, halting legs. "And?"

"And he means no evil," Abdel said from behind him. Scar turned to look at Abdel, and Jaheira stopped, just at the edge of his vision. Scar took a step back, instinctively.

"What did you find?" he asked.

Jaheira stepped back too, staying just out of his range of vision. Abdel smiled.

"Iron-poisoning potions?" Abdel joked. "Is that what you expected to find?"

Scar stepped back again and to the side, and Jaheira obliged him, moving into his vision even as Abdel took three long, slow steps to Scar's side.

"What did you expect to find, old man?" Jaheira asked him, her voice full of ominous import.

A sweat broke out on Scar's forehead. He was unarmed, dressed only in thin wool trousers and a cotton blouse. He felt naked.

"What is this, Abdel?" he asked, and before he got the name out he realized: "You're not Abdel."

The sellsword stopped walking, and Scar turned to face him. Jaheira stepped lightly behind him.

"Of course I'm Abdel," the big man said, reaching slowly, teasingly, for the broadsword hanging from his back, "for now, at least."

There was the screech of steel on steel and Scar knew it was Jaheira drawing her long sword.

"Damn you," Scar cursed and stepped to the side faster than anyone would expect a man of his years and girth to move, "to all Nine Hells and back again!"

Abdel's sword met Jaheira's in the space that was, less than a second ago, occupied by Scar's head. Abdel grunted, and the woman swore when her blade broke neatly in two. Abdel pulled up short of killing her, and they both spun on Scar. Jaheira's sword was now no longer than a decent dagger, and flat on top, but the blade and jagged edge were still sharp, still deadly.

"What have you done with them?" Scar asked, backing up, his feet wide apart. "Do you inhabit their bodies?"

"Do we?" Jaheira asked, a devilish gleam in her eyes.

"If we do," Abdel added, "and you kill us, your friends' spirits will drift—"

Scar hopped forward, startling both the impostors, but the two recovered quickly, and Abdel made a fast, tentative stab that drove Scar back again. The mercenary leader circled, going toward the door. Abdel stepped up to block it, and Jaheira went the other direction. Scar backed up against the wall, his eyes darting to random spots around the room. Both impostors tried to track his gaze but soon gave up.

Abdel smiled craftily and said, "Panicking, old man?"

Scar swallowed loudly and said, "Kill me, then, if that's what you came for."

"Oh, that is indeed what we came for, fool," Jaheira hissed, "but we were asked to find something out first."

"And you thought I'd tell you anything?" Scar asked, his voice dripping with incredulity, his eyes still darting around the room, not focussing on any one thing, especially the broken tip of Jaheira's still-sharp sword.

"We can kill you with a thousand cuts, old man," Abdel said, "or a single one."

"So if I tell you what you want to know, you'll kill me quick?"

"Aye," Jaheira said, keeping her distance, but still trying to keep to the edge of Scar's vision.

"If I had a gold piece for every time that offer was made to me, assassin," Scar said lightly, "I'd have enough to hire Elminster to protect me."

Neither Abdel nor Jaheira thought that was the least bit funny.

"As you wish," Abdel said, then blinked in Jaheira's direction.

The woman came in fast, and Scar tried to flinch back but was already against the wall. The back of his head knocked against the stone blocks and bounced back into Jaheira's swing. The jagged edge of the broken blade gouged a deep cut over Scar's left eye and he hissed at the pain. Jaheira skipped back three steps, flicking the blood from the edge of the blade. Scar put his hand to his head. Blood flowed freely, and he tried to blink it out of his eye. The warm fluid stung.

"Bitch," Scar scowled, "I'll kill you for that."

Jaheira ignored him and asked, "Why did you send us to the Seven Suns?"

"Did you kill Abdel and his woman?" Scar asked in return.

Jaheira came at him again, slicing high and across. This time Scar stepped into the attack. Jaheira had her arm up too high, exposing too much of her body, and Scar slammed into her. He grabbed her arm from underneath and used the woman's momentum to flip her tail over teacup and smash her roughly to the wood floor. He could see Abdel coming in fast and dived head first for the broken tip of Jaheira's sword that lay a few feet away.

Jaheira spat out a feral, inhuman growl and spun to stand up. Abdel fouled in her twisting legs and came crashing down next to Scar, the heavy broadsword bounced out of the impostor's grasp and slid away, coming to a stop at the edge of the brick hearth. Scar grabbed the broken blade and ignored the pain of the sharp edges cutting into his hand. The mercenary leader hopped up to a crouching position and grabbed for the box under his bed.

Abdel stood up and took the time to retrieve his sword.

"Just kill him," Jaheira spat. "To the hells with the Iron Throne!"

Scar heard heavy footfalls and grabbed the rough leather handle of the iron box at the same time. Abdel came in and down fast, and Scar spun on his rump to avoid the first downward stab. The sword tip bit deeply into the wood planks but didn't break. Scar pulled his knee to his chin and kicked out. Abdel saw the kick coming and jumped back out of the way, though the kick wasn't intended for him. Scar's bare foot smashed into the side of the iron box and the box scraped deep furrows into the wood floor as it slid out from under the bed. Scar didn't see it stop. Jaheira stomped on his forehead with a booted foot, and the old mercenary's head exploded with pain and light. The sound of his head hitting the floor echoed in his skull, and he had to fight to stay conscious. He felt the woman's knee on his chest and put a hand up to guard his face. Jaheira dragged a bloody scrape across the old mercenary's palm and Scar hissed again. He slashed with the broken blade, and it cut deeply through the woman's heavy trousers and into her leg. It was Jaheira's turn to hiss, and Scar took advantage of her momentary weakness, and he threw her off him.

"I'll bleed you dry!" she shrieked at him, but Scar ignored the threat and rolled forward and up, diving ahead with all his weight and strength. He saw Abdel's foot, and the impostor backed off again, but as before, Abdel wasn't Scar's target. There was a flash of white-hot pain and a loud shriek of metal on metal when Scar brought the broken sword tip down on the iron padlock, and the blade and lock shattered all at once.

Scar rolled, knowing he'd been heading in one direction too long, and his instincts proved correct. Abdel's blade came down hard again, and again only took splinters from the now ruined floor. Scar pushed the box open and grunted when a jagged piece of the shattered blade, that was still stuck in his bleeding palm, was driven deeper.

Abdel's sword came down again, and this time it pierced Scar's heavily muscled thigh. The old mercenary grunted at the pain and wanted to cry out but couldn't. Abdel's heavy boot landed square on Scar's chest. The old mercenary was driven hard to the floor, but the push only helped him lift the weighty axe out of the box. He slashed down in a wide arc and caught the impostor Abdel in the groin. There was a gout of blood, and the young sellsword fell. The axe was stuck in the already dead body, and it slipped easily out of Scar's weakening grip. He sighed heavily, content to at least have taken one down.

Abdel hit the ground quivering, and when the impostor's head lolled over on its lifeless neck, the face changed. Scar was face to face with some inhuman thing. It had a wide oval head with impossibly large, soulless eyes and smooth gray skin the color of old ash. He saw the axe come free of the dead thing's body, and he rolled to sit up.

He was going to say something—some last words, but he didn't have time. The air was smashed from his lungs, and he fell back hard. The impostor Jaheira drove the big battle-axe deeply into Scar's chest, then out the other side, pinning the man to the wood floor. Scar felt the blood bubble in his throat and saw the demonic gleam in the woman's eyes as her face became his own, then there was only blackness and eternity.

* * * * *

Julius stared straight ahead and mouthed the word "corporal" three times, then offered the empty corridor a self-satisfied smile.

"Stop that grinning, corporal," Sergeant Maerik grumbled. Julius jumped, and his face flushed. He hadn't seen or heard the sergeant approach. Maerik stood in front of Julius and stood on his toes to stare the younger, taller corporal in the eyes. Their noses were almost touching.

"Where are you, son?" the sergeant asked quietly.

"Sir," Julius began, then paused to force down a swallow in a dry throat. "Sir, in the ducal palace, sir."

"Where in the ducal palace, corporal?"

"Sir, in the residence wing, sir."

"Do you mean the place where the grand dukes live?"

"Sir, yes, sir."

"Where Grand Duke Eltan lives?"

"Sir, yes, sir."

"The Grand Duke Eltan who's facing a ducal election?"

"Sir, yes, sir."

"The Grand Duke Eltan who has more enemies than any one man in the Gate?"

"Sir yes, s—"

"Then *wake up*, you idiot," the sergeant shouted.

Julius tensed his abdomen, concentrating on holding his bladder. "S-sir," he stammered, "y-yes, sir."

"As you *weren't*, corporal." Maerik scoffed, then turned down the corridor and off a side passage, his boots making no sound on the cold marble floor.

Julius breathed a sigh of relief. He'd only been assigned to the ducal palace for a week now, and though he'd been in battle before, even fought wererats in the darkest part of the wharf, this was the most tense duty he'd ever pulled. He wasn't worried that an assassin might get in, not this far into the ducal palace, but he was afraid that what just happened might happen again, and again, enough times for his newfound rank to find its way back down to footman.

He shifted the halberd over to his left side and mopped sweat from his brow. It was late—or early—and his eyes felt heavy, dry, and tired. A tiny sound made him jump, and he glanced sharply down the dimly-lit corridor to see a mouse scurry off into the darkness. He sighed, then jumped again when a heavy hand landed squarely on his shoulder.

"Heads up, soldier."

The man was instantly familiar to Julius. Scar had led the attack on the wererats, and Julius was at the briefing he gave, then fought at the experienced warrior's side for a few precious moments in the sewer drain.

"C-captain Scar," Julius said, standing as straight as he could. "I—uh—I wasn't told . . ."

Scar scowled at him and said, "Why would you be?"

"I—" Julius started to say. Scar held up a hand to stop him.

"Go to the stables and ready the grand duke's steed," Scar ordered casually, "I'm getting him out of here before dawn."

Julius was so surprised he just stood there with his mouth hanging open. Something was going on, something big. Not on my watch, Julius thought, why on my watch?

"Are we unclear on something, corporal?"

"N-no, sir, I just—"

"Move your ass, kid." Scar said, and the look in his eye was enough to propel Julius down the corridor as fast as his shaking knees would take him.

He ran for a while before he realized that, as he was prone to do in the labyrinthine palace, especially at night, he'd gotten himself lost. He prayed strenuously to Tymora, who answered his prayer with the luck goddess's typical sense of humor.

"By Umberlee's undulating bosom, boy," Sergeant Maerik belted out, "what in the name of every other god are you doing here, you addle-pated son of a flea-bitten—!"

"I'm lost," Julius said before he had any chance to even think how amazingly bad an idea it was to say that.

Sergeant Maerik punched him in the face.

"I'm sorry," Julius squealed even as he fell hard on his rump. Blood tricked from his still vibrating nose, and his halberd clattered on the floor next to him.

"This is hardly the time to leave your post, you butt-sniffing dolt," the sergeant shouted. "Captain Scar's been murdered, and the whole company's being called up."

"But I just saw him," Julius blurted.

"Saw who, you tick?"

"Scar," Julius said, scrambling to his feet. "It was Captain Scar who told me to go to the stables and get Grand

Duke Eltan's horse—"

"Scar was *here?*" Maerik asked, his eyes wide. "This night?"

"Sir," Julius said, straightening his blood-dripped tabard and scanning for his fallen polearm, "not half an hour ago, sir. He was going into the grand duke's residence."

Maerik went pale and grabbed Julius roughly, dragging him down the corridor at a run.

"Not on my watch!" the sergeant cursed. "Why does it always have to be *my* watch!"

* * * * *

Julius and Maerik skidded to a halt at the wide double doors that led into the grand duke's private residence. Julius had had a difficult time keeping up with the sergeant, and when they stopped Julius was panting, almost gasping for air.

The grand duke stepped out of his chambers holding a huge battle-axe the likes of which Julius had never seen— or even dreamed of. The man was dressed in a long nightgown that was soaked with blood. His eyes and hands were steady. His broad, serious face was also smeared with blood, and some of it dripped from the tip of his long handlebar mustache. His crystal-blue eyes blazed under bushy gray eyebrows that matched the short-cropped hair still disheveled from bed.

Maerik fell to one knee, and Julius followed suit, unable to take his eyes off the gold-and-mithral axe.

"M'lord," Maerik said, "I—"

"Captain Scar has been murdered," the grand duke said simply. Maerik stood, and Eltan reached back to push the tall door open. On the richly-carpeted floor inside lay the gray body of some inhuman thing, still leaking blood on the expensive wool.

"Aye, m'lord," Maerik breathed. "He was found in his chamber."

Julius gagged at the sight of the dead thing's eyes.

Eltan's strong, aging features were grave. "Have the captain's body taken to the High House of Wonders," he said, his voice low and full of import. "I will dress and meet you there."

Chapter Twenty-One

"Sounds like your friends are here," Jhasso said, trying to peer through the little window in his cell.

"Or yours," Jaheira offered.

The sound of battle was unmistakable, though far off and muffled by at least one floor. Abdel could hear the ring of steel on steel, the stomp and scuffle of feet, a body falling, then another. His arms tensed, and he tried again to pull the bars out of the window. They shifted this time but only a little. He felt like a rat in an innkeeper's trap, and he wanted out.

"No," Jhasso answered Jaheira. "I don't have any friends."

"Not if there's been a doppelganger you making enemies all over the city for as long as you say you've been in there." Jaheira agreed.

"Damn them," Jhasso said, "I thought they were all in Waterdeep."

The three of them, all cold, exhausted, and teetering on the edge of claustrophobic insanity, just stood there listening to the sound of battle.

A door burst in suddenly, and the sound was close. Abdel turned his head and pressed his cheek into the bars trying to see anything. There was a warm orange light at the end of the hallway, and Abdel could see twisted, flickering shadows on the stonework, shadows that danced to the tune of ringing steel, stomping feet, and desperate grunts. A body fell, and the steps rushed toward the cells. A young man wearing a blood- and sweat-stained tabard bearing the sign of the Flaming Fist stopped in front of Abdel's cell. Blood dripped from a halberd that was easily heavier than the young soldier.

"Are you Jha-Jhasso?" the soldier asked breathlessly.

"He's in the cell behind you, troop," Abdel answered at the same time Jhasso called out, "Let me outta here, kid!"

The young soldier looked confused and frightened. "I have to get somebody," he said.

"You're not leaving us here!" Jaheira called, and the young man stopped at the sound of a woman's voice.

"Fear not, madam," the soldier said. "I'll be back for you!"

With that—and followed closely by some rude remarks from all three captives—the young soldier hared off up the corridor. They could hear voices and more footsteps going up the stairs and away into the diminishing sounds of battle.

"He's coming back for us, right?" Jhasso asked.

"He better damn well," Abdel said. "If not, I'm going to stick my fist so far up his—"

"Listen!" Jaheira said, and Abdel and Jhasso held very still. The fight was obviously over. Abdel could hear the muffled sounds of male voices and heavy footsteps approaching. A door opened and there was the unmistakable sound of a man in heavy metal armor rapidly descending the stairs.

"Here, Gondsman," a steady, commanding voice said. Abdel could see a sturdy older man in shining, blood-spattered plate mail. His face was unfamiliar, but his accoutrements were unmistakable. This man was a grand duke, and his crest bore the sigil of the Flaming Fist. Could this be—?

"Grand Duke Eltan," the young soldier who first found them said, confirming Abdel's suspicions, "I found the key, m'lord."

"Very good, Julius," Eltan answered. "When the priest is finished, let these people out."

Philip Athans

"Let us out now, for Gond's sake," Jhasso whined.

Abdel saw a stout man in saffron robes stop at the door of Jhasso's cell and peer in. The priest went to each of the three doors in turn. Abdel met his gaze when the priest came to his door, but couldn't make eye contact. The man's eyes were strangely out of focus, like he was looking at a point somewhere in front of or behind Abdel.

"The men are human," the priest said to Eltan, "and the woman is a half-elf."

"Open them," Eltan said, and in seconds the three of them were free.

When Abdel stepped out of his cell Julius looked up at him and swallowed. "S-sorry," the young soldier said.

"No need to be sorry, corporal," Abdel said with a smile, "there're doppelgangers about."

"Indeed there are," the grand duke agreed, looking Abdel up and down suspiciously. "Two of them killed Scar."

"No," Jaheira breathed.

"And at least one has taken my place," Jhasso said. "I hope I still have a business to run, Eltan."

The grand duke looked at Jhasso impatiently and said, "You'll answer only for what you're responsible for, Jhasso. For now, just stay out of the way."

Jhasso nodded, obviously content to be let out of whatever was going to happen next.

"Your . . . duke-ness . . ." Abdel stammered, exhaustion and grief making his mind muddy.

"My name is Eltan," the grand duke said sternly. "You must be Abdel."

"I am," Abdel answered. "Scar was my friend. I'd like the opportunity to kill the things that took his life."

"Scar beat you to one," Eltan answered, "and I had the pleasure of disemboweling the second, but something tells me there's more killing to be done, my good man, if you've a mind to kill."

Abdel nodded. He had a mind to kill.

* * * * *

Abdel and Jaheira were given very little time to clean up, and Abdel spent most of that time eating. He was given back his sword and chain mail, neither the worse for wear. They met in the foyer of Grand Duke Eltan's residence in the ducal palace. Abdel smiled at Jaheira, who was wearing a simple but flattering black gown lent to her by Grand Duchess Liia Jannath herself. Abdel felt bad then that he hadn't changed himself. He hoped at least he wasn't offensive in look or smell.

A sleepy butler showed them into the grand duke's study, and Abdel knew no one there would spare the time to smell him. The air in the room was serious, like a general's tent on the eve of battle.

"Abdel," Eltan said motioning them into the richly-appointed room, "Jaheira, enter."

Eltan was sitting at his desk with his arm resting on the wide mahogany surface. A thin man with wiry gray hair and strange glass disks in wire frames resting on his nose, was bent over the grand duke's arm, carefully stitching a nasty cut. Eltan winced when the healer pulled the thread tight and cut off the end.

"You were wounded," Abdel said unnecessarily.

"Aye," Eltan said, smiling, "my two hundredth cut in battle. I should throw a party."

Abdel smiled and stood quietly next to Jaheira while Eltan gave orders in hushed tones to three Flaming Fist officers who stood on the other side of the big desk. Finished, he sent them off to the temple of Gond where they were to elicit the aid of priests who apparently had the ability to recognize a doppelganger when they saw one.

As the officers filed out and the healer collected his implements into a leather satchel, the grand duke motioned Abdel and Jaheira forward.

"I understand," Eltan said, "that you fought beside my friend Harold Loggerson more than once."

Abdel looked confused. "M'lord?"

"Scar," Eltan said, his voice full of emotion. "You never knew his real name?"

"No," Abdel said. He glanced at Jaheira, embarrassed but not sure why. "No, m'lord. Perhaps we were not such good—"

Eltan stopped him with a hand and said, "No, no. You can count on the fingers of one hand the people who know that name. Sit, we have much to discuss."

Eltan looked tired. His eyes were circled by gray marks that were turning almost purple. His cheeks were sunken and his eyes red. He was still wearing most of his armor as if he were too exhausted to remove it, or knew he would have need of it soon. Jaheira sat first, then Abdel, and both of them couldn't help but admire the soft leather of the big chairs with a gentle touch.

"Not quite the general's tent, eh sellsword?" Eltan remarked, winking once at Jaheira.

"You—" Abdel started to say, before he realized no response was necessary.

"This city is blessed with a number of fine temples," Eltan said, "and cursed with a number more, I suppose. When word of Scar's death came to me I had him brought to the High House of Wonders in hopes that my good friend Thalamond might be able to breathe life back into the old war dog's lungs."

Abdel had heard this was possible, but it was a power most priesthoods reserved for the most dire of circumstances. Jaheira looked at Abdel, and he saw she was impressed as much by the sort of friends Abdel attracted as by the scope of the situation they now found themselves in.

"They couldn't do it, I'm afraid," Eltan said. "His soul had fled, or . . . well, whatever." The grand duke took a moment to compose himself, then said, "They allowed me to speak with him, though, if you can believe such a thing is possible. He vouched for you, as only Scar could. He told me he'd sent you two snooping around the Seven Suns's pier, that there was some connection between them and some group that is responsible for our troubles with the iron mines."

"Yes, m'lord," Jaheira said. "I was sent by the Harpers to look into this." She paused to look at Abdel, who smiled slightly and nodded. "The Iron Throne wants to start a war between your people and mine."

"A war with Amn?" Eltan asked. "To what end?"

Jaheira shook her head and said, "I don't know. That was what Scar sent us to that pier to find out."

"My city is crawling with doppelgangers," Eltan said, "we're being pushed into war with Amn, our resources are being sabotaged, and no one knows why?"

Jaheira reddened, sensing Eltan's mounting frustration.

"I know where the Iron Throne meets," Eltan said, and as if in answer a sharp sound of metal hitting the marble floor startled all of them. They looked up at the healer, who smiled sheepishly from the corner.

"You can go, Kendal," Eltan told the man, "I'll be fine."

"I will need to change that dressing, m'lord," the healer said, "tomorrow morning."

"Very well," Eltan agreed with an impatient wave. "Off with you."

The door closed behind the healer, and Abdel asked, "Where is this place?"

"Here in the city," Eltan said. "You can come along if you like. I could use a man who can operate outside the walls of the Gate. If Scar trusted you, that's good enough for me." He looked at Jaheira and said, "I've met Harpers before, miss, but I won't hold that against you."

Jaheira blushed and they stood to go.

* * * * *

" 'We will be monks again, for a time,' " Julius read from the dog-eared notebook. " 'Return to the meeting place under the pillars of the Wise God.' "

The young corporal looked up at the grand duke, Sergeant Maerik, Abdel, and Jaheira. Julius was squatting next to the tall, wiry man dressed in black leather that Abdel had killed. There seemed to be only two men left in the Iron Throne's subterranean lair. Eltan and his forces were one step behind them.

"Candlekeep," Abdel said quietly.

"Can they get in there?" Eltan asked. "My understanding was that Candlekeep rarely if ever opens her gates. How could a whole cabal of conspirators use Candlekeep as a meeting place?"

"Gorion could have answered that," Jaheira said, looking sadly up at Abdel.

The sellsword nodded slowly. "My father was a monk," Abdel said to Eltan. "He raised me behind the walls of Candlekeep, and he set me on the path I've been walking for what seems like a lifetime now. He led me to Jaheira." He turned to the half-elf and asked, "Was he working for the Harpers?"

Jaheira shook her head and said, "He was a friend."

"I can sooner go to war with Amn and win than storm the gates of Candlekeep," Eltan sighed. He wasn't defeated, he was thinking.

"Seems a handy clue," Maerik piped in, and Eltan looked at him sharply. The sergeant took half a step backward and said, "My apologies, I—"

"Don't apologize, sergeant," Eltan said. "This notebook was a rather important text to leave behind."

"The Iron Throne has done sillier things, m'lord," Abdel offered. "How could they want us to know they've gone to Candlekeep?"

"If it's true what you—" Julius started, then stopped at a sharp look from Maerik.

Eltan held up a hand and said, "Go on, corporal."

Julius smiled weakly and said, "M'lord, if we can't get into Candlekeep, maybe they want us to—want *you* to know they're out of your reach."

"They're taunting me?" Eltan asked.

Julius shuddered. "I'm just—"

"It's possible," Jaheira said. "We—the Harpers—have thought there's one man behind this whole thing. A dwarf the Iron Throne had made a slave told us this man's name. He's a wealthy merchant from Sembia named Reiltar. I have reason to believe this man Reiltar is the—is a son of Bhaal."

Abdel looked at her with eyes wide. There it was again, the name of this dead god of murder and the idea that he'd left behind sons. Maybe, Abdel thought, I should have pressed Jaheira for what else she knew. Jaheira looked at Abdel with a red, almost frightened face.

"The son of Bhaal?" Eltan asked, incredulous. "The dead *god* Bhaal?"

Jaheira nodded, and Julius stood on shaking legs.

"That's madness," Maerik commented. "M'lord, who are these people?"

Eltan looked at Maerik, then at Jaheira, and said, "How could you know this?"

"There are others," Jaheira said. "Other offspring of Bhaal. The Harpers have been watching some, have lost track of others. No one knows how many have survived."

"And one of them wants to start a war with Amn?" Julius asked, forgetting his place.

"Murder," Jaheira said, "on a grand scale."

Abdel swallowed in a suddenly dry throat. Gooseflesh rippled across his arms and chest, and he felt his body shudder. Murder, Abdel thought while holding back a smile with great effort, on a grand scale.

Chapter Twenty-Two

"Murder," Tamoko said, "on a grand scale."

Sarevok smiled at her—smiled that demon smile—but Tamoko did not step back. To her surprise, Sarevok seemed pleased.

"Murder, yes," he said. His voice echoed in the underground chamber, and there was an unsettling shriek of steel on steel as he dragged a long, thin dagger absentmindedly across his black metal breastplate. A spark flew, but there was not a mark on the armor.

"This is not . . ." Tamoko paused, then sighed in frustration. She wasn't reluctant to speak, but was still not completely fluent in the common tongue of Faerûn. "It is not . . . acceptable. Acceptable."

Sarevok's yellow eyes flashed, and he turned back to the empty frame, eyeing it casually, as if it showed a scene of only passing interest.

"Tamoko, my dear girl," he said finally. "When I found you, you were killing every day, for money. You murdered as a way of life."

She bristled at the comparison, and her outrage gave her courage. "There is no shame in the life of an assassin."

"You killed innocent people," he pressed. "That is murder."

"Innocent people have nothing to fear from the assassin's blade," she said. "Innocent men do not associate with men who might hire an assassin. If I am sent to a man, that

180

man has made the reason, one way or another."

"So," Sarevok said, turning to her with a self-satisfied grin, "you only killed corrupt men."

"Yes," she said, her chin held high, falling into his trap.

"On the orders of corrupt men."

She flushed and looked away. Sarevok chuckled and turned to the frame.

"You may enter," he said evenly.

Tamoko turned at the sound of the opening door, and a doppelganger strode slowly, reluctantly into the room. Its huge, lifeless eyes darted around the chamber's spartan furnishings, then took careful stock of Tamoko who stood rigidly at Sarevok's side. The woman was dressed simply in loose-fitting trousers and a matching black tunic. Her thin, curved katana hung in its sheath at her waist. She regarded the doppelganger coldly, having no love for these creatures who were without selves.

"You are an idiot," Sarevok said to the doppelganger, and the creature dropped instantly to its knees.

"Please, master," it begged in a voice neither male or female, devoid of character or substance. "Spare me to serve you again. I will do anything . . . take on any form Your Majesty requires."

"That soft old goat Eltan has priests—*PRIESTS!*" Sarevok exclaimed in a voice like the inside of a thunderclap. The doppelganger skittered back on its haunches in a desperate attempt to avoid the voice—like it had sent a shock wave across the still chamber. Tamoko jumped and felt a tingling to her very core at the power in her lover's manner. Sarevok paused for a long time, letting the doppelganger shudder and whimper once before he continued, "Priests of the tinker god Gond, and who knows what else, wandering the city of Baldur's Gate, praying over and over for this true sight of theirs. Do you know why?"

"We can hide, master," the doppelganger whimpered. "Please, just—"

"Do you know why?" Sarevok asked again, his voice calm and steady.

Philip Athans

"Sire, please—"

"If I ask you the same question a third time, doppel-ganger, you'd best hope the answer is written on the inside of your brain, because if it isn't and I've ripped your head off for no good reason . . . I shall be disappointed."

Tamoko drew her sword slowly, making a show of the sound and the reflected candlelight. She loved Sarevok, with her entire soul, lost as it might be, and though her confidence in him and her certainty that he was worthy of her adoration was more than wavering, she'd be all too happy to put down one of these soulless abominations on his behalf.

The doppelganger saw that much, at least, written plainly in her eyes.

"They search for us," the creature said. "They search for us with their true sight. But they won't—"

"Shhhhh . . ." Sarevok hissed lightly, holding a long finger in front of his lips. He smiled that evil wolf smile and stepped closer to the cowering creature. Tamoko saw a tear roll down the doppelganger's smooth gray cheek.

"Of course they will, doppelganger, just as I knew they would. I was hoping they wouldn't start so soon, though, and it is in that way that you have disappointed me."

"Oh," the doppelganger sobbed through quivering, hair-line lips, "no—"

Sarevok turned and made eye contact with Tamoko for less than half a heartbeat, and the assassin skipped forward, swinging her sword high over her head.

She came in fast and steady—steady as always. She flashed her sword over her head in a rapid whirling motion designed to distract her victim—opponent—the distinction made Tamoko pause in her thinking but not in her movement. She brought her sword slashing down, driven purely by instinct honed from talent and practice. She didn't really make a conscious decision to strike. Her blade met steel with a spark and a clang that sent vibrations up through her arm and snapped her into the now.

The doppelganger had managed to transform in the eye

blink it took for her to attack. She hopped back lightly and quickly, withdrawing as much on instinct as she'd attacked. She needed time to assess the situation at hand. Her victim truly had, all at once, become an opponent.

Tamoko rankled at the sight of the transformed doppelganger. It was her. She tipped her head to the side in what some might have thought was a salute. Tamoko meant it as a promise—the promise of a slow and dishonorable death.

"Outstanding," Sarevok said with obvious relish.

Tamoko ignored him and locked her gaze on her opponent. The doppelganger stood and took on a wide stance. It looked deeply into Tamoko with her own eyes, and with each passing heartbeat it grew more like her. Tamoko exhaled sharply and charged it.

She shouted out in her own language the name of each attack, though she was not conscious of the moment she began formal fencing. Her conscious, creative mind was pushed aside by training, experience, and a code more ancient than even Sarevok could imagine. Her sword whipped through the air with a chorus of whistles and shrieks that made the blade seem to take on a life of its own. The doppelganger managed to parry one attack after another, and it was soon dancing lightly on its toes in much the same way as Tamoko. It was still defending, though, and Tamoko didn't think it understood she wasn't really attacking but feeling her opponent's skills and weaknesses, gathering information on more than just the best way to kill it.

In less than a minute Tamoko knew the doppelganger was running through her own experiences in rapid chronological order. She felt the creature make the breakthrough she had spent an entire summer working up to with sensei Toroto in the Temple of Fist and Light. She felt more, though. This doppelganger was afraid of Sarevok—an easy assumption—but it was also afraid of birds—irrationally afraid. Tamoko smiled and whistled once, a robin's call, and the thing opened itself, and Tamoko sliced at its throat. It had made it to the following autumn of her life, though, the season she spent walking backward, and it stepped out of danger and even made a bold attack that Tamoko only barely managed to put aside.

Her sword flashed even faster, and soon she had achieved her pure state. The sword's pommel came away from her hand and slid through an envelope of energy that surrounded her in a cocoon of pure, unmuddied martial prowess. The doppelganger's left hand came away from its own sword, but it wasn't ready, no power it possessed could make it ready to fight on anything even approaching the level it found itself in.

Tamoko batted its sword away and took its head off in a single zigzagging swing that was too fast for even Sarevok to see. The headless body convulsed through its retransformation, but Tamoko didn't watch. She closed her eyes and forced her mind and spirit back together, forced herself back to the plane of life and time.

She turned around, and Sarevok was coming at her fast. He was reaching for something at his waist, and she exhaled slowly. His breastplate came away, and he was suddenly right there. She dropped her sword and before she heard it clatter on the stone floor she felt his hands on her. She grabbed at him, and their tongues met and she let him take her, though this time, she felt something missing.

* * * * *

Abdel heard Jaheira splash in the shallow pond near their campsite. Still two days from Candlekeep, the woman was taking a rare opportunity to wash away the grime and sweat of the road. The sun had passed under the horizon, and though the sky was a deep shade of indigo, their modest campfire was Abdel's only source of light. Looking up in the direction of the pond, hidden from his sight by a line of closely-spaced trees, Abdel opened his pack and reached inside.

He couldn't see Jaheira, but as long as he could hear her, he knew she was safe. He pulled out the book and sighed when he finally held it in both hands. The leather that made the book's binding was human skin. Abdel didn't know exactly when he came to realize that, but now it seemed so obvious he couldn't imagine ever having been confused by it.

He opened the cover, and the first page was blank. Abdel's heart raced, and he looked up again. He was still alone, and that was the only way he'd allow himself to even hold, let alone open, that book. His palms sweating in some arcane mix of fear and excitement, he turned the first page. There was a skull painted there, surrounded by what might have been either flames or drops of water. The writing was ornate and still meaningless to Abdel, but at the same time it was somehow familiar. He thought it might be the same way a young, illiterate child might feel, seeing the same written language all around him every day, but not being able to suss it out.

His mouth was dry, and he turned the next page. The line drawing there made his heart race, and he closed his eyes against the horror of it even as his skin tingled with the irrational excitement, even as—

"What's that?" Jaheira asked, and Abdel jumped and a soft, startled sound escaped his open mouth. The book bobbled in his hands, but he grabbed at it, closing the cover with a loud crack.

"Are you all right?" she asked him. He looked up and saw her standing next to the fire. She was wrapped in Abdel's well-worn traveling blanket, and her hair was wet. It curled coyly. In the orange light of the fire, the skin of her face looked soft. She smiled at him, but her brow was furrowed.

Abdel looked down, and a tear dropped onto the ghastly cover of the book. Jaheira pulled in a sharp breath and crossed to him, knelt in his lap and put a cool, soft hand to the side if his face. He set the book aside and took her in his arms.

"What's happening to me?" he asked her, not really understanding the question himself.

"You are becoming Abdel," she answered cryptically.

Their lips met for just the briefest moment, but Abdel pushed her gently away. She met his steady gaze with a knowing look and sighed, stepping back off of him. She sat near the fire and looked into the flames, waiting.

"Why did you call me Abdel Adrian?" he asked. "I'd never heard that name before Khalid spoke it. Did Gorion tell you that was my name?"

"It is your name," she told him flatly. "It was the name you were born with."

Abdel let out a long breath and grabbed the book. He wanted to throw it into the fire as much as he wanted to study it and keep it with him forever. He grimaced and put it back in his pack.

"It's time for you to tell me, Jaheira," he said, looking at her looking into the fire.

"You are not who you were born to be, Abdel," she said sadly, but the smile she flashed at him was full of hope. "You can make your own way in this world, and your father, your brothers and sisters, don't have to turn you off that path."

"What do you know of my father?"

"What the Harpers have always known," she said. "What the priests of Oghma and the paladins of Torm have always known. When I told Eltan that Reiltar is a son of Bhaal, I wasn't sure . . . I wasn't as sure of that as I am that . . . that you are a son of Bhaal."

Abdel scratched his head, and Jaheira seemed surprised at the gesture.

"Xzar told me that, too," he said. "I didn't believe him then."

"But now?"

"I am a sellsword, Jaheira, a hired thug. I guard caravans and warehouses and fat merchants. I have a good sword arm, and I'm taller than most, but I'm no god."

"No," she agreed, "but your father was. Your mother, I don't know, but your father was the god of murder."

"And my brother—half brother at least—is Reiltar, leader of the Iron Throne?"

"Perhaps," she said. "We suspected that another son of Bhaal was behind this attempt to bring war between Baldur's Gate and Amn, but we don't know his name. It could be a sister, even. You have half sisters, you know."

He smiled and laughed, but it was an empty expression.

"And Abdel Adrian?" he asked.

"Netherese, I think," she answered. "Abdel means 'son of' and Adrian 'the dark.'"

"Son of the dark," he said. "Appropriate, I suppose, if not flattering."

"Do you take pleasure in killing anymore, Abdel?" she asked him pointedly.

"No," he answered without thinking, then paused.

She looked at him, but he couldn't look at her. His face flushed, and he shifted his weight uncomfortably on the chill ground.

"I used to," he said finally. "I used to get this feeling, like . . . well, a feeling anyway. Since Gorion was killed, since I met you, I've lost that feeling."

"You're changing," she said. "You've changed."

"Maybe, but I'm no god."

"You're so sure," she said.

"I enjoyed killing for killing's sake, and I was good at it," he told her. "In my line of work, that describes a lot of people. Even a god couldn't have that many children. I have no . . . traits, no powers. If a god's blood ran through my veins wouldn't I be able to fly, or turn invisible or something?"

Jaheira chuckled, but there was no humor in the sound. "Maybe you have his eyes," she said, "or his nose."

"I can imagine he had a big nose," Abdel joked.

"You had a human mother, Abdel," she said softly, almost in a whisper.

"And she was a good woman," he decided, based less on the facts at hand than on what he wanted to believe.

Jaheira looked at him in the dark for a long time, then said, "She must have been."

Chapter Twenty-Three

"Beuros, you squirmy little piece of—" Abdel started to say but stopped when Jaheira put a hand on his arm.

"Good sir," she said, glancing at Abdel who sighed explosively and turned away from the gate, "you obviously know my companion here, you know him to be a resident of this fair city and the son of one of your own. Please understand that we have urgent business here and—"

"Go away," Beuros the gate guard said sternly. "Go away or I'll be forced to—"

"You'll be forced to what," Abdel roared, "you thrice bedamned—"

"Go away!" the guard squealed and shut the little window in the big, sturdy oaken gate.

"This is ludicrous," Jaheira said to no one in particular. "What kind of city is this?"

Abdel kicked a stone on the gravel path that ended at the gates of Candlekeep, the place that had been his home for most of his life, and watched it skip away. He sighed again and looked up at the sky, noting the increasingly graying clouds obviously heavy with rain.

"I've never been refused entrance to Candlekeep," he said. "Never in my life."

"Gorion was alive then," Jaheira said without really thinking. "He was in there to let you in."

Abdel looked at her and forced a smile. She didn't notice, being too busy examining the gates with a tactician's eye.

"It's not a city," he said.

She looked at him with a furrowed brow.

"It's not a city," he said again, "it's a monastery. A library."

She nodded and shrugged as if that fine distinction didn't matter. "The Iron Throne is gathering in there," she said, "whatever it is. We need to get in there."

"Give me a book," Beuros's voice sounded suddenly, making Jaheira jump. They looked up at the little window, a good ten feet off the ground in the tall gates. All they could see of Beuros was his pimply face and crooked yellow teeth, a graying stubble and a dense, intractable expression. Abdel had known Beuros most of his life.

"Beuros—" Abdel started to say.

"Ah," Beuros interrupted, "a book, or a scroll, or a tablet, or a . . . something with writing on it. Give me something of use to Candlekeep and you can come in."

Now it was Abdel's turn to furrow his brow in confusion and frustration. He regarded the little man coolly.

"Why this all of a sudden, Beuros? What's going on in there?"

"The business of Candlekeep," the guard answered haughtily. "The business of learnedness."

Jaheira smiled and said, "That's not even a word, you little—"

"A *book!*" Beuros interrupted again, fixing an angry gaze on the half-elf woman.

"I don't have—" Abdel started to say, then stopped when he realized he did indeed have a book, a book that terrified him but that he doubted he'd be able to part with.

"Give us a few minutes, Captain Steadfast," Jaheira said sarcastically, making a dismissive brushing away hand gesture in Beuros's general direction. The guard harrumphed and withdrew behind his little shutter.

"Abdel," Jaheira said, crossing the few feet to him just as it started to rain lightly, "you still have that book, don't you?"

Abdel looked away, tense and fearful, though he couldn't

put his finger on why.

"Abdel?" she asked. "You still have it, don't you? The book that Xan found in the bandit camp, I mean."

Abdel nodded, avoiding her eyes.

"Well then just give it to Lord Peephole here, and let's get on with it. We've been on the road—again—for almost a tenday, and it's possible that the people we've gone through all Nine Hells and more to try to stop are in there right now, laughing at us."

Abdel let a long breath whistle out through his nose, then finally he looked up at Jaheira. He didn't say anything, just slipped his pack off his back and fished inside it. He didn't even glance at the book when he slid it out.

"Beuros!" Jaheira called, looking at the little door. It took a while for Beuros to finally make his presence known, and when he did Jaheira was surprised to see him genuinely curious. Jaheira figured she and Abdel had been more persistent than most.

"A book?" the guard asked, then grinned widely when his eyes lighted on the old tome in Abdel's now outstretched hand. "Well, well . . ."

"Let us in first," Jaheira said, easily able to read the greed in Beuros's eyes.

Beuros laughed, and it wasn't a terribly pleasant sound. "Not on your life, missy. Tell him to slide it through the slot."

Abdel could hear Beuros perfectly well without Jaheira having to relate the guard's words. The sellsword studied the space that was the peephole eight feet or more above the gravel-covered ground.

Jaheira said, "If there was a window a bit—" but stopped talking when a slot, easily able to accommodate the book, opened up on the door at Abdel's waist height. Abdel and Jaheira blinked, obviously both seeing the slot for the first time.

"Slide it in there, Abdel," Beuros said softly, finally using Abdel's name.

"I knew you knew me you bastard," Abdel grumbled,

crossing the short distance to the gate with the book held out in front of him.

Jaheira's eyes narrowed, and she was about to ask Abdel if he was all right. The sellsword had stopped abruptly just as the edge of the old book touched the slot. He was obviously reluctant to let it drop.

"You can't even read the language it's written in, for Mielikki's sake," Jaheira said. "Give him the heavy old thing, and let's get in there."

"Indeed, Abdel," Beuros said, "listen to this young woman, and give me the book. I need a gesture of good faith."

Abdel couldn't let go. It was like his fingers had locked, like his fist had gone into some death grip, and the book was his last hope for life—or was it his last hope for just the opposite?

"Abdel?" Jaheira asked, her voice now carrying an edge of fear at the sellsword's sudden reluctance.

Abdel sighed once more and let go of the book, letting it drop through the slot. Beuros's face disappeared from the peephole again, and he was gone for a long time.

* * * * *

"Beuros, you squirmy little piece of—" Abdel started to say, but stopped when the strange woman put a hand on his arm.

"Good sir," the woman said, glancing at Abdel who sighed explosively and turned away from the gate, "you obviously know my companion here, you know him to be a resident of this fair city and the son of one of your own. Please understand that we have urgent business here and—"

"Go away," Beuros said sternly. "Go away or I'll be forced to—"

"You'll be forced to what," Abdel roared, "you thrice bedamned—"

"Go away!" Beuros said again and shut the little window in the big, sturdy oaken gate.

Philip Athans

Beuros was one of many charged with defending the gates of Candlekeep, the place that had been his home for his entire life. He'd known Abdel for almost as long and never liked him. Abdel was the adopted son—foster son really—of Gorion, a priest and a scholar, one of Beuros's favorite teachers. Beuros had been pushed around by the young Abdel, as had many of Beuros's friends. When Abdel left Candlekeep, years before, to seek out his own life as a mercenary or hired thug, or whatever his slow wits and strong arms had bought him, Beuros, like many others in the monastery, was nothing but happy to see him go. He'd returned a few times, once quite recently, to visit Gorion, and that time had actually left with the old monk. That had been at least a dozen tendays ago, though it seemed shorter to Beuros. As far as he was concerned, anytime Abdel came back to Candlekeep was too soon. Now he'd returned with some woman—a half-elf, and she was dressed for battle. Beuros could believe almost anything about Abdel, up to and including the distasteful notion that the bully had somehow managed to trade the learned Gorion, a man worthy of respect and beyond reproach, for this mercenary trollop half-breed.

Beuros was a bitter man, small in the body and small in the spirit, but he was a part of something in Candlekeep. He studied, he read—and occasionally understood—and copied the texts of the greatest library on all Toril. Beuros belonged here, where everyone—including Gorion—knew Abdel was never really at home.

Now, having to take on one of his least favorite responsibilities, he sighed and looked up at the sky, noting the increasingly graying clouds obviously heavy with rain. Guarding the gate consisted almost entirely of turning away travelers. Virtually no one was welcomed at Candlekeep, and like many of the monks, scribes, priests, and scholars there, Beuros liked it that way.

"I've never been refused entrance to Candlekeep," Beuros heard Abdel say through one of the many magical means at his disposal—magic that helped guard Candlekeep from an often hostile outside world. "Never in my life."

"Gorion was alive then," the half-elf woman said, and Beuros's heart skipped a beat. "He was in there to let you in."

So Gorion was dead. Beuros wanted to weep at the loss but held back the tears with a great sniff and cleared his throat. Beuros wondered if maybe it was true what was said about Abdel when he was a child—that Gorion had adopted him as some kind of changeling. Rumors abounded about the young Abdel, that he was some kind of demon spawn, a cambion or an alu-fiend, or the son of some evil wizard, maybe descended from a long line of corrupt Netherese archwizards. It was hard for Beuros and his friends to believe this since demonology was a part of their regular studies, and Abdel failed to exhibit any of the powers normally associated with the infernal, but still. Abdel grew to enormous proportions and exhibited both a strength and a thirst for violence that didn't seem entirely human, at least not to the mild-tempered monks of Candlekeep. It certainly crossed Beuros's mind that Abdel had perhaps killed Gorion himself, and the gate guard could think of no greater offense to the law and will of Candlekeep.

The name Tethtoril came immediately to Beuros's mind, and he quickly made use of one more of the minor magic items available to him. He spoke Tethtoril's name into a cone of golden foil and trusted the device to convey the message to the aging monk. In the meantime, he had to try to stall Abdel, though he doubted it would have been easy to get rid of the man even if he tried. Abdel and the woman were still outside the gate, conversing quietly. Beuros opened the peephole.

"Give me a book," he said, obviously startling the woman, who jumped. They looked up at the little window.

"Beuros—" Abdel started to say.

"Ah," Beuros interrupted, "a book, or a scroll, or a tablet, or a . . . something with writing on it. Give me something of use to Candlekeep, and you can come in."

The sellsword furrowed his brow in confusion and frustration. Beuros wasn't at all surprised that Abdel didn't have any form of written record with him. It wouldn't have surprised the man to hear that Abdel had forgotten how to read.

"Why this all of a sudden, Beuros? What's going on in there?" the sellsword asked.

"The business of Candlekeep," Beuros answered directly. "The business of learnedness."

The woman smiled evilly and said, "That's not even a word, you little—"

"A *book!*" Beuros insisted, insulted that this half-elf by-blow would question his learnedness.

"I don't have—" Abdel started to say, then stopped, a look of dumb realization coming over his face.

"Give us a few minutes, Captain Steadfast," the woman said sarcastically, making a dismissive brushing away hand gesture in Beuros's general direction. The guard ignored her and closed the shutter.

Beuros wiped sweat from his brow and wondered what he was doing, and what was keeping Tethtoril. Abdel and the woman were talking again, and Beuros had a dreadful feeling in the pit of his stomach. What if Abdel managed to call his bluff? He heard the woman call his name, and brimming with apprehension, he opened the shutter once more.

"A book?" Beuros asked.

He saw then what Abdel was holding in his big, callused hand. It was a book all right, and the sight of it set Beuros's heart racing. It was bound, no less, in human skin, and bore on it a symbol he hadn't seen in a long time, a symbol crafted from a human skull. Whatever this tome was, it was unusual to say the least. Evil, no doubt, but certainly a subject worthy of study from a purely detached perspective. If it was some dark text, Faerûn would certainly be better for having it kept safe within the walls of Candlekeep.

"Well, well . . ." Beuros started to say.

"Let us in first," the woman interrupted.

Beuros laughed and said, "Not on your life, missy. Tell

him to slide it through the slot."

Beuros activated the trigger for the secret panel that would open the more accessible slot in the gate while the sellsword studied the space that was the peephole eight feet or more above the gravel-covered ground.

The woman said, "If there was a window a bit—" but stopped talking when she finally noticed the slot—easily able to accommodate the book—open up on the door at Abdel's waist height.

"Slide it in there, Abdel," Beuros said softly, not realizing he'd used Abdel's name for the first time in years.

"I knew you knew me you bastard," Abdel grumbled, crossing the short distance to the gate with the book held out in front of him. The sellsword stopped abruptly just as the edge of the old book touched the slot. He was obviously reluctant to let it drop.

"You can't even read the language it's written in, for Mielikki's sake," the woman said, making Beuros smile. "Give him the heavy old thing, and let's get in there."

"Indeed, Abdel," Beuros said, "listen to this young woman, and give me the book. I need a gesture of good faith."

Abdel wouldn't let go

"Abdel?" the woman asked dully.

The sellsword sighed once more and let go of the book, letting it drop through the slot. Beuros climbed down and picked up the book. It was heavy, and the touch of the cover was at once ghastly and exhilarating.

"What have you got there, Beuros?" Tethtoril asked from behind him, making the guard gasp and spin to face him.

* * * * *

Less than an hour later Abdel and Jaheira were siting in Tethtoril's private chamber watching him make tea. The walk across Candlekeep's meticulously landscaped bailey brought back such a flood of emotions, Abdel had all but shut down. Tethtoril's reaction to the news of Gorion's death made Abdel live through it again. Jaheira, sensing what this visit was already doing to Abdel, clutched at his arm. She seemed impatient, but Abdel didn't think about why. All thoughts of the Iron Throne had fled his mind.

"I won't ask you where you got that book, Abdel," Tethtoril said, handing a cup of tea to Jaheira, "but I'm glad you decided to bring it here. It was the right thing to do."

Abdel waved off the cup that Tethtoril offered him, and the aging monk took a sip from it himself.

"I don't even know what it is," Abdel admitted. "I couldn't read it."

This seemed to take Tethtoril by surprise. "You tried?" he asked.

Abdel looked at him quizzically and shrugged.

"That book of yours, son," the monk said, "is one of a very, very few copies remaining of the unholy rites of Bhaal, Lord of Murder."

Abdel flushed, his head spinning. He'd been attracted to the book, wanted desperately to absorb it, understand it, but had at once been ashamed of that feeling and driven to keep his attraction to it a secret. Abdel still doubted it meant he was the son of this dead god, but the presence of Bhaal's influence must have been a factor in his life—his life before Gorion.

"Then I'm happy to be rid of it," Jaheira said, looking only at Abdel. "What I told you is true, Abdel."

Abdel sighed through his nose and forced a smile.

"Your father," Tethtoril said quickly, obviously uncomfortable with what he was about to say, "left something in my care. He told me that if he ever met an . . . untimely . . . if he died before he'd had a chance to . . ."

The monk held back a sob but couldn't continue.

"What is it, brother?" Abdel asked, finally looking up at Tethtoril.

"A letter," the monk said, then cleared his throat. "A letter and a pass stone—a stone that will give you free run of Candlekeep."

"A letter?" Abdel asked, and his mind spun, remembering

the scrap of parchment Gorion had clutched to his body with his last bit of mortal strength. "I saw it," he said. "Gorion had it with him when he died."

"Impossible," Tethtoril said. "I have the letter right here."

Chapter Twenty-Four

Abdel read the letter aloud, and Jaheira didn't look at him almost the whole time.

" 'Hello My Son,

" 'If you are reading this it means I have met an untimely death. I would tell you not to grieve for me, but I feel much better thinking that you might. If you can, it will mean I have done the best any father could hope to do.' "

Abdel stopped reading for a moment. If Jaheira had glanced at him right then she would have seen the cords standing out in his neck, his throat was so tight. Gorion had done his job and done it well. The son of the god of murder was—if only for a moment—speechless with grief.

" 'There are things I must tell you in this letter that I should have told you before, but if my death came too soon and I have not been given the chance, you must know these things, and know them from me. I know you better than anyone on this world. You must believe what I have written here with the knowledge that, though there have been things I have not told you, I would never lie to you—not about this.' "

Abdel stopped reading again and looked at Jaheira, who didn't turn toward him. "He's going to tell me what you told me," he said, his voice barely above a whisper, "isn't he?"

Jaheira nodded, then Abdel sighed and read on.

" 'As you have known all your life, I am not your true father, but you have never known your sire's name. It is a name spoken only in fearful whispers, for so great was the terror of it that even though its power has fled the multiverse, it has meaning still. You are the son of . . .' "

Abdel sighed again, and his face tightened into what might have passed for a smile or some tight, twisted, silent laugh. A single tear rolled down one cheek, and still Jaheira didn't look at him.

" 'Your father is the entity known as Bhaal, Lord of Murder. A thing of evil, so vile it's nearly impossible to believe the multiverse itself could stand its hateful presence.

" 'You do not remember the Time of Troubles, when the gods walked Faerûn. Like other great powers, Bhaal was forced into a mortal shell. As is possible, I have read, with divine beings, Bhaal was somehow forewarned of the death that awaited him during this time. He sought out women then, of every race, and forced himself upon them or seduced them. Your mother was one of these women, a mortal . . .' "

There was a silence then that hung in the air for what seemed to both of them like hours. Abdel looked at Jaheira with tear-blurred eyes and saw her cover her face with her hands. She sat on the corner of the rickety iron cot that had been Abdel's bed since he was but a toddler. The scroll he'd made in the first year of his schooling hung on the wall above her like some kind of cruel reminder of the lie that had been his human life. He continued reading, though he knew what was coming next and, worse than that, knew he didn't know what to do about it.

"'Your mother was one of these women . . . a mortal ravaged by murder incarnate.'"

He stopped this time only long enough to clench one big fist almost tight enough to draw blood under his jagged fingernails. His voice as tight as his fist, he read on.

"'Your mother died in childbirth. I had been her friend and knew the paladin who brought you to me. I felt obliged, at first, to raise you as my own. As the years went by and I saw in you—every day—the promise of a life beyond some divine destiny, I came to love you as only a father can love his son. I have but one hope now, and that is that you will always think of me as your father.'"

I do, Abdel thought, hoping Gorion could hear him.

" 'The blood of the gods runs through your veins. If you make use of our extensive library you will find that our founder, Alaundo, has many prophecies concerning the coming of the spawn of Bhaal. Perhaps these prophecies will help you find your way.

" 'There are many who will want to use you for their own purposes. You had many half brothers, and nearly as many half sisters. Over the years an order of the paladins of Torm—among which I have some friends—and the Harpers, and some other individuals—I'm not even sure who—have kept track of you, and as many of your half siblings as possible. We've lost touch with some, we know some are dead, and we've rediscovered one. This one may be your half brother, and you may want to believe that he is family, that he can be a brother to you, but I beg you, do not. He means you only ill, and he was not raised in the calm, studious atmosphere of Candlekeep, but by a series of faceless cultists still clinging to the hopeless servitude of a dead god.

" 'This one calls himself Sarevok.' "

Jaheira gasped, and Abdel looked at her. She was looking at him finally. Her eyes were red, brimming with tears, and wide with confusion and surprise.

"Not Reiltar?" she whispered hoarsely.

" 'Sarevok,' " Abdel said, then looked back at the letter, then up at Jaheira again. "Do you know that name?"

She shook her head and looked away, so he read on.

" 'This one is the worst danger. He has studied here at Candlekeep and thus knows a great deal about your history and who you are. I have left you a token that will give you access to the inner libraries. You can find the secret entrance in one of the reading rooms on the ground floor. Do not tell any of the monks about your pass stone as they will take it from you. The inner libraries contain a secret route that leads out of Candlekeep. Use this only in the most pressing situations.'

"And he signed it, 'Your loving father, Gorion.'"

"Abdel—" Jaheira wasn't able to finish. The door burst open and men came in. Abdel reacted, like he always did, and put his hands up fast to guard his head.

The first blow was a solid one that nearly broke Abdel's left forearm. He stood and used the strong muscles in his legs to help propel the staff he'd been struck with up and into the low ceiling. It snapped in half, sending another jolt of pain across Abdel's forearm. He ignored it and grabbed the broken end of the staff as it began to fall and returned the attack without even looking at the target. He'd been reading a letter that sent his life spiraling down a pit with very little hope at the bottom of it, a letter that presented more mysteries than it solved. The death of Gorion was a wound suddenly reopened, but Abdel didn't let himself fall all the way back. When he hit the man on the head with the broken end of his own staff, it was with enough force to stun him, but not kill him.

Jaheira was on her feet too, but she had no weapon. Abdel's broadsword was resting on an old wooden cabinet— a piece of furniture Gorion had given him and where he'd kept his clothes when he was just a boy. Abdel saw someone pick it up, and he clenched his teeth tightly. These men, maybe half a dozen of them, were dressed in the all too familiar chain mail and tabards of the guards of Candlekeep.

The man he'd hit fell heavily on the floor in front of the big sellsword, and Abdel used the broken staff like a club to parry one swipe, then another, then another, from two guards coming at him with stout oaken cudgels.

"Submit!" a commanding voice bellowed from somewhere just outside the narrow door as the guards continued to spill into the room. "Submit to the justice of Candlekeep, and it will all go that much—"

Abdel took another guard down with a fast, short jab to the temple with the rounded end of the staff.

"—easier for you both!"

Abdel heard Jaheira grunt and looked to see her doubled over. The guard who'd hit her in the stomach with a staff was smiling, and Abdel didn't like that smile one bit. Jaheira rolled her shoulder and pinched the end of the staff against her body, sending it into the leering guard's gut. The man coughed once and stepped back. Abdel was hit on the arm with a cudgel, and it felt like his whole body was shaken. He punched out at the guard, who flinched back far enough to save himself from the fist, but not the broken staff, which came in low from Abdel's other hand and crashed into the side of his knee. There was a loud pop, and the guard screamed and fell to the floor.

Jaheira pulled back on the staff still pinned to her side, and the guard let go. She staggered back half a step, and the guard punched her squarely in the side of the jaw. It was a tight-fisted, full-out punch that men rarely, if ever, threw at women, and the sight of it made Abdel's blood boil almost as much as the sight of Jaheira falling heavily to the ground, blinking, stunned, and rapidly losing consciousness.

Abdel didn't think, he stabbed. Spinning the broken staff through his fingers, he brought the pointed, splintered end to bear and grunted. The guard who'd punched Jaheira was still grinning when he turned to see Abdel coming at him. He didn't have even the split second it would have taken him to wipe the grin off his face before he was impaled on the broken staff. The sharp wedge of wood split the guard's chain mail like cotton, and the weakened wood shattered and splintered as it passed through the guard's guts and out his back, making a tent out of the unbroken chain mail behind.

One of the other guards screamed in shocked horror, and Jaheira passed out, a sad look passing briefly over her face before it went still and slack-jawed. Two men jumped Abdel from behind, and the touch of their cold chain mail sent a shiver through him. He managed to bat one away with a fast elbow that shattered the guard's teeth and sent him back on his rump, mumbling curses and beginning to cry. The other guard was stronger, and Abdel couldn't immediately shake her.

"It's murder now, for certain," the guard growled into Abdel's ear, as if justifying to herself that she would have to kill this man she'd known all her life.

"Pilten!" Abdel gasped "What—?"

"Sleep!" the voice from the corridor shouted, and Abdel's head spun.

He was trying to say, "No," as he fell, but all that came out was a grunt. He could feel something rattle his throat that might have been a snore, but he didn't feel his head hit the floorboards.

* * * * *

He was unconscious for a matter of minutes—long enough to be chained securely at the wrists and the ankles. He came to when they were dragging him down the corridor, the guards taking pleasure in the occasional retributive shot with the blunt staves and cudgels they carried. Abdel realized he'd killed one of the guards and let his neck go limp. Something in him wanted to take the punishment the guards were meting out, but that something was very new in him.

* * * * *

". . . and the guard makes nine," Tethtoril said from the other side of the barred door. Once again Abdel and Jaheira were caged like animals. They were together this time—unusual even for the more humane dungeons of Candlekeep—and unchained. The bruise on Jaheira's face was already starting to fade. Tethtoril had called on the power of Oghma to heal her as they were dragged to the dungeons. She was awake, horrified, and bemused.

"We didn't kill those men," she said, her voice betraying her growing anger. "We came here to prevent—"

"Is this yours?" Tethtoril interrupted. She gasped when

she saw the bracelet he was holding. If she'd allowed her-self time to think, she might not have said what she said next.

"Yes, where did you find it?"

It was the bracelet that Xan had dropped in the bandit encampment, the same camp in which he found that most unholy tome of Bhaal. The look on Tethtoril's face made Abdel's heart sink. The man was disappointed in him. Abdel admired Tethtoril, had admired him all his life, and though he had no idea who these other eight men were he was accused of killing, he did kill the guard who'd struck Jaheira. Not even Tethtoril could save him from that.

"The guard . . ." Abdel asked weakly, with very little hope. "Is there any chance?"

Tethtoril put a hand to his forehead and pretended to be thinking about the question. He obviously didn't want the guards to see him cry. When he'd gathered himself, he pulled from the same leather bag from which he'd produced Jaheira's bracelet a wide-bladed dagger. The blade sparkled in the lamplight, and the blood drying on it glistened around the edges where it met the shiny silver.

"Before I was shown this," the old monk said, fixing a stern, hurt, disapproving stare on Abdel, "I might have thought so."

"Tethtoril," Abdel said, "you can't think . . ."

Abdel didn't finish the thought because he understood that of course Tethtoril could think him capable of killing any number of men. He knew Tethtoril recognized the dagger—he'd been in the room when Gorion had made a great show of presenting it to him. Abdel only now recognized the voice that had put him to sleep as Tethtoril's. The old monk had seen him disembowel a guard for striking Jaheira a hard but recoverable blow. Of course Tethtoril could think him capable. He was capable.

"Pilten," Tethtoril said, and the guard Abdel had known when they were both children stepped forward. "Take these and . . . all of this . . . and secure it."

Pilten nodded once in acknowledgment, spared Abdel a

disappointed look, then took the bundle that included Abdel's sword, the letter from Gorion, the pass stone—Tethtoril made a point of showing Abdel that he'd put it in the leather bag—and the incriminating evidence and walked away.

"Go with her," Tethtoril said to the others, "all of you."

The other guards were reluctant to leave the old monk.

"I will be quite all right," he said, lifting his chin in an expression of simple authority. The other guards shuffled off, and there was the sound of many doors closing.

"I will do what I can," Tethtoril said to Abdel, sparing a glance at Jaheira, "but you've left me little to work with."

"Send word to Baldur's Gate, perhaps," Abdel said, "to Eltan?"

Tethtoril nodded, though there was very little hope showing in the old monk's face.

"I've disappointed you," Abdel said quietly.

Tethtoril forced a weak smile and nodded.

Chapter Twenty-Five

Abdel touched his nose and, like the rest of him, it had turned to glass. The surface was smooth and cold, and there was a distinct tinkling sound when he opened his eyes. His head reeled at first. He wasn't used to being so high up. The horizon was wider and deeper. There was a huge, dark-green blanket of forest stretching for what must have been miles.

The forest was filled with people in rough black robes. At first it sounded to Abdel like the people were humming, but then he realized they were chanting—they were chanting his name.

"Ab-del, Ab-del, Ab-del," over and over again in a steady cadence that melded together into a single voice, a voice that was familiar to Abdel, a voice that repelled him.

He took a step back and was surprised when it seemed like whatever structure he was standing on moved back with him. This made his head spin all the more, and a sigh escaped his crystal lips. He put one foot forward to try to balance himself but couldn't. It was then that he realized he wasn't standing on a tower—he was the tower.

He fell forward, unable to move his cut glass body, which must have weighed thousands of tons, either quickly or gracefully. He must have been a hundred feet tall or more, and it took him a long time to fall, the trees rushing up at him. When his center of gravity shifted enough, his shins started to crack. The sound of it was loud and would still

have been disturbing even if it wasn't his legs. As his face
rushed toward the ground and he came closer and closer to
her, he saw Jaheira.

She was looking up at him, her eyes bulging in abject
horror. He was falling on her—a shattering glass titan that
would crush her at the same time it ripped her to shreds.
He couldn't stop himself from falling, and she didn't seem
able to run. She screamed his name, and it sounded as
angry and frustrated as it did fearful. She held up her
hands, and Abdel tried to scream out her name, but his
voice caught in his glass throat and shattered it. His head
fell off and hit Jaheira hard enough to drive her into the
ground as it shattered into a trillion screeching fragments.

* * * * *

Abdel came awake with a start, and Jaheira was holding
his shoulders, her face close to his. She looked angry and
smelled awful.

Memory flooded back to him in torrents, and he remembered being put to sleep by Tethtoril—was it Tethtoril?—
and being dragged to the dungeons under Candlekeep and
thrown into a cell with Jaheira. He remembered Tethtoril
promising to help, then himself telling Jaheira to be
patient. He remembered curling up on a surprisingly comfortable cot and watching Jaheira do the same on the other
side of the room. He remembered a guard blowing out the
little oil lamp, then he was asleep and dreaming he was a
hundred-foot-tall god shattering over the woman he loved.

"You don't smell very good," he said, forcing a weak
smile.

Jaheira sighed impatiently and said, "It's not me."

She turned to the bars, and there was the ghoul, Korak.

"Abdel," he said in the voice of the chanting people of
Abdel's nightmare. "Abdel, I help you."

The reeking undead thing held up a heavy iron ring hung
with a dozen or more big keys. Clinging to the ring was a
severed hand already turning gray, its knuckles still white

in its death grip.

"He's been following us," Jaheira said, backing off so Abdel could stand. He brushed straw from his bliaut and rolled his shoulders, hearing them pop and grind from a cold night on the dungeon cot.

"You killed the guard?" Abdel asked the ghoul directly.

Korak smiled, held up the ring again, and said, "I help you. I want to help you."

"Go away," Abdel said, even as the ghoul started trying keys in the big lock.

"I'm not convinced this is a good idea either, Abdel," Jaheira said, "but I'm not sure we have much choice. Murderers are executed here like everywhere else, aren't they?"

There was a loud clank and a squeak. Abdel looked over to see Korak swing the gate open.

The ghoul smiled a black-toothed smile and said, "Come."

"If you step one foot in here, Korak," Abdel said, "I will kill you with my bare hands."

"Abdel," Jaheira said, ignoring the ghoul, "if they could get to Scar—with doppelgangers—if they could get into the ducal palace in Baldur's Gate . . . they could get in here."

"Tethtoril will help us," Abdel protested. "I've known him all my life. He's a good man, and he won't hang either of us."

"If he isn't already dead," Jaheira said sternly.

Korak hovered in the open doorway and said, "Coming now?"

"That was Tethtoril who locked us in here last night," Abdel assured her. "If it was a doppelganger why wouldn't he just kill us?"

"Would Tethtoril?" Jaheira asked. Abdel's only answer was a confused look, so she continued. "If that was a doppelganger it would have to behave the way Tethtoril would behave. It could be up there right now, gathering more false evidence against us—evidence of crimes committed by doppelgangers who look just like us—evidence that it'll use to convict us and execute us. To everyone else it'll all seem perfectly rational, perfectly just. We'll be blamed for everything . . . the Iron Throne, Reiltar or Sarevok, or whoever is behind this will have won."

Abdel didn't want to believe that possibility, but he had to at least consider it. He turned away and breathed too deeply of the air now fouled by the presence of the rotting ghoul. He coughed and looked up in time to see Korak hold up one finger then skip away, taking the oil lamp he was holding with him. The cell was plunged into darkness, and the absence of light helped to clear Abdel's mind.

"So we can't trust anyone," he said simply.

"I don't think we can," she replied as simply. "We can trust Gorion's letter, though. You have a half brother named Sarevok, who I'm guessing is Reiltar's—the Iron Throne's—'man' in Baldur's Gate."

The light came back quickly with Korak, and the ghoul dropped the precarious load he was carrying, letting it clatter on the flagstones outside the cell. Their armor was there, Abdel's broadsword, and the pass stone. Abdel was happy when he realized Korak had used a key to open the cell, so the ghoul didn't know the power of the stone. It would be their ticket out.

The last item Abdel pulled from the sack was his dagger, the wide-bladed silver dagger Gorion had given him so long ago. It felt good in his grip, not because it could rip any man's guts out, but because it was given to him by someone he cared about, and who cared about him.

"You lost your sword," he said to Jaheira. She looked up at him and nodded. He turned the dagger around in his hand and offered her the handle.

"Thank you," she whispered, taking the weapon. "I'll take good care of it."

They stood, and Abdel took Jaheira lightly by the elbow and whispered into her ear, "Didn't we decide this ghoul was working for the Iron Throne?"

Jaheira shrugged and whispered, "I haven't the slightest idea, but we can always kill him later."

Abdel smiled sadly and guided her to the open cell door.

Even in the most curious summer afternoons of Abdel's youth, he'd never seen this side of Candlekeep. Under the monastery, for what seemed like endless layer upon endless layer, was a series of catacombs and sewers that was like an infinite labyrinth. It didn't take Abdel long, who didn't have much of a sense of direction underground, to get lost completely, and he and Jaheira soon found themselves in a position they'd both promised themselves and each other they'd never be in again. They were blindly following the vile-smelling Korak.

"This one must have been important," Jaheira whispered. The sound of her soft voice echoed through the narrow passageway like a drawn-out hiss. She motioned with the dagger to a niche in the catacomb wherein sat an ornately carved mahogany casket. There was a brass plaque carefully nailed to the side but tarnish and cobwebs made it illegible. Above the niche was a shield on which was painted an elaborate coat of arms that Abdel didn't recognize.

"Eventually this should lead out to the sea," Abdel said, ignoring her observation.

She smiled at him in the flickering torchlight and was about to say something when the ghoul's voice echoed back at them, "No time to stop." Korak sounded nervous. "No time at all!"

The zombies fell on him from all sides at once.

Jaheira breathed in sharply as if she were about to scream, and Abdel's heart skipped a beat at the sight of the ghoul being torn to pieces by a good half-dozen walking corpses who each looked worse off than even the rotting ghoul. Korak screamed a pitiful, thin wail that bounced around in the tunnel along with the sound of tearing and shuffling and splashing and cracking. The zombies were as silent as the dead they were.

One of the undead things turned slowly and looked at the half-god and the half-elf. The thing's ashen face betrayed no sign of life, let alone emotion, but it recognized their presence and came forward. When the pieces of Korak stopped twitching, the rest of them followed suit, and they advanced on Abdel and Jaheira as one.

"We need to go," Jaheira, already backing up, said.

Abdel thought about it for a long time—two steps of the zombies—then said, "Yeah, I think so."

More zombies appeared from side passages. Abdel stopped counting at eight and just turned tail to run, following closely behind Jaheira. They turned a corner in the dark, damp, musty, narrow corridor, and their way was blocked by a rusted iron gate. Abdel swore loudly, and the echoes momentarily drowned out the loud, reverberating hiss of the zombies dragging their desiccated feet along the stone floor.

"Break it open," Jaheira suggested weakly. Abdel grabbed the bars and felt big flakes of rust powder in his grip. He pulled hard on the gate and it gave a little, sending a hundred different echoes cascading through the passageway. The first zombie rounded the corner.

In a panicked voice Jaheira whispered, "Abdel . . ."

He turned at the same time he drew his sword, bringing it around close to his body to avoid cutting Jaheira. The zombie came in slow, tangled in the tatters of the long robe it was wearing. This one had been a woman, maybe centuries before it became this shuffling, undead thing.

Jaheira stabbed at it with the silver dagger, and a big chunk of its midsection just fell away. It staggered back, never making eye contact with either of its living prey and then came back again. When it was within arm's length it reached its rotting claws up and took a slow, clumsy, but strong swipe at Jaheira with its hands. Abdel took its head off easily, but Jaheira had to jump out of the way to avoid being cut herself, and she dodged directly into the next zombie in line.

It grabbed at her forearm in what looked like an attempt to keep itself from falling, but the zombie wasn't capable of that kind of high-level decision making. It meant to claw her, and using the weight of its fall as much as the strength in its dead, reanimated arm, it took three deep gouges out of Jaheira's shoulder. The half-elf screamed and pushed back with both legs, coming into the rusted gate hard in an attempt to avoid the zombie's second scraping set of claws. The zombie fell away as Jaheira hit the gate and continued through when the bars, which had rusted through after centuries of neglect, gave way behind her.

Jaheira had expected the gate to hold her so was surprised enough at finding herself landing rump-first on the damp stone floor that she didn't see Abdel cut in half the zombie that had scratched her. Abdel kept his sword in his right hand and fumbled in his belt pouch with his left hand. He pulled out the pass stone and turned, moving past the prone Jaheira, even as another zombie appeared around the corner. Jaheira stood up, turned, and ran.

"Follow me!" Abdel said and didn't look back. He could hear her staying close behind him. He held the stone in his left hand and let it pass an inch or two from the wall.

"Do you know . . ." Jaheira panted, ". . . where we're . . . going?"

Abdel answered, "No, but I know Candlekeep."

He knew this wouldn't make sense to Jaheira, who didn't respond.

"The whole thing," Abdel said as he ran, "is full of secret doors. It's practically made of secret doors. I've never been down here, but I see no reason why—"

He stopped at the sound of grinding stone, and Jaheira collided with his back with a grunt. A doorway slid open in the stone wall to their left. Abdel winked and stepped through into the soft, damp breeze that carried on it the scent of the sea.

Chapter Twenty-Six

"Candlekeep will take care of them for you," Duke Angelo said, handing the semicircular glass to Sarevok. "They will never be seen again."

Sarevok smiled, and Angelo looked away. As one of the dukes of Baldur's Gate, an experienced mercenary commander, and a half-elf who'd already lived longer than most humans would ever dream of, Angelo had met all kinds—but no one like Sarevok. This imposing man made the air in his apartment in the ducal palace heavy with—what? Angelo couldn't put his finger on the word: malice? avarice? destiny?

"What do you call this?" Sarevok asked, his voice even in casual conversation was deep, resonating, and commanding.

"Brandy," Angelo answered. "It's quite new. I think you'll find it to your liking."

Sarevok smiled, and Angelo managed to look away casually, as if he weren't terrified of that grin. He crossed the big room to the fireplace, his feet whispering over the rug he'd had brought to him from Shou Lung at the cost of so many gold pieces they had to be conveyed east by magical means. The decorations and furnishings in this room could buy a small city, and Angelo took great pride in his varied collection of artifacts from the four corners of Toril. He took the poker from next to the fire—heavy mithral from the dwarven mines of the Great Rift—and prodded the fire absentmindedly.

"Interesting," Sarevok said, and Angelo looked up to find him holding an empty glass. "Cherries?"

"I believe so," Angelo answered, then changed the subject abruptly in an effort to hurry Sarevok's departure from his home. "My command of the Flaming Fist is secure. This Abdel of yours, and his woman, are known and wanted in this city. I don't suppose you can tell me how you got this information?"

"Oh," Sarevok laughed, "of course not, but I assure you they are indeed working in the employ of the Shadow Thieves."

"And this . . . what is it . . . cabal?"

"Guild, really," Sarevok replied.

"This thieves guild is Amnian in origin," Angelo said, studying the fire. "Surely they're outlaws in Amn as well, then."

Sarevok put down his glass with a hollow clink. "Think of them as privateers," he said. "Outlaws in the service of Amn."

"This is not to be tolerated," Angelo said, as if looking for agreement from Sarevok.

"Indeed," the imposing man said, "it is not."

"So what does it mean?" Angelo asked. "War with Amn, then?"

"Do you fear war?"

Angelo looked at Sarevok sharply, and a cold sweat broke out under his fine clothing. He thought for the briefest moment that Sarevok's eyes flashed an inhuman yellow, as if lit from within, then his guest smiled again.

"I fear needless war, yes," Angelo replied. He turned away and looked at the portrait of himself that hung above the fireplace. The artist had done an admirable job with Angelo's long, thin, vertical features. The duke kept his goatee trimmed to match the portrait, though current fashions were passing it by. The painting, unlike the man, still showed a trace of the warrior he once was. He met his own stare and felt like withering from it as much as from Sarevok's.

"If men are asked to fight, and no good reason is given them, they don't fight with their hearts."

"Their hearts do not concern me, Angelo. I need arms and legs."

Angelo took three steps and sank heavily onto a divan near the fire. He touched the calfskin cushion. It felt like a baby's skin and had cost him enough to buy a hundred children. Suddenly it didn't seem as impressive as when he'd purchased it in Waterdeep.

"Will your men fight?" Sarevok asked, his voice as loaded as the question.

Angelo nodded, hoping to reassure himself.

"Then tell them it is because Amn wants this war," Sarevok said calmly. "They poison our iron mines, try to strangle our neighbors to the south, they mean to have Baldur's Gate, the river, the mines . . . all of it. Is that enough?"

Angelo smiled and said, "More than enough, my friend. Add to that these Shadow Thieves working their mischief here in the Gate herself . . ."

"When I am named grand duke," Sarevok said, "there will be no more Amnian cutthroats defiling our great city . . . if we have to kill every man, woman, and child in that cursed realm to ensure it."

Angelo swallowed in a throat turned dry.

* * * * *

It wasn't even a whole shadow that caught Abdel's eye but the edge of a shadow. It was the third time he'd caught a glimpse of it since they'd returned to Baldur's Gate, sneaking into the city at night, unsure of their status in that city or any other on the Sword Coast. They were considered murderers in Candlekeep. Now they were being followed.

"You're sure?" Jaheira said softly. She'd noticed him tense at the glimpse of shadow.

Abdel nodded and said, "Just keep walking. We need to see Eltan."

"He might be the one following us," Jaheira said, "or having us followed."

Abdel didn't say anything. He was going over the options in his mind, and he made a decision quickly. Jaheira grunted in protest when he pulled her into a narrow, lightless alley.

"Shortcut?" she quipped.

He drew his sword in answer, and Jaheira grew as serious as he.

"If I have to kill whoever—or whatever—is following us, I don't want to do it in the street."

It took them an hour or more to reach the ducal palace, staying in the shadowy alleys the whole way. They heard footsteps once, saw another shadow, then another, before they reached their destination. Most of the time Abdel was the one who noticed their tail. He couldn't explain it even to himself, but it was as if he could smell her. Her? Abdel shook the thoughts out of his head, sheathed his sword and, Jaheira at his side, approached the guards at the gates of the ducal palace.

"Halt," one of them called, his voice conveying the growing tension in the city both Abdel and Jaheira had felt in the air this time. There was a heaviness about Baldur's Gate. "Who goes there?"

Abdel held his hands out next to him and walked up the little incline to the gate slowly. "I seek an audience with Grand Duke Eltan," he said simply.

The guard who stepped forward was a stocky young man who filled out his chain mail well. He held a well-polished halberd in a way that told Abdel he knew how to use it. Torches lit the area around the gate, and Abdel could see at least five more guards.

"And who are you?" the guard asked.

"A friend," Abdel answered.

"Eltan—" Jaheira said, "Grand Duke Eltan knows us. He sent us to . . . on a mission, and we need to report back."

"The grand duke is dying," the guard said. "You can make your report to the captain of the watch in the morning."

Jaheira looked pointedly at Abdel who closed his eyes and sighed, clenching his fists tightly. One of the other guards moved timidly out of the shadows, and the sound of his feet on the gravel made Abdel look up.

"Abdel?" the approaching guard asked, "Jaheira? Is that you?"

The first guard tensed visibly and shifted the weight of his halberd.

"Julius?" Jaheira said, her half-elf eyes allowing her to see the second guard's face.

"Torm save us," the first guard exclaimed, "it's the Shadow Thieves!"

"No—" Jaheira started to say, but Julius rushed at her with his halberd out in front of him. Now even Abdel could see his angry, frightened face as he charged. The first guard came at Abdel, and the sellsword stepped lightly to one side and grabbed the pole of the halberd in a tight grip. The guard let go of the polearm and drew a sword so quickly Abdel realized he must have practiced it. Only Abdel's chain mail saved him from a quick disemboweling.

Abdel spun the polearm around and was surprised by the thoughts that seemed to explode in his head. These guards thought they were Shadow Thieves—a group Abdel knew to be Amnian. Whatever story the Iron Throne had managed to create about them in Candlekeep had obviously stretched to Baldur's Gate—and in strange ways. In Candlekeep he had proven the Iron Throne right when he killed the guard. Abdel, even as he swung the halberd at the guard, decided not to make it that easy for the Iron Throne again.

Jaheira was ready for Julius's clumsy charge and stepped past the head of the polearm too. She punched Julius square in the nose, his own momentum compounding the blow. There was a sharp, snapping sound and a warm wetness over Jaheira's fist, and Julius went down.

Abdel dodged a slice from the first guard's sword and heard the other four running up rapidly even as a hollow horn blew in the otherwise quiet night. They'd have the whole palace down on them soon enough. Abdel spun the halberd around again and faked a jab at the guard's head. The guard dodged the attack, but put his head in line for a sideswipe that knocked him down—and out—with a solid clunk. Abdel threw the halberd sideways at the approaching guards and turned to see Jaheira already running for the safety of the dark alleys. The guards chased him only halfheartedly, and Abdel wondered if it was that they didn't want to abandon the gates, or if the dark alleys of their own city frightened them. Maybe it was a bit of both.

* * * * *

Abdel passed rats, garbage in piles, sleeping houses, and shops closed for the night. At intervals he would whisper-shout Jaheira's name into the darkness. A few times he thought he heard her footsteps or saw her shadow. He passed through an alley between two expensive looking townhouses. There was a beggar asleep in the alley who looked like nothing more than a pile of rags, snoring softly. Abdel held his breath, as he'd learned to do when passing beggars. He'd been walking a long time though, and he breathed in just slightly as he passed. The smell wasn't right. It wasn't a beggar's smell, and Abdel recognized it right away. He kept walking though, forcing himself not to hesitate. When he got to the end of the alley he stepped to the side and stopped, pressing his back against the wall and looking to his left at the alley entrance. Afraid of making any noise, he didn't pull his sword.

The face of the person who'd been following them since they'd returned to Baldur's Gate came around the corner slowly, eyes like slits in the darkness. Abdel spun around and grabbed for the stranger. He caught half a handful of smooth, cool fabric then his arm was batted away, the blow making his wrist tingle though it came so quickly he didn't see it. He felt something on his shoulder, and his vision went dark for the briefest moment. He stepped back and spun around at the sound of a voice from above.

"I am not your enemy."

The voice was quiet, precise, and the accent was unrecognizable.

"Abdel," Jaheira whispered behind him, and the sellsword gasped and spun, going half for his sword. Jaheira squeaked in surprise and jumped back.

"Don't do that!" she said, too loudly, then flinched again when Abdel put a hand up to silence her. He turned around and looked up at the balcony. The stranger moved up onto the stone rail and stepped off, falling what must have been fifteen feet and landing as softly as if it had been an inch. It was a woman, short and thin of frame, dressed in a close-fitting black garment unlike any Abdel had ever seen. Her face was hidden behind a mask that showed only her eyes, eyes the sellsword thought must have been eastern—Shou, or maybe Kozakuran.

"Who's that?" Jaheira asked. The stranger stepped back into the darkness of the alley, motioning Abdel to follow. The sellsword tipped his head to one side, but didn't follow her.

"My name is Tamoko," the woman said from the shadows.

"Why are you following us?" Abdel asked.

Jaheira drew her blade but didn't move forward.

"I know you are not Shadow Thieves," Tamoko said quietly. "I know you are not attempting to start this war, but avoid it."

"What war?" Jaheira asked. "War with Amn?"

"Grand Duke Eltan is dying," Tamoko said, still ignoring Jaheira. "The healer is not what he seems."

With that Tamoko stepped back into the shadows. Abdel rushed forward with Jaheira at his side and though they were at the entrance to the alley in less than a second, the dark woman was gone.

Chapter Twenty-Seven

If they hadn't spent as much time in the company of the festering ghoul Korak, Abdel and Jaheira wouldn't have been able to stand being in the alley as long as it took the guards to finish searching the place for them. The fish stew that filled the rusting metal bins they were hiding next to couldn't have been very good, even before it was thrown away. Abdel looked at Jaheira's face and in the predawn darkness of the alley he could see she was almost gagging with every breath.

"What's keeping them?" Jaheira asked in a voice dripping venom and impatience.

"It's a big place," Abdel answered. "The Blushing Mermaid goes on forever . . . almost, with wings attached to wings attached to wings. If they really think we're in there, it could take a long time."

Jaheira held a hand over her mouth, but Abdel could still hear her say, "Well, I guess the longer they're in there, the more thorough a search they give the place, the less likely they'll be to think they missed us and come back again. Besides, the reek is the only thing keeping me awake right now."

Abdel nodded and looked up at the sky, which had turned a dark blue with the approaching dawn.

They didn't have much longer to wait, and when the guards came out it was hard to miss them. They were a noisy, boisterous lot who seemed to have spent more time in the Blushing Mermaid drinking than searching. Abdel and Jaheira forced themselves to be patient until the guards' voices faded down the maze of crooked streets.

They slipped into a side door and got only a passing, disinterested glance from a halfling cook who was standing on a little wooden stool, stirring a huge black caldron full of that vile fish stew. They made their way out of the kitchens and into the tavern proper. Abdel held back behind a greasy curtain, letting Jaheira slip into the common room alone. He watched her cross the dark, low-ceilinged barroom inhabited by only a scattering of wee hour drinkers. A few of them were passed out on or under tables. One table was occupied by a group of nearly a dozen sailors, still singing some sea shanty and clapping while a woman, who looked so tired she might have been the Goddess of Tired, danced for their amusement and the odd tossed silver piece.

Not even the sailors noticed Jaheira slip into the room, so Abdel followed her to a table far away from the loud group. When he passed the bar a young man in loose-fitting ring mail looked up at Abdel with bleary eyes.

"Julius," Abdel said, stopping abruptly enough to draw the momentary attention of a couple of the sailors. Abdel looked back at them, and they turned away from his steely gaze. He reached out and took the young guardsman by the shoulder.

" 'Ey," Julius slurred weakly. He reeked of stale beer and sweat.

Abdel dragged Julius to the table where Jaheira was staring at them both expectantly. Julius sat down heavily— was sat down actually—on one of the little stools, and his head bobbed loosely on his neck.

"Finish me off, why don't you?" he murmured, making passing eye contact with Jaheira. His nose was swollen and purple and big bruises were forming under both his eyes. He had jammed bits of blood-soaked cloth up both nostrils, which only made his voice weaker, comical.

"Julius," Abdel said gravely, "we need some time. You're not going to turn us in, are you?"

Julius sat swaying gently for a few moments, trying to choose one of the Abdels he saw. Abdel glanced over his own right shoulder to try to see what Julius was looking at.

"To the Abyss with 'em all, my big, giant friend. They busted me, d'you believe that? They busted me to footman," the young guard said.

"Julius," Jaheira said, having to just hope he could understand her. "The guard at the palace told us Eltan is dying. What's been going on here?"

"Eltan Schmeltan . . ." Julius murmured. "He can kiss my—"

"Julius," Abdel said roughly, and the young guard laughed sloppily and tried to sock Abdel in the arm playfully but just waved impotently in the air.

"Yeah . . . yeah . . . Eltan," Julius said around sudden, violent hiccups. "He's taken . . . he's taken . . . he's taken . . ."

"Ill?" Jaheira provided.

"Yes," Julius said, scratching at his hair like a dog. "That too."

"Julius," Abdel said, but the young guard didn't look up, he just snored loudly. "Julius!" Abdel shouted, and the sailors all looked at him. The dancing woman sat down and sighed.

"Hey, swabby," one of the sailors called, "keep it down."

Abdel ignored the sailor and shook Julius awake.

The guard smiled and said, "They busted me to footman, so now I gotta wear this damned ring mail. I hate ring mail. It—"

The door to the street burst open, and an enormously fat woman surged into the tavern, panting and sweating.

"Whoa," Julius said and nearly fell off his chair. The woman crossed to the bartender and told him something Abdel couldn't hear, though the woman's face told him the news was urgent and grave. Even the sailors were looking at the bartender in anticipation.

"Hey up!" the bartender shouted, sliding to the center of the long bar. "Hey up!"

Even some of the passed-out drunks, whose eyes were

growing red and puffy, looked up at the bartender.

"Dawn breaks over a sad city," the bartender said, his voice gravelly and loud, "for Grand Duke Eltan is dead!"

The woman who'd been dancing for the sailors gasped and began to cry. The sailors regarded her for a few seconds, some seeming legitimately worried, then they all shrugged in turn and started talking about what a bastard their first mate was.

Abdel turned to look at Jaheira. Her face was a stone mask—as hopeless as he'd ever seen her.

"Angelo," Julius murmured. "I have to take orders from Angelo."

"Angelo?" Abdel asked, "The half-elf?"

Julius nodded loosely and said, "Aye, sir. He's taken over the Flaming Fist. Now there'll be nobody to stop the ducal election from going to whatsisname."

"Who?" Jaheira asked.

"Sarevok," Julius said sluggishly. "It'll be Grand Duke Sarevok."

* * * * *

Abdel was hesitant to follow Julius's stammered, mumbled directions, but had little choice. As another day dawned over Baldur's Gate, Abdel and Jaheira stole cloaks off a wash line and went through the waking streets with hoods drawn over their faces. They kept to opposite sides of the street, assuming the guards would be looking for a couple, but kept each other in the corner of their vision all the way.

They followed Julius's directions and came around the back of the ducal palace, keeping to the still shadowy alley facing the rear gate from which Julius claimed the ducal healer would eventually emerge. There was something about the healer—Kendal was his name—that Abdel didn't like the first time they'd met him. Now they had this strange eastern woman tell them there was something amiss with the healer the very night that Eltan, under

Kendal's care, died of some mysterious ailment. Abdel only hoped Julius, who was passed out in the Blushing Mermaid when they left him, wouldn't remember telling them where to go, or even remember meeting them at all, and tell his superiors.

Abdel forced himself not to think about what else Julius had to say. If it was true that his half brother Sarevok was here in Baldur's Gate, was Reiltar's man on the Sword Coast, was responsible for the whole bloody mess, what was he going to do? If Sarevok became grand duke, if Eltan was dead and even Tethtoril had turned against him, what could the two of them do against—

The door opened, and Abdel and Jaheira stepped silently back into the shadowy alley and watched Kendal stride quickly, casually, out into the street. The sellsword and the half-elf glanced at each other and followed the healer into the maze of slowly waking streets. Kendal took what could only have been a purposefully meandering path through the streets. Though it wasn't difficult to follow him, both Abdel and Jaheira were becoming more and more wary of being caught out in the open. It was with some relief that they saw Kendal ditch into a dark, thin alleyway. They followed him into the shadows and stopped when they saw him change.

By the time Kendal reached the end of the alley—less than a dozen yards at most—he'd blurred around the edges and faded into a new form altogether. What came out the other end of the alley was a young woman, carrying not a bag of medicines, potions, and such but a basket of fresh cut flowers.

Jaheira breathed out through her nose, and Abdel took her by the elbow and nudged her gently forward. The doppelganger continued on its way—actually paused twice to sell flowers to passersby—then slipped into another alley without ever looking behind it. Abdel and Jaheira circled around quickly and were at the other end of the alley before the doppelganger emerged, this time in the form of a burly laborer in mud-stained coveralls.

Abdel and Jaheira hid behind an apple cart and watched the doppelganger disappear down another side street. They moved quickly along the next block, hoping to cut the doppelganger off, but when they cut through an alley, back to the street they'd seen the creature turn down, there was no sign of the laborer. The street was all but empty. The sun had barely peeked over the city wall.

"Damn them all," Abdel whispered.

"I hate those damned doppelgangers," Jaheira said.

"As do I," replied a voice from behind them.

They turned and saw what could only be the slight eastern woman from the night before. She was dressed in shimmering black silk that Abdel thought must have cost her a king's ransom. The sword that hung loosely from a cord around her neck was thin and curved gracefully. The hand guard was a simple oval with a cloth-of-gold-wrapped pommel long enough for two hands. Abdel had never seen a sword like it.

"It is a katana," Tamoko said, noticing Abdel noticing her weapon.

Abdel nodded once and said, "And you're a doppelganger."

Tamoko smiled sadly. "I understand that that possibility would exist," she said, "but I am not."

"Who are you?" Jaheira asked, her brow furrowed.

Tamoko nodded in the direction of an alley and stepped in, this time making no attempt to hide herself. Abdel and Jaheira reluctantly followed. Jaheira drew the silver dagger, and this elicited a tiny, knowing smile from Tamoko. Abdel almost returned the smile. This strange woman's face was not unlike Jaheira's. Her ears showed no trace of elf blood, but her features were strangely sylvan.

"I can take you to the Iron Throne," Tamoko said simply.

Jaheira laughed in response and said, "Can you really? And will they wait to kill us there or pounce on us in the street?"

"They will not expect anyone to be coming in from this entrance. You will be able to kill them all and—"

"This is ludicrous," Jaheira interrupted. "Abdel . . ."

The sellsword held up a hand, and Jaheira's look all but burned into his flesh.

"My friend is right," Abdel said to Tamoko. "We have no reason to trust you . . . or anyone in this pit of shapeshifters."

"I am your brother's lover," she said, locking her eyes onto his. Abdel felt the truth radiate from them. She was speaking so simply, so plainly, and never wavering. He had no real reason to, but he believed her.

"Sarevok?" Abdel asked, the name almost tripping on his tongue.

Tamoko nodded once. "I can help you, but you must not kill him."

"This is madness," Jaheira scoffed. "This lover of yours is going to start a war. Thousands of people are going to die. He's already killed two of the most powerful men in Baldur's Gate, and others . . ." Jaheira stepped forward and bent the elbow of her sword arm just slightly. Tamoko fixed her gaze on the tip of Jaheira's blade. Abdel could feel what was about to happen and didn't like the feeling one bit.

"No one believes us," Abdel said then, just letting the words pour out. "They've accused us of murder, of being Shadow Thieves, of being Amnian spies, of the gods only know what else. They've killed all of our friends, all of our contacts. We're alone against this man—my brother if that's what he is—who by nightfall will be the next grand duke. There might be people left who can help us, but they will need proof." Abdel spared a long, telling glance at Jaheira and added, "They will need *written* proof."

Jaheira looked at him and sighed. He wasn't sure if she was angry at him for dealing with this strange woman who might be a doppelganger or worse, or if she realized that he meant to return to Candlekeep with some evidence, some way to garner Tethtoril's forgiveness. Abdel himself felt silly and weak for thinking the latter, but he was happy to feel that way.

"If the Iron Throne is revealed," Tamoko said, her gaze

coming off Jaheira's blade and over to Abdel's eyes, "Sarevok will have to flee the city. I will go with him. We will . . ."

"Abdel . . ." Jaheira said. He couldn't read her tone.

"The threat of war will be at an end," Tamoko said.

"And you will reform this brother of mine?" Abdel asked. "You'll turn him away from . . . from our father's . . ."

"I will," Tamoko said flatly.

"Abdel," Jaheira said, "he's not you."

Abdel looked at her and smiled, "No," he said, "Sarevok is not me. I had a chance. I had you."

Jaheira sighed and turned away, unable to argue though she knew he was making a mistake big enough to kill them all.

"I will not kill Sarevok," Abdel said to Tamoko.

The assassin bowed deeply, forming nearly a ninety-degree angle at her waist.

She stood and said, "You will have your evidence."

Chapter Twenty-Eight

Abdel stood over the doppelganger he'd just killed and watched Tamoko fight. He was in awe of her skill, her speed, her agility, and her detached, pristine calm. He couldn't imagine having to fight the woman. Abdel knew he was good—knew now that a god's blood ran in his veins even—but he was a bumbling novice next to this woman.

She sliced open the neck of a city guardsman and dark blood pumped from the wound. It transformed back into its gray, inhuman form as it fell. Its comrade fought on, knowing it had no choice but to at least attempt to save its own miserable life. It went for her eyes, then tried for her knees, it fought with desperation and panic and a complete lack of sportsmanship. Tamoko, who seemed so studied, took it all in stride and met each attack, however cheap, with strong, unhesitating, calm.

She batted away the doppelganger's short sword so hard it spun from the creature's grasp.

It stopped, put its hands to its side and said, in the voice of its Amnian soldier form, "I yield."

Tamoko took its head off so fast the doppelganger had time to blink once or twice at its own headless corpse.

"That is all that we will find here," she said, sparing the transforming doppelganger not the slightest emotion. "The rest are elsewhere in the city."

"Where?" Jaheira said, wiping doppelganger blood from her own blade.

"You wanted proof," Tamoko said.

"I don't want to leave any more of these things alive in the Gate," Abdel replied, waiting for the location of the other doppelgangers.

Tamoko stood firm and said, "There will always be doppelgangers in this city," Tamoko obviously took no joy in her opinion. "There will always be doppelgangers in every city. It is how they live."

"Great," Jaheira muttered, "that's just—"

Abdel put a hand on her arm, and Jaheira sighed.

"She's right," he said. "We came here for evidence."

Jaheira looked up at Tamoko and raised her eyebrows. The assassin bowed and gestured to a corner of the cellar. This particular cell of doppelgangers—all in the employ of Sarevok and the Iron Throne—made their home in the cellar of an abandoned manor house on Windspell Street. The cellar was dark, smelled bad, and was crowded with old crates and stacks of rotten firewood. There were six cots and four dead doppelgangers. Abdel looked in the corner Tamoko indicated and saw a stout wooden chest. Jaheira insisted on staring at Tamoko while Abdel dragged the chest into the feeble light of the doppelgangers' oil lamp.

Tamoko knelt next to one of the dead creatures, and Jaheira winced when the assassin stuck her finger into the doppelganger's bloody mouth. She obviously didn't find what she was looking for, so she knelt next to another one.

"What are you doing?" Jaheira asked her.

Tamoko fished about in the doppelganger's mouth for a moment and produced a wet, slimy iron key. Jaheira shook her head in amazement, and Tamoko flashed an almost imperceptible smile.

The assassin tossed the key to Abdel, who used it to open the chest.

"What is it?" Jaheira asked him, still keeping her eyes on Tamoko. "What's in there?"

"Scrolls," Abdel replied.

Jaheira looked at him. He was kneeling in front of the chest, his back to her.

"Scrolls?" she asked.

"Evidence," he answered, turning to face her. He looked at her and smiled, but his smile quickly faded as he looked past her, then turned his head to scan the room. Jaheira followed his gaze to nothing. Tamoko was gone.

* * * * *

The chest was heavy, and Abdel was tired. He carried it a long way through the streets of Baldur's Gate and brushed aside Jaheira's offers to help. They had decided their course of action in the cellar, and they were both more than a little nervous. Abdel got the feeling Jaheira wanted to say something to him, and he felt like he should say something to her. They settled on small talk.

"She's something, isn't she?" Jaheira asked conversationally, watching the midday crowds go by as they walked.

"Tamoko?" Abdel asked unnecessarily.

Jaheira nodded and said, "I've never seen a fighting style like that before. It was . . . beautiful."

"I think she's from Kozakura," Abdel offered.

"She's beautiful," Jaheira said, her voice quavering ever so slightly.

Abdel got that feeling from her that told him to stop. He set the chest down gently next to a sweet-smelling bakery. An old woman harrumphed as she passed, having to walk around the big chest.

"She might be able to . . ." Abdel started to say, but Jaheira just tipped her head to one side and smiled, knowing what he was going to say.

"I hope so, Abdel," she said. "I really do, but I find it hard to believe."

"She has no hope?" he asked, wanting to draw something out of her but not sure what.

Jaheira smiled and put a hand on his heaving chest. He was sweating from carrying the evidence, but she didn't care. "She might love him," Jaheira said. "If she does, that might . . ."

She stopped talking and just stood there, looking at him.

"I love you," he said, not sure why he thought he needed to say that just then, but he needed to.

She smiled a strangely sad smile, but her eyes sparkled. "I love you," she said.

He smiled, but not at her. He smiled at the feeling that washed over him then. It was like the feeling he used to get before a particularly threatening fight or just before a kill. It wasn't as long ago as it seemed, but once Abdel was afraid that the feelings he had for Jaheira came from what he now knew to be his father's side, the part of him that was a murderer. Now, he realized that feeling wasn't the same, that the love he felt for her was pushing the Bhaal out of him, replacing his need to kill with his need for her.

Jaheira's expression changed, and she laughed lightly at the sight of all this thinking. He didn't realize it, but his face had betrayed his inner dialog all too well.

"Pick up that chest," she said playfully, "we have people to see."

"Yes ma'am," he replied. "Let's go turn ourselves in."

* * * * *

"Oh no," Julius breathed. "Get away from me!"

The young footman waved his halberd weakly at Abdel and Jaheira. The bruises under his eyes were a livid purple, but he'd taken the cloth out of his nose. His eyes were bright red, and his face was pale. He didn't look well, and now he was scared on top of it all.

"Why," he asked the heavens, "on my watch?"

"Julius," Abdel said as he put the chest down on the gravel path leading to the gates of the ducal palace, "we've come to turn ourselves in."

Jaheira slid her sheathed blade out of the loop on her belt and tossed it casually to the ground in front of Julius's feet. Attracted to the odd confrontation, the other guards started to gather around.

"You're going to kill me this time, aren't you?" Julius

231

asked, his voice as serious as it was weak.

Abdel removed the broadsword from his back and tossed it to land on top of Jaheira's weapon on the ground in front of Julius. The young footman jumped back.

One of the other guards asked, "You know these people?"

Julius ignored his comrade and said to Jaheira, "You might as well kill me. They can't bust me any further down . . ." he turned his gaze to Abdel and finished, ". . . except maybe the dungeon."

Abdel put his hands on top of his head, smiled, and fell to his knees.

"Footman Julius," he called in a voice loud enough for everyone within a block of the palace to hear, "I, outlaw Abdel, surrender to you."

Jaheira followed suit, saying, "And I, outlaw Jaheira, do the same."

"Why," Julius asked the other guards, "is it always my watch?"

* * * * *

Julius, with a parade of other guards to back him up, led Abdel and Jaheira through the wide, high-ceilinged corridors of the ducal palace. He stopped at a set of tall double doors on either side of which stood two nervous halberdiers.

Julius nodded at them and said, "Duke Angelo is expecting us."

They pulled open the doors, and Jaheira gasped at the sight of the chamber within. It was an enormous room filled with ornate furnishings and artifacts that simply oozed wealth. It was like some exotic museum. Abdel had seen some things similar to the pieces here inside Candlekeep but not all in one room.

There were six people already there, but only one man— a half-elf actually—stood when Julius led Abdel and Jaheira in. Abdel had heard of Duke Angelo only in passing. He was said to be a good man. Not as good as Scar, maybe, but if he hadn't been replaced by a doppelganger, a man who would listen to reason. Two guards put the heavy chest down a few paces into the room. Abdel and Jaheira followed Julius and the other guards' lead and bowed to the duke.

"These are the . . ." Julius said, ". . . them, m'lord."

Angelo smiled at Julius and said, "Footman . . ."

"Julius, m'lord."

"Julius," Angelo said, nodding, "you'll make corporal for this."

Julius looked relieved, but didn't smile. "Th-tha-thank you, m'lord," he stammered.

"Abdel Adrian," Angelo said, "I have heard a great deal about you."

"Duke Angelo," Abdel said with a nod.

While the two guards who'd brought in the chest opened it, Abdel studied the other occupants of the room. There were two women, both tall and dark and impeccably dressed, dripping with gold and dazzling gems. They both regarded Abdel as if he were a specimen to be studied. Two of the men were middle-aged bureaucrats—politicians— common even in cities like Baldur's Gate. They looked at Abdel as if he was an entirely different kind of specimen.

The third man was obviously one of the mercenaries who'd made Baldur's Gate his home. He was dressed in simple, utilitarian clothes, and there was no sign of jewelry. His face was serious, expectant, and well chiseled. Though he was seated, Abdel could tell this man was tall, easily as tall as Abdel himself, and solidly muscled. His eyes were dark but gleamed oddly in the daylight streaming through the windows. This man never looked at anyone or anything but Abdel.

"I am told you have brought with you your reason for turning yourselves in," Angelo said, his voice alive with curiosity. "I have it on good authority"—and he glanced at the big man—"that you are both members of the Shadow Thieves, and spies of Amn here to incite war through sabotage and—"

"We're none of those things," Abdel said, "and the contents of this chest will prove that."

The big man stood and approached slowly, still keeping his eyes on Abdel. The sellsword almost thought the big man's eyes flashed yellow, but—

"A chest full of scrolls?" Angelo asked.

"Yes, m'lord," Abdel answered.

Jaheira cleared her throat and added, "M'lord, on these scrolls you will find plans for mines both familiar and unfamiliar to you. You will find an alchemical recipe for a potion designed to ruin iron ore. You will find—"

"Evidence of a Faerûn-spanning conspiracy," Duke Angelo finished for her, "that only you two Amnian agents are aware of, is that it? Did I get that right?"

"We have surrendered ourselves," Abdel said, fighting to keep still, fighting not to betray his nervousness. "We are at your mercy for as long as it takes you to study the contents of this chest. There is a man in Baldur's Gate who is working for an organization called the Iron Throne." Abdel stepped forward, in front of Jaheira. "The Iron Throne is responsible for the troubles with the iron supply, not Amn. These men, if men they are, use doppelgangers to kill the very best of us—Captain Scar and Grand Duke Eltan among them."

Angelo seemed ready with another quip, but he couldn't pull his eyes away from Abdel's.

"And this man in Baldur's Gate?" he asked.

"This man is named Sarevok," Abdel answered.

Then things started happening too quickly for all but two of the people in the room to really follow.

Angelo looked sharply over his shoulder at the big mercenary, whose eyes did flash with a distinct yellow light. Duke Angelo said, "Sarevok?" at the same time that the mercenary's hand flashed forward, and there was a lightning bolt of energy, thin and blue-white. It cracked in the air of the room, and Abdel twitched to the side faster than even he thought he was capable of. The electricity flashed past him. The eyes of the fancy women and the stuffed men bulged, and one of them spilled his drink.

There was a scream behind Abdel, followed quickly by a

thud and Angelo's voice asking, "Sarevok?" again.

Abdel reached for his sword, but of course it wasn't there. The big man twisted his fingers and muttered something Abdel couldn't understand, and Abdel realized two things at the same instant: This man was Sarevok, and he was casting a spell.

Abdel leaped forward and brushed Sarevok's hands aside as he went for his half brother's neck. The spell spoiled, Sarevok bellowed in rage and brought his hands up to break Abdel's stranglehold. Abdel answered that with a head-butt that bounced the back of Sarevok's skull against the wall. Neither of them had remembered Sarevok falling backward, with Abdel on top of him.

Abdel thought of Jaheira, then his promise to Tamoko, and his fingers relaxed just enough that Sarevok managed to push him away and to the side, almost breaking Abdel's neck in the process. As he rolled onto his back, Abdel could see two guards—one of them Julius—rushing to put out a fire. The fire was burning on Jaheira's chest.

"Jaheira!" Abdel screamed, and he spun at the movement next to him, though at that instant he cared about nothing more than the half-elf woman who lay sprawled and burning on the floor. Sarevok stood and bounded toward the big glass window. Abdel let him go.

Angelo shouted, "Sarevok!"

Abdel slid across the polished floor to Jaheira's side. There was an enormous crash as Sarevok leaped through the window. Duke Angelo slid to the floor next to Jaheira, and Abdel reached out to grab him.

Angelo called out, "Get a *priest!*" but Abdel didn't hear him. He was too busy screaming into the lifeless eyes of the woman he loved.

Chapter Twenty-Nine

Abdel stabbed the doppelganger so hard his hand followed his broadsword through the creature's body. He could feel the thing transform while his arm was still inside it, but even that sensation wasn't shocking enough to distract Abdel from what he'd come here to do. Thanks to Sarevok's own, nearly compulsive, record-keeping they'd been able to find the entrance to the subterranean labyrinth of old sewers and catacombs the doppelgangers had been using to infiltrate nearly every corner of the city of Baldur's Gate. All the tunnels led in one direction. As Abdel tossed aside the dead doppelganger, he peered into the murky darkness and somehow knew they were close, but didn't know exactly what they were close to.

"This way?" Duke Angelo asked Abdel, his voice clipped and professional. The press of soldiers from Angelo's Flaming Fist, men who fought in the memory of Scar and Eltan, almost pushed the half-elf forward.

"This way?" Abdel said finally, "Yes, I think so, but I can't be sure."

"Maerik," Angelo called.

The stocky sergeant pressed through his comrades, nodding expectantly.

"Take your men and Ferran's," Angelo ordered, "back to the last side passage. Err to your left."

Maerik said, "Yes, sir," and was off faster than even Angelo expected. These men were fighting for their homes now.

"Temil," Angelo said to a short, thin, gray-haired woman in flowing satin robes, "you and your men go left up there and try to circle around. I'm going with Abdel and taking Julius's men with me."

The mage smiled and swept her robe around in a flourish. Her men followed her warily, obviously not used to taking orders from a sorceress, but knowing their duty.

Abdel didn't wait for Angelo to catch up. He was off down the passage fast, stepping lightly on his toes, ready for anything. Angelo followed more cautiously, and his men slowed him down. Abdel heard their voices and their footsteps growing more distant as he moved on, but he just couldn't wait for them.

When Tamoko stepped out in front of him he slid to a halt, and he realized who she was before he killed her.

"Tamoko," he said, "where is—"

She drew her strange curved sword as fast as anyone Abdel had ever seen draw steel. Her eyes blazed at him, but Abdel couldn't tell what she felt at that moment. She was injured. Her black silk clothes were stained a darker black. Abdel knew as much by the smell as anything that she was bleeding, and bleeding badly. A trickle of blood was running down the right side of her face from under her black hood. She was breathing heavily, and Abdel saw her fighting not to stagger as she advanced on him, one pained step at a time.

"Tamoko . . ." he said, and she shook her head. Abdel saw a tear trace a line down her left cheek.

"I was . . . *orokashii*," she said, "I was disloyal . . . I was disloyal."

Abdel put his sword up, ready to defend, but not to kill.

"He killed Jaheira," he told her, though he wasn't sure exactly why.

"I know," Tamoko whispered. "Of course he did."

"He needs you," Abdel told her, "but he doesn't deserve you."

"It is I who does not deserve him," she said and attacked.

Abdel was staggered at his own ability to block her

Z-shaped assault. It was fast—for any other swordsman but her. She stumbled at the end of it, throwing herself off balance in what must have been the first time in years, maybe ever.

"I won't kill you," he told her.

"I have to kill you," she replied and attacked again, this time taking a nick out of Abdel's side. He roared more with frustration than pain. She stepped back quickly, and her knees gave out all at once. Her chin hit the flagstone floor, and Abdel heard her teeth clack together. She put her arm out to stop her fall a good second after she'd already hit the floor.

"He killed you too," Abdel asked her as she lay there on the floor trying to move, then just trying to breathe. "Didn't he? For helping us?"

Angelo came up behind Abdel and asked, "What is this—" but Abdel stopped him with a hand to his chest.

"Tamoko?" Abdel asked the dying woman.

From the floor, she said, "I release you . . . from your vow. I cannot . . . he must . . . *shiizumaru* . . . he must die."

"Tamoko," Abdel said, but by the time he finished saying her name, she was dead.

* * * * *

It wasn't absolutely necessary, for the completion of the ritual, for the other sixteen priests in the inner sanctum of the High House of Wonders to be chanting. It was an aid in concentration for High Artificer Thalamond Albaier, though, and a chance for the lesser priests to see the greatest of all Gond's miracles.

The fact that the woman lying sprawled and lifeless across the marble altar had elf blood in her veins didn't help, but the high artificer had been asked to perform this ceremony at the request of the new leader of the Flaming Fist, so he was doing everything in his substantial power to see that it happened. The candles that burned in the room were blessed of Gond, the air was scented with incense grown in the greenhouses of Wonderhome itself, and the artificers and acolytes gathered there chanted in disbelief at seeing this ritual performed three times in as many tendays. The first two times, the outcome had been Gond's will but had gone against the wishes of the high artificer and his secular friends.

This time, perhaps it was the wavering in the high artificer's own faith that made the difference. Gond might have thought a demonstration was due.

A sharp, jagged breath was drawn in, followed by a hollow wail that made every hair in the chamber stand on end.

"*Abdel!*" Jaheira screamed as she was born once more onto the face of Toril.

* * * * *

Abdel had no idea how far underground he was. He followed the passageway, leaving Tamoko's body behind, with Angelo and an increasingly anxious group of Flaming Fists. They were good men, but this was a bad situation, and all Abdel could do was trust in Angelo's ability to lead them. A lot of people—all of Baldur's Gate—would have to start doing that.

The passageway ended in a small, low-ceilinged chamber with one other exit. A wide archway opened to a much larger chamber, and the unmistakable orange glow of torchlight lit the space beyond.

Abdel took a deep breath. Through that archway, he knew, he would find his half brother, a man he'd seen only once before, and only for the length of time it took his brother to kill the woman he loved. Abdel didn't want to kill anymore, had even naively hoped that Tamoko would be able to show Sarevok that there was human blood in his veins too, but now he'd come here for one reason and one reason only.

He stepped through the archway with sword in hand, and a sizzle of cold electricity passed through his body at the sight of the chamber beyond.

The space was enormous, and though Abdel was no engineer or miner, he couldn't imagine what was keeping the ceiling—and what must have been two hundred feet or more of earth and bedrock above it—from falling in. The rows of stone pillars that lined each of the long sides of the rectangular chamber looked more ornamental than practical. Carved into the stone of the pillars and the walls alike were scenes of unimaginable horror. Screaming faces of men, women, children, and beasts leered out at Abdel, their faces frozen in a moment of pure agony—the moment of traumatic death. Only an artist who had visited the deepest pits of the Abyss could have carved such faces.

The far end of the room was dominated by a stepped dais, several yards on a side, that rose perhaps twenty feet off the flagstone floor. An altar fit for sacrifices and carved with the same tormented faces dominated the top of the dais. Torches set into wall sconces fashioned from hideous wrought-iron gargoyles lit the chamber with an unsteady illumination. Candles dripped blood-red wax onto the floor of the dais, candles set in golden candelabra twisted into the forms of dying women.

Sarevok was waiting for him. He stood behind the hideous altar, and a semicircle of figures stood around him, men in black robes, their hands poised in front of them in odd gestures that might have been some attitude of prayer.

Sarevok's armor reflected every nuance of their father's evil. Fashioned from what must have been iron—iron as black as midnight—the plates covered every inch of the tall man. Blades whose razor edges gleamed in the dancing light rose from exaggerated randers like miniature wings and flared from his vambraces like the raking claws of some clockwork raptor.

Set into the center of this cruel suit was a sigil Abdel recognized from the cover of the cursed book: a skull ringed by drops of blood. Sarevok looked like some huge, black iron beetle.

This time Abdel couldn't attribute the eerie glow in his

half brother's eyes to any trick of the light. They blazed yellow from behind a mask of jagged teeth-like ribbons of steel. Horns that must have been ripped from the skull of a demon curved from the sides of the otherwise impenetrable helmet.

"Abdel Adrian," Sarevok said, his voice rolling through the chamber.

Abdel expected him to say something more, but Sarevok only laughed. The sound set the robed figures off, and they rushed headlong at the mercenaries coming timidly into the room behind Abdel.

"To arms!" Angelo screamed, and a wild, incoherent battle cry rose up from the throats of the mercenaries.

The black-robed cultists chanted and murmured. Waves of darkness, blue glowing missiles, and bursts of flame scattered the first rank of Flaming Fists.

The men quickly regrouped, and a few of the cultists went down to ordinary steel. Then it was just all-out havoc. Abdel thrilled to it. He let himself have that feeling—just this once more. Sarevok still stood in place and none of the cultists would come within ten feet of Abdel. The brothers locked eyes, and Abdel brought his sword up in a salute he didn't think his brother deserved. He offered the salute to the memory of the people in his life that Sarevok had killed: his true father, Gorion; his only love, Jaheira; and his friends Khalid, Xan, and Scar.

Sarevok smiled a wolf's grin, and they came at each other.

Abdel advanced quickly and made it more than halfway across the room before he had to slash through a robed figure that had stumbled in front of him. Sarevok came down the steps of the dais two at a time and brought a huge, black, two-handed sword up and over his head as Abdel leaped over the fallen cultist.

The sound their swords made when they smashed together made Abdel's ears ring. There was a momentary flash of what might have been respect in Sarevok's eyes when his brother's sword took the full force of his strike.

The sound of steel on steel echoed through the giant room. Men screamed, women screamed, dozens died. There was a dull, rumbling sound, searing heat, and red-orange light—a fireball going off close to Abdel and Sarevok. Neither of the sons of Bhaal let it distract them.

Sarevok whirled his sword down and to the left, and Abdel nearly didn't meet it with his own blade in time to keep from being sliced in half. Abdel batted his brother's sword away, getting the distinct impression that Sarevok wanted just that. He couldn't stop himself from stepping in close, but Abdel realized he'd been seduced into the move in time to crouch, his tired knees creaking in protest. Sarevok let one hand come off his sword, and his blade-lined forearm whistled over Abdel's head.

In too close, Abdel had to roll on his rump to get out of the way. Sarevok tried to step on him once while he was still on the ground, and Abdel swiped at the armored leg as it came down. His broadsword spanked off Sarevok's black-iron jamb with a shower of sparks and a sound that made Abdel's gums curl. He hit his brother's leg hard enough that Abdel realized the armor had to be enchanted. He'd taken the leg off armored men with the same attack in the past.

Abdel was on the ground and vulnerable, but Sarevok took three long steps backward, bringing his sword up in front of him in the guard position.

He can't bend down, Abdel thought. That armor might help me.

Springing to his feet, Abdel grunted and went at his brother again. Abdel intended to rush in, drawing Sarevok's defenses high, then slide down between his brother's legs and attack him from below, where he was vulnerable. In the din of battle, though, Abdel didn't hear his brother's quickly mumbled incantation. Sarevok's hands had come off his sword, which hung straight in the air in front of him as if suspended from above. His fingers worked a complex pattern in the air in front of him.

Instinctively, Abdel ducked and covered his face with one powerful arm. Clenching tightly to his sword, he rolled on

the floor and spun to the side as the space between him and
his brother burst into a bright rainbow of multicolored light.
The magical effect fanned out in front of Sarevok and held
itself in a triangular pattern, almost three-dimensional,
that sliced through the air just above Abdel's head. There
were screams, and sounds like popping, and a wave of the
smell of burning flesh that seemed too closely timed to the
spell not to be a result of it. Cultists and Flaming Fists alike
were dying. Pain flared across Abdel's back, then burned
into his side when he stood and ran, cutting a wide semicircle around to his brother's left. There was an eerie sizzling
sound coming from his chain mail tunic, but Abdel knew he
would die if he didn't force himself to ignore the sound, the
pain, and the injury, however serious it was.

Abdel didn't know any spells and had no tricks up his
sleeve. If he was going to kill Sarevok—and he was determined to do just that—he would have to hack him to death.
When he came at Sarevok again, Abdel got the feeling his
brother was surprised that he'd survived the burning spell.
Abdel took advantage of the half-second's hesitation and
slashed strong and hard at Sarevok's neck, hoping to end
the fight quickly and decisively.

Sarevok's hands found his floating sword, and he turned
into Abdel's attack. Abdel braced himself for the force of the
two blades coming together and grunted in surprise and
pain when it was their hands, not their blades, that met in
the middle. The force of the blow drove one of the half-inch
spikes lining Sarevok's gauntlets into the back of Abdel's
left hand, then ripped through skin and bone as the attack
followed through.

Both Abdel's and Sarevok's swords flew into the dense
air of the battle-filled chamber. Sarevok swore and took
several steps back, sparing a glance up at his tumbling
sword. He held out a hand to catch it, and Abdel was about
to do the same, when, without really making the conscious
decision to do it, he flung himself at his brother and hit
him, body to body with force sufficient to drop a rothé.

Abdel could hear Sarevok's breath punch out of him, and

they hit the floor together. Sarevok almost seemed like he wanted to fall on his back. He spun Abdel up and over himself in a single fluid motion that launched the big sellsword into the air. Sarevok's sword hit the flagstones several paces to his right, at the feet of a Flaming Fist footman who was watching the two brothers' fight in wide-eyed horror.

Abdel's hand found the pommel of his own sword after it had bounced once on the flagstones with an alarming clang, but before he hit the ground. He landed on his knees and brought the sword up in time to block a hard, fast punch from a still rolling Sarevok.

Abdel stood and, panting, sword in front of him and ready for anything, slid two steps away from his brother, who did the same.

Sarevok glanced to the side and ran at the footman, who met the charge with a frozen, terrified stare. Abdel screamed at him to run, but the man just stood there. Sarevok scooped his sword up from the ground and spilled the footman's guts in a single motion and was already coming back at Abdel before the soldier's body hit the ground.

Abdel recognized many of his own instincts in the way Sarevok fought. The thought that they'd both inherited common traits from their infernal sire unnerved Abdel enough that Sarevok had the opportunity to cut the tip of his right ear off. The pain was like a splash of searing hot water in Abdel's face, and it was as effective as cold water in snapping Abdel back into the fight. He answered Sarevok's cut with a flurry of slashing attacks—across, back, up, down, across, and back again—and Sarevok took a defensive step backward.

It went on like that for what seemed to Abdel to be the rest of his life. He never felt tired, was past exhaustion—he was fighting for his life, and it wasn't in him to let himself waver in the slightest in order to rest. That would be as alien to him now as the thought of letting Sarevok live would be. Abdel pressed again, and Sarevok fought back out of desperation, but Abdel never connected. Sarevok got in another lucky cut, but it was superficial, most of its force spent on Abdel's blood-spattered chain mail.

The sound of the melee around them started to diminish, but neither Abdel nor Sarevok took notice. There was a flash of blue-white light from somewhere, the impossible sound of a thunderclap, and the smell of ozone, then a chorus of screams. Abdel had to sidestep quickly to avoid treading on a severed head that rolled into his path.

"Kill me!" Sarevok screamed. "Kill me if you can, brother! One more death in the glory of our father, who shall rise again on the blood of the murdered!"

"No!" a voice from behind Abdel screamed.

It was Angelo. Abdel saw a man in the tabard of the Flaming Fist, who had begun to advance, hesitate, looking back at Angelo. The duke knew. He understood it was between the brothers now.

Abdel knew the Iron Throne had been defeated, the war avoided—the war that never seemed like a war, won. That gave him the strength he needed—just that little bit of strength—and his next blow came in not too hard for Sarevok, but too hard for his brother's blade.

Sarevok's sword burst into shards of glittering black steel, and Abdel didn't waste a heartbeat. He brought his foot up high into his half brother's chest and stomped him down like a bug. Sarevok bounced when he hit the floor, his armor clattering in protest. As he came down on top of Sarevok, Abdel spun his broadsword in his right hand and reversed the blade, so he was stabbing down with it. The tip of the blade plunged through Sarevok's armor. Abdel twisted it up to gouge the man's neck and almost punctured the skin before he hesitated, sweating, panting, bleeding. All the anger, and all the emotion, and all the regret, and all the uncertainty rushed out of Abdel in a torrent.

"You may not have accepted our father's gift, brother, but there are others—like me—who are willing."

"I will find them too then, *brother*," Abdel spat, making that promise in the memory of Jaheira.

"And murder them?" Sarevok asked, the yellow light already fading from his eyes, as if in anticipation of death.

"Like you'll murder me now? Enough deaths, and Bhaal will be reborn. I won't bring him back with my war, but maybe you will with yours. Our father's blood runs true in your veins."

"Yes," Abdel said softly, "just this once more."

He leaned all his weight onto the blade and held it down until Sarevok was dead.

R.A. SALVATORE'S WAR
OF THE SPIDER QUEEN

THE NEW YORK TIMES BEST-SELLING SAGA OF THE DARK ELVES

DISSOLUTION BOOK I
RICHARD LEE BYERS
While their whole world is changing around them, four dark elves struggle against
different enemies. Yet their paths will lead them all to the most terrifying discovery
in the long history of the drow.

INSURRECTION BOOK II
THOMAS M. REID
A hand-picked team of drow adventurers begin a journey through the treacherous
Underdark, all the while surrounded by the chaos of war. Their path will take them
through the heart of darkness and shake the Underdark to its core.

CONDEMNATION BOOK III
RICHARD BAKER
The search for answers to Lloth's silence uncovers only more complex questions, allowing
doubt and frustration to test the boundaries of already tenuous relationships.

EXTINCTION BOOK IV
LISA SMEDMAN
For even a small group of drow, trust is the rarest commodity of all.
When the expedition prepares for a return to the Abyss, what little trust there is
crumbles under a rival goddess's hand.

ANNIHILATION BOOK V
PHILIP ATHANS
Old alliances have been broken and new bonds have been formed. While some finally
embark for the Abyss itself, others stay behind to serve a new mistress – a goddess with
plans of her own.

RESURRECTION BOOK VI
PAUL S. KEMP
The Spider Queen has been asleep for a long time, leaving the Underdark to suffer war
and ruin. But if she finally returns, will things get better... or worse?

For more information visit **www.wizards.com**

THE YEAR OF ROGUE DRAGONS

BY RICHARD LEE BYERS

Dragons across Faerûn begin to slip into madness, bringing all of the world to the edge of cataclysm. The Year of Rogue Dragons has come.

THE RAGE

Renegade dragon hunter Dorn has devoted his entire life to killing dragons. As every dragon across Faerûn begins to slip into madness, civilization's only hope may lie in the last alliance Dorn and his fellow hunters would ever accept.

THE RITE

Rampaging dragons appear in more places every day. But all the dragons have to do to avoid the madness is trade their immortal souls for an eternity of undeath.

THE RUIN

May 2006

For more information visit **www.wizards.com**

HOUSE OF SERPENTS TRILOGY
By The New York Times best-selling author
Lisa Smedman

VENOM'S TASTE

The Pox, a human cult whose members worship the goddess of
plague and disease, begins to work the deadly will of Sibyls' Chosen.
As humans throughout the city begin to transform into the freakish
tainted ones, it's up to a yuan-ti halfblood to stop them all.

VIPER'S KISS

A mind-mage of growing power begins a secret journey to Sespeth.
There he meets a yuan-ti halfblood who has her eyes set on the scion
of house Extaminos – said to hold the fabled Circled Serpent.

VANITY'S BROOD

The merging of human and serpent may be the most dangerous
betrayal of nature the Realms has ever seen. But it could also be the
only thing that can bring a human slave and his yuan-ti mistress
together against a common foe.

www.wizards.com

FORGOTTEN REALMS

THE FIRST INTO BATTLE,

THEY HOLD THE LINE, THEY ARE...

THE FIGHTERS

MASTER OF CHAINS

Once he was a hero, but that was before he was nearly killed and
sold into slavery. Now he has nothing but hate and the chains of
his bondage: the only weapons he has with which to escape.

GHOSTWALKER

His first memories were of death. His second, of those who killed him.
Now he walks with specters, consumed by revenge.

SON OF THUNDER

Forgotten in a valley of the High Forest dwell the thunderbeasts,
kept secret by ancient and powerful magic. When the Zhentarim find
out about this magic, a young barbarian must defend his reptilian
brethren from those who would seize their power.

BLADESINGER

Corruption grips the heart of Rashemen in the one place they thought
it could not take root: the council of wise women who guide the people.
A half-elf bladesinger traveling north with his companions is the people's
only hope, but first, he must convince them to accept his help.

For more information visit **www.wizards.com**